COU of BITTER THORN

ALSO BY KAY L MOODY

The Fae of Bitter Thorn

Heir of Bitter Thorn
Court of Bitter Thorn
Castle of Bitter Thorn

The Elements of Kamdaria

The Elements of the Crown
The Elements of the Gate
The Elements of the Storm

Truth Seer Trilogy

Truth Seer
Healer
Truth Changer

Visit kaylmoody.com/bitter to read the prequel novella,
Heir of Bitter Thorn, for free

COURT

of

BITTER

THORN

KAY L MOODY

THE FAE OF BITTER THORN

1

Court of Bitter Thorn
The Fae of Bitter Thorn 1
By Kay L Moody

Published by Marten Press
3731 W 10400 S Ste 102, #205
South Jordan, UT 84009

www.MartenPress.com

Cover by Angel Leya
Edited by Justin Greer

ISBN: 978-1-7324588-8-8

CHAPTER 1

S words came first.

Love could come later—maybe never—but Elora would die before she went a day without lifting her sword. Her father usually sparred with her, but now that he was too busy arranging her marriage to a rich, old merchant, she'd just have to find a new partner herself.

Her blade sliced through the brittle red leaves that clung to a bush by her home. Each gave a soft crunch before drifting to the cracked dirt below. The chilly air cooled her brow as she swung the sword again.

The leaves would have fallen on their own in another week or two. That made it less satisfying to chop them away, but it was also less destructive.

When only bare branches remained on the bush, she took her sword to the trunk of a nearby tree. The sharp metal of her sword cut into the rough wood. Chips of bark flew as she ripped her sword away to do it again. It didn't take long for the trunk to be covered in gashes. Her mother would have sighed at the sight of it. Her father would have chuckled.

None of it made Elora feel any better. She let out a huff as she sliced the tops off a lovely clump of wildflowers.

Was it normal to be so angry while waiting to meet one's betrothed?

The mere thought caused her simmering emotions to bubble up. Though her bottom lip trembled, she refused to acknowledge anything but the sword in her hand. It cut through the air, this time slicing another bush that had red leaves trying to hold on for dear life.

Even after the leaves had been eradicated, her sword continued to spin and slice. The muscles in her arms ached, but that wouldn't stop her from swinging the blade like her life depended on it.

Anything to keep the tears at bay.

When her sword glanced against a tree instead of against its intended target of a bush, a shudder ripped through her shoulders. Pain stung through her throat when she tried to swallow. Her arms slumped to her sides, feeling heavier than usual. Hard pants puffed from her mouth while drops of sweat trickled down her neck.

Gripping her sword hilt tight, she pressed her forehead against the nearest tree trunk. Its familiar scent of rich bark and sticky sap wafted into her nose. Would her new home have trees that smelled the same?

Her lip was trembling. Again.

With a sniff, she shoved herself away from the tree and slid her silver blade inside its sheath. The belt that was wrapped around the bottom of her leather corset held the weight of the sheath and sword, distributing it evenly across her hips.

Even in the brisk air, her skin felt too warm. She wrinkled her nose at the limp fabric covering her arms. The long-sleeved underslip might have been lightweight, but it always got in the way when she used her sword. Her woolen skirt she didn't mind. She'd learned to fight in a skirt years ago. The leather corset actually helped her sword skill since it acted as a torso support and as a kind of armor. But the linen underslip?

She would have sliced the long sleeves right off if she hadn't been certain her mother would faint at the sight. And perhaps Elora *should* have been more concerned about her appearance, considering she was about to meet her future husband and all.

At least the rich purple dye in her skirt had lasted longer than her family's wealth. And at least it still fit her. Her light brown hair hung freely down her back in gentle waves. It wasn't a common hairstyle: no braids, combs, or even a ribbon. But she had only been able to make so many concessions when getting ready that morning. Hopefully her betrothed liked long hair.

A lump pricked her throat, which would have been easier to ignore if tears hadn't puddled in her eyes at the same moment. She blinked them away before they could fall. It didn't change how her corset seemed too tight and her heart seemed too heavy.

Ignoring those things, she traced a finger over the leather wrapped hilt of her sword. There was no reason to be emotional anyway. This was a marriage, not a death sentence. With her eighteenth birthday a month away, she had been hoping for a *little* more time at home. A little more time to be free.

But her father's forge was close to ruin, and her marriage was the only thing that could save it—and her family.

Mother always said Elora was lucky for being so beautiful. Now her beauty would buy a husband who could save her parents and two younger sisters from financial ruin. All she had to give in return was her entire self to a complete stranger.

Lucky indeed.

The veins in her hand pulsed as she gripped her sword hilt tighter. She forced deep breaths in and out of her nose, urging her heart to stop racing. It refused. Why could her heart do whatever it wanted but her head still had to accept marriage?

Before her thoughts could spin too far out of control, she reached under her corset for a reminder of her one last goal. She wanted to win her very own sword fighting tournament. Of course, women were not allowed to participate, but she had been preparing for this goal for weeks. To hide in plain sight at the tournament grounds, she just needed the right clothes.

With a gentle tug, she pulled a piece of parchment out from under her corset. Handling the parchment gently, she smoothed out the creases as she traced a finger over the drawing. Thin pencil lines and colored paint combined to portray a knight in full armor. Her father had recently acquired a full book of drawings that depicted life in a nearby castle. The images and descriptions of the gardens and clothing were captivating, but this drawing of the knight was her favorite.

Letting her finger linger over the knight's sword, she carefully studied his stance. Years of sword training with her father taught her plenty about correct stance. Still, the man in the drawing somehow seemed nobler and more gallant than her.

Straightening her back, she unsheathed her sword and attempted to stand in the same position. As it had been doing a lot lately, the air hung stagnant all around with no hint of breeze. She made her own wind by swiping the sword diagonally in front of her body.

In her mind, the leather corset and woolen skirt were gone. Instead, she imagined herself wearing a heavy suit of chainmail with a belted white tunic on top. Matching clothes sat in a dusty trunk in her father's forge. His old tournament clothes *might* be recognized by others in their village, but they were the only men's clothes she had access to. They would have to do.

Her eyes remained closed as she struck her sword forward in lethal jabs. After a moment, she peeked through one eyelid at the drawing of the knight. She adjusted her feet to match the stance and closed her eyes to move again.

When she slashed her sword through the air again, she didn't just imagine herself in the clothes. Now she imagined herself standing across from Theobald, the greatest sword fighter and sword maker the land had ever seen. His prowess was well known due to all the tournaments he'd won.

Theobald was also her father, though she imagined a slightly younger version of him to fight against.

Age had caught up to him now, but her father had once boasted incredible sword skill. During her childhood, he spent as many days forging new swords as competing in dangerous sword fighting tournaments. She remembered sitting on her mother's knee in a crowded arena while her father effortlessly beat any opponent who crossed him.

When Elora's skirt rippled around her legs, her arms dropped to her sides again. The illusion vanished in a heartbeat.

Even with the right clothes, she still might not get away with sneaking into a tournament. And too many people would be angry if they found out. That gloomy truth always crept around the corners of her mind, but she did her best to ignore it. No matter what everyone else thought about a woman wielding a sword, she *had* to participate in a tournament. At least once.

For a single moment, the air sizzled around her. Hairs prickled at the back of her neck while the sensation of being watched flooded through her. Before she could glance into the woods, a strong gust of wind blew the drawing of the knight out of her hand. Her eyes flew open as she jumped to snatch the parchment from the air.

Instead, another gust carried it past the clearing where she had been practicing. In only a moment, it drifted toward the front of her family's cottage. Despite the dirt and leaves she had to trudge through, Elora raced toward her drawing without question.

As a tangible reminder of the tournament she hoped to win, nothing could stop her from protecting that parchment.

Her feet tripped over crunchy leaves and dry twigs. The page finally stopped flying when it wrapped itself around the front leg of a chestnut brown horse. Her husband-to-be had arrived on that same horse not long ago. He and her parents were still discussing the particulars of the upcoming marriage. The horse probably wouldn't appreciate a stranger grabbing at its leg, but she *needed* that paper.

Heavy thumps pounded in her chest as she reached out. Her fingers pinched over the page just as the horse snorted with a distressed neigh. Its teeth chomped down, nearly taking a chunk of out her arm. She had stepped back just in time.

Despite the pounding pulse that strummed through her, a smile tugged at her lips. She held the drawing against her heart for a beat before folding it and tucking it neatly underneath her corset.

The horse continued to neigh, but her relief seemed to calm it slightly. She took a step back and lowered her head. Reaching out a flat palm, she let the creature sniff her until its muscles relaxed.

"Elora." Her mother appeared through the front door of their cottage wearing her finest blue shawl. She gave a pointed grimace at Elora's dust-covered hem before turning back toward the inside of the cottage. "I discovered the cause of the horse's fright. Elora must have been eager to meet it."

While the sound of footsteps neared, Elora shook her skirt to loosen most of the dirt. Her back had only just straightened when a man appeared in the doorway beside her mother.

The beam on her mother's face could have brightened a moonless night. "Elora, meet Dietrich Mercer, your betrothed."

A curtsy came automatically. Elora could only hope it hid the scowl taking over her features. By the time she rose from the curtsy, her father had joined the others. He closed the door of the cottage behind him as the three of them stepped toward her.

Mr. Mercer was shorter than her father and had less defined features. His round belly poked out above his belt. He did have a fine head of curly blonde hair, which paired nicely with his bright blue eyes. But it looked as though the most intense sport he had ever performed was writing a letter. At least he wasn't as old as her father. The man was much closer to her father's age than to hers, but he still had a *bit* of youth in him.

Heat flushed into her cheeks when he nodded his head in return. Somehow, she managed to stop herself from reaching for her sword hilt. Instead, her sweaty palm stroked over the horse's chestnut mane. "I apologize if I acted out of turn, but your horse caught my eye. Such a beautiful creature."

Mother always said flattery could smooth over anything.

Mr. Mercer must have agreed because the slightest smile twitched at his lips. "You have a good eye." He glanced up and down her body as he spoke, but at least he had the decency to pretend he was eyeing his horse. "This mare has strong legs that have carried me through many villages. It can carry a cart full of wares all by itself."

"How impressive." Her mother touched a hand to her necklace as her jaw dropped.

That caused a bigger grin on Mr. Mercer's face before he turned to look at Elora again. "But I usually take two horses, so I don't put so much strain on this one."

"What a humane thing to do." Somehow, Elora had adopted her mother's dulcet tone. Getting married to a stranger was the last thing she wanted, but she didn't want to upset her betrothed during their first meeting either.

Mr. Mercer stepped forward to rub between the horse's eyes. He gave her the briefest glance before staring back at his horse. "Once we marry, perhaps we could go horseback riding together. I have a lovely meadow where the flowers bloom beautifully."

His blue eyes flicked toward her again, this time looking brighter than before. She allowed one corner of her mouth to tilt up in a smile. "I'd like that." The most surprising thing about her statement was that it actually held truth.

The words seemed to give him courage. He reached into the leather pouch hanging from his horse's saddle. "I brought you a book from my library."

A tiny gasp escaped her when he dropped a thick leather-bound book into her hands. "You have a library?"

His chest puffed out as he nodded. "Yes, your father said you'd like that."

She glanced back at her father whose thinning brown hair looked wispy over his head. He gave a short nod that said more than words could have. He had promised to find her a good husband, and so far, things weren't as bad as they could have been.

Her father cleared his throat and gave a pointed look toward her betrothed. "And you said you had a bit of woods where she can practice her sword fighting every day, correct?"

Red burned through Mr. Mercer's neck and face. He ducked his head and looked studiously at his horse's mane. "Uh, yes. I can provide for your," he glanced at Elora through the side of his eye, "eccentricities."

She tightened a fist but did it beneath the folds of her skirt. Her father had promised to find her someone who would let her continue to practice her sword skill. She should have known her betrothed would only barely be able to tolerate it.

Still, *eccentric* was one of the better words used to describe her skill. Most people considered it downright unseemly for a woman to know how to wield a sword.

Mr. Mercer cleared his throat and looked deeper into his horse's mane. "As long as the sport doesn't interfere with her childbearing."

Her muscles stiffened at once. It was lucky her betrothed continued to stare at his horse. He wouldn't have liked the scowl that screwed up her face. It wasn't that she found marriage or children inherently disgusting. But this conversation made her feel less like a person and more like an object in some business arrangement.

When her mother invited everyone back inside to discuss the details, only Elora's body accompanied them. Her mind was off imagining a tournament. In it, she wore chainmail and boots, and no one criticized her for carrying a sword. Then again, in her father's old clothes, no one knew she was a woman either. The thoughts brought a smile to her lips.

They could make her get married, but they *couldn't* take away her dream. Before her wedding, she'd sneak into a tournament. No matter what the cost.

That same strange sensation of being watched prickled over her skin again. Rather than fearing it, she found herself longing for it. Maybe someone new in her life was just what she needed. She'd welcome any number of new people... as long as she could fight them with her sword.

CHAPTER

2

Grime gathered in the edges of the forge. Elora collected her father's tools and set them in a pile next to him so he could clean each one. While he worked, she wiped away the dirt and soot that covered the wooden counters and walls.

The tip of her boot bumped an old trunk under one counter. She spared a quick glance toward it while her father shook out a rag. The dust on the trunk's surface had been undisturbed for many months at least. *Good.* Her father wouldn't even notice when she stole his old clothes out of it. She couldn't do it while he sat in the forge with her, but maybe she could sneak in that night after everyone had gone to bed. With her wedding drawing nearer, she was running out of time to get into a tournament like she had always dreamed.

Plucking a tool from the ground, her father scrubbed it with the polishing rag. "Mr. Mercer promised to recommend my skills in every village he visits. As a merchant, he has extensive influence. I expect I'll have plenty of work before winter comes."

She nodded at her father's words but kept wiping the counters without a word. How wonderful that her *imprisonment* with the merchant would improve her father's business. As soon as the thought struck her, a wrinkle scrunched up her nose. She loved her father more than anyone. She *was* grateful her marriage could help him. But why couldn't she help without being tied down to a boring life she didn't even want?

"I know he isn't perfect." With such a sturdy build and rough hands, it felt out of place when her father used a tender voice. "But Dietrich Mercer is a good man. Those who know him personally only have good things to say about him. And he is very wealthy."

How could she be ungrateful when her father had tried so hard to find her a good match? "I suppose he seemed kind." Her heart tightened as she forced the words out.

The muscles in her father's arms rippled as he cleaned the grime away from his hammer. "I know he acted uncomfortable about your sword skill when you met him, but he promised me it wouldn't be a problem. He said he would let you continue to practice every day if you wanted. He even said he'd let you teach his scullery maid so you can have a sparring partner."

Apparently, the soreness in her throat was a permanent fixture these days. She swallowed over a hard lump, but the tightness only grew. In a soft voice, she braved the response she'd been forming for weeks. "I know it's a good match but... Is it wrong for me to dream of something more? Having sword skill isn't enough, I want a chance to *use* that skill." Her chin trembled through each of the words.

Dropping his hammer, her father came near.

18

When she spoke again, her voice broke. "Is marriage the greatest adventure I'll ever have?"

Her mother appeared in the doorway of the forge just as her father pulled Elora into a tight embrace. Emotion spilled out of her before she could stop it. Tears soaked her father's wool tunic. His shoulders had caught so many of her tears, but soon, she'd have only a stranger to turn to in times of pain. As kind as Mr. Mercer acted, he didn't seem the type to offer great comfort.

How could anyone replace her father's strong arms and steady heart?

Her mother must have come inside the forge because now she stroked Elora's arm. "Don't you remember the story of when your father and I left the castle? I was a court musician, the finest harp player in generations. Your father was the renowned castle blacksmith. But when we married each other, we chose to move to the country so we could raise our family away from the dangers and politics of the castle."

The words did nothing to temper Elora's tears. Her two younger sisters had always found their parents' story romantic, but to Elora, it just seemed sad. Her parents had once lived exciting lives, and they gave it all up for each other. It only further confirmed her belief that marriage was the opposite of adventure. It could never beat the thrill of a tournament.

When the tears slowed, her father held Elora by the shoulders and looked her in the eye. "Your betrothed promised he would buy you a new book in every village he ever visits."

Her mother offered a smile as she nudged Elora in the arm. "And his merchant business has afforded him a large estate. Even if you hate him, you'll always be provided for."

Elora wrenched her shoulders away from her father's grip. She wrapped an arm over her stomach and began pinching the skin on her opposite elbow. "But what if he doesn't treat me well?"

Despite her father's insistence, Mr. Mercer hadn't acted happy about the sword fighting.

A crease formed in her father's forehead. "Dietrich has a good reputation. His neighbors—"

But her mother cut him off with a wave of her hand. "Take comfort, Elora. If Mr. Mercer does anything to hurt you, your father will just stab him."

The sound that escaped Elora's mouth wasn't quite a gasp, but it wasn't quite a laugh either. "Mother!" What a change for *her* to be the one scolding.

Her mother shrugged, but it didn't hide the smile dancing beneath her lips. "Only if his actions warrant it, of course. Mr. Mercer knows your father's reputation." She hooked an arm through her husband's and looked up at him with a wink. "He knows what your father is capable of."

Her father shook his head at the words, but he also stood a little taller. With a smirk, he gestured toward Elora. "She's better than me with a sword now, Cecily. She could stab him herself if needed."

Her mother responded by fluttering her eyelashes. "Yes, you did tell me that, didn't you?" She pulled his arm closer. "But I know you could still take him easily."

Elora covered her eyes with one hand as she let out an exasperated sigh. Being in love was probably wonderful and all, but did her parents have to be *so* ridiculous around her?

By the time she moved the hand away from her face, her parents had stepped apart.

"The point is," her mother said while reaching out to squeeze her hand, "even after you marry, you will always be our daughter."

The world felt warmer then. Or softer maybe. Comfort surrounded Elora despite the harsh realities all around. Swallowing over the largest lump in her throat yet, she reached out to embrace her parents. They responded with even tighter hugs.

Footsteps shuffled across the floor. When Elora pulled away from her parents, she saw her two younger sisters standing in the doorway to the forge. It wasn't unusual for everyone to be in the forge, but they did come here a lot more lately. They were trying a little too hard to keep Elora in good spirits. Still, the effort brought comfort.

With a prim stance, Elora's middle sister, Chloe, held her hands behind her back and fluttered her eyelashes. She had inherited more mannerisms from their mother than either of the other two sisters. "Will you come with Grace and me into the village, Elora? The bookstore is supposed to get another book of poems today, and I'm dying to take a look."

Without missing a beat, Elora narrowed one eye. "And will Alistair be at the bookstore too? Are you sure you aren't going just to see him?"

Right on cue, Chloe's fair skin turned a bright red. It stood out against her softly curled blonde hair. "It's not just because of Alistair." Her lips pursed as she tried to suppress a smile. "But I won't complain if he is there."

Alistair Rolfe was only one of many young men Chloe had her eye on. She didn't love any one of them more than the others. Rather, she was in love with the idea of being in love.

Why couldn't Chloe be the oldest and have her marriage arranged? She was *dying* to get married. At fifteen, she didn't have too much longer to wait.

From behind Chloe, Grace's bright face appeared. Her reddish-brown hair was swept up in a loose bun. It was her attempt at appearing older than her actual age of twelve. "Please come, Elora. I want to tell my friend how you've finally started learning the harp duet with me."

Grace acted a bit childish, but her enthusiasm for life couldn't be denied. She was also more driven than her two older sisters when it came to music. Despite being the youngest, she was the most accomplished harp player between them. Only their mother had greater skill.

Mention of the duet brought a pit to Elora's stomach. She had just recently promised to learn the duet and only because her time was running out. Soon, she'd be married and living in an all-new village. With her impending marriage, she didn't have long to perfect the duet she had always promised Grace she would learn.

A smile accompanied her red cheeks as Chloe skipped across the floor and hooked an arm around Elora's. "Please, please, please? You know Mother won't let us visit the village without you."

"You should go." Father brushed a knuckle across Elora's cheek and pointed his chin toward the doorway. "It will give you time to look over this letter."

He pushed a folded piece of parchment into her hands. It felt as heavy as iron. Even before looking, she knew it had come from her betrothed.

Her mother placed a hand over Elora's and gave her a gentle nod. Even at her age, her mother's blonde hair only looked slightly duller than Chloe's. "Mr. Mercer would like you to pick the wedding date. He asks that you send your response soon."

Elora's heart sank as she clasped the letter in her hand. The very strong desire to burn the letter came over her. If the drawing of the knight had still been under her corset, she would have reached for it. Now it was inside her room in the cottage. Instead, she glanced at the trunk holding her father's old tournament clothes. Her breath caught at the sight of it.

Soon.

When her father pulled something from his pocket, his face said *peace offering*. A moment later, he dropped a leather pouch filled with coins onto her palm. She must have made a face at the sight of it because her father pushed it toward her and turned away.

Apparently, she wouldn't be allowed to ask where the money had come from. Considering her mother's neck—which almost always sported a necklace—was now bare, Elora had a pretty good guess. Nausea twisted through her at the thought.

Chloe tugged her toward the door before she could think about it too much.

A tiny squeak of protest came from their mother as they reached the doorway. With lips pursed to a straight line, her mother's face scrunched up in a wince. "Must you wear your sword into the village, Elora? Couldn't you leave it here in the forge?"

The tears that had spilled earlier threatened to make another appearance. Elora's heart pounded in her chest. Of all times, *now* was not the best moment to be reminded how unseemly she was for having skill with a sword. Not when she had to choose a wedding date for a marriage to a man she barely knew.

She glanced toward her father. As always, his eyes softened at the sight of her distress. He let out a resigned sigh. "Oh, let her take the sword. She already has a husband picked out, what harm could it do?"

That prompted a series of giggles from Chloe and Grace as they finally left the forge. Neither of them had ever been interested in sword fighting. And they never seemed eager to get their father to fight for them the way Elora did. But they did find it highly amusing that their father always took Elora's side and never their mother's.

Luckily, their mother found it charming how her husband always had a soft spot for their oldest daughter. Even *she* let out a soft chuckle as the sisters left the forge.

By the time Elora and her sisters made it to the road, Chloe was already thick into an explanation about the epic poem she had most recently read.

"It says Faerie has but one rule, and that is to never give away your heart. Well, technically, the first rule is to never enter a bargain, but everyone seems to break that one, so I don't think it counts. Besides, giving away one's heart seems so much worse." Chloe swept a blonde cluster of curls over one shoulder while letting out a long sigh. "If I ever met a fae, or even a dwarf, I would almost certainly fall in love with it."

Grace let out another giggle as she clasped her hands under her chin. "I'd like to meet a dryad. Didn't you read us a poem that said dryads are wise? Maybe a dryad could teach me why mother's fingers move more delicately across harp strings than mine do."

Elora shook her head as they moved up the beaten path that led to the village. The stagnant air barely seemed able to hold a chill. "I can tell you why mother's hands seem more delicate. It's only because she has more experience than you, Grace. You are already better than Chloe and me. It won't take long until you're just as good as Mother."

With a mischievous smirk, Chloe leaned closer to their youngest sister. "But it would be more believable if you heard it from a dryad, wouldn't it?"

Grace clapped both hands over her mouth as she tried to stifle yet another laugh.

Shaking her head again, Elora said, "Faerie is only a myth." As she spoke, her thumb absently reached out for her other hand. She rubbed her thumb over a strange scar that sat on the fleshy part of her hand between her pointer finger and thumb. Not that long ago, she would have scolded Chloe for putting such fanciful notions into their youngest sister's head. But now?

Elora's thumb stroked over the lopsided-circle scar as even more fanciful thoughts filled her own head. She imagined herself in chainmail and swinging a sword. She imagined fighting for her life with nothing but her leather corset as armor. For some reason, her thoughts turned back to a tree she had recently climbed.

That tree had been just tall enough and just far enough away that it took her years to finally make it to the top. When her father had first explained that she had to get married, she finally took the plunge and climbed the tree to the very top. It had filled her with a sense of freedom and accomplishment. It made her want to finish all the little things she had intended to do before getting married.

Things like learning the duet with Grace. Buying a frame for Chloe's favorite epic poem. Getting through a harp lesson with her mother without throwing a fit. That last one should have been the easiest, but she had yet to manage it. For some reason, harp lessons always made her irritable.

But her biggest goal of all was still winning a tournament.

"Did you fall asleep?" Chloe asked with a grin. "You look as if you're dreaming."

Elora pinched the scar on her hand before dropping her hands away. Yes, maybe Faerie and all its wonderment was a myth.

But she had never wished harder for it to be real. Her heart skittered at the idea of a Faerie tournament. Even a stroll in Faerie would probably be more exciting than anything in her life had been so far.

She couldn't respond to her sister's question. Instead, she pulled the letter out from under her corset while her fingers shook.

Both of her sisters flashed each other forlorn glances.

"Read us the letter," Chloe said.

Grace's loose bun bounced as she nodded. "We can help you choose a wedding date." Her head ducked down while her lips pinched into a knot. In a softer voice, she added, "If it's too hard for you."

Elora clenched her jaw to keep it from trembling. Hopefully her sisters wouldn't see through the disguise. Since she *had* to choose, a summer wedding had always seemed nice. With a nod, she unfolded the letter and prepared to read.

CHAPTER 3

S o much for a summer wedding.

    Apparently, Elora's betrothed wanted to get married before winter. He had villages to visit in the early winter and didn't want a wedding interfering with his business. That left only six weeks from which to choose a wedding date.

The distraction provided by her sisters had been welcome at first, but now their giggling seemed incessant. When they got to the bookstore, Chloe did indeed get a chance to speak with Alistair Rolfe. The young man made her blush furiously after only a few sentences.

After some demure chuckling and eyelash fluttering from Chloe, Alistair retrieved the poetry book she had been so anxious to see. She pored over it with more love in her eyes than even the young man had elicited.

Elora rested her back against the wall, tapping her foot as she waited. It might have been easier to endure if Grace hadn't been busy chatting away with her friend at the Coopers' next door.

When Mrs. Rolfe began stacking books that had to be put away on the shelves, Elora jumped at the chance to help. The woman gave a long glance at the sword hanging on Elora's hip, but she managed to keep her mouth shut about it.

"Thank you, dear." Mrs. Rolfe pointed and directed while Elora put the books away. "I heard about your engagement."

Heat rushed into Elora's cheeks. She tried to smile. Unsuccessfully. "Yes, we just have to decide on a wedding date. Mr. Mercer wants to be married before winter."

The woman nodded absently, and her eyes wandered across the bookstore. A grin twitched at the corners of her mouth when she spied her son and Chloe with their shoulders pressed together while they pored over the poetry book. Mrs. Rolfe turned back to Elora and gestured toward another shelf.

Before the woman handed Elora another book, her face brightened. "I don't know if your parents ever told you, but they helped my oldest son become a knight at the castle. If it weren't for their recommendation, he never would have gotten the placement." Her face beamed as she touched a handkerchief to the corners of her eyes. "After my husband passed, I never would have been able to keep this bookstore going on my own." She gave a little sniff. "But with my son's financial help, I have been able to make it."

The story didn't come as a surprise. Elora's parents always helped whenever and whoever they could. But what had been intended as a compliment only made her more frustrated than ever. If her parents were so good at helping people, why couldn't they help their own daughter avoid an unwanted marriage? The guilt associated with such thoughts stung a little less each time.

When she and her sister left the bookstore later that day, Chloe had even more red in her cheeks and a newly copied poem to read. Elora, on the other hand, felt emptier than ever. They retrieved Grace from the Coopers' next door and continued down the dry, crusty path that led to their cottage.

Chloe found it necessary to read her poem as they walked. "It says, 'Against a fae who magicks in bargains, one can rarely win the fight.'"

The boiling in her gut probably had something to do with it, but Elora felt more eager than usual to pick a fight. She threw a sideways glance toward her sister. "A fae who *magicks in bargains?* That doesn't make any sense."

With a carefree shrug, Chloe only brought the poem closer to her nose. "Alistair says there are scholars who believe the words were misprinted. They think it was supposed to say 'a fae who *bargains in magic.'*" She let out a heavy sigh. "But I love the way it sounds. *Magicks in bargains?* It seems so whimsical. The entire poem is fascinating. After that line it says, 'Only the truest weapon against him can win, and that is always—"

Her words were cut short when she stubbed her toe on a rock protruding from the cracked dirt path. It served her right for keeping her eyes on the poem instead of on the road.

Bitter thoughts twisted in Elora's mind. Suddenly, she wanted to burn that stupid poem. But only after she jumped inside it and lived it out herself.

If only that were possible. Fighting against a fae sounded deliciously adventurous.

The sound of clashing swords interrupted her thoughts. She had been so deeply engrossed in her imaginings that for a moment, she had thought the swords were part of her daydream.

When she glanced to the side, the true source became clear.

"I didn't know there was a tournament today." The words had barely left Grace's mouth before Elora dashed down a less worn path to the benches where spectators sat. From behind, her sisters grumbled as they slowly caught up to her.

They didn't have much to complain about because the tournament was clearly almost over. The tiny spark of excitement that dared flicker in Elora's chest had already been snuffed out.

On the tournament grounds, two sword-wielding men swung their weapons at each other. Even from her distance, she could see sweat dripping down their cheeks.

Their movements came slow and labored, an indicator that the tournament was nearly finished. They each heaved their weapons about, letting out huffs and grunts as they moved.

"Are they even good?" Chloe said with clear disdain.

Even little Grace narrowed her eyes at the two men. "Why are they so slow? When you and Father fight, you jump around faster than grasshoppers."

Brushing away her blonde hair, Chloe nodded. "And I know sword fighting is a man's sport, but why do they have to lumber around like that? You make sword fighting almost look elegant."

One corner of Elora's mouth pricked upward. It was entirely possible that her sisters were being overly complimentary. Everyone had been nicer to her lately, which only reaffirmed her belief that marriage merited condolences, not congratulations.

Still, her sisters' words *did* lift her spirits. They even nodded thoughtfully when she gave a long explanation about how easily she could have beaten the two competitors.

Her eyes grew wider with each swipe of the swords. A deep longing ached in her chest at the sight. The muscles inside her itched to be on that field, swinging her own sword. Thrill buzzed through her so potently, she could taste it. One word thrummed through her mind over and over.

Soon.

"I see that look in your eye."

Sucking in a breath, Elora turned to the man who had just spoken. He wore a threadbare blue tunic with a silver embroidered trim that had long since frayed. Bastien. He ran the tournament and had been getting weapons from her father for years. His dark brown hair fell over his forehead as he brought his eyebrows together.

Feigning innocence was probably her best move. "What look?" she asked.

He jabbed a callused finger at her. "You're thinking about disguising yourself in boy's clothing so you can stride in here and participate in a tournament."

His words froze in the air between them while fear very likely shimmered in her eyes. Could he tell how difficult it was to let out a throat-clearing cough? She touched a hand to her collarbone, as she had seen her mother do so many times. "I wouldn't dream of—"

"You'd never get away with it." He cut her off without so much as a nod to acknowledge her words. The vein in his forehead pulsed harder with each word. "Your father marks every weapon he makes with that raised shield and chevron symbol."

With a single step forward, Bastien had moved close enough to tap one finger on the pommel of her sword. "But only his weapons and yours have a star inside the shield and chevron symbol."

Just like that, her heart dropped. The symbol. Why had she never considered the symbol? Everyone knew about the raised shield and chevron her father used to mark the weapons he forged. Only a few knew about the added star he used to mark his own weapons.

She should have realized Bastien would recognize it. Finding a different sword might be impossible. Every sword she had access to had some form of her father's mark on it. And anyway, her sword was almost like an old friend. She had used it for years. A part of her wondered if she could even fight at all with a different sword.

Victory etched itself all over Bastien's face as he rolled back on his heels. "I'd recognize you the moment you walked onto the field, even if you wore boy's clothing."

A scowl was the only response she could muster. Her teeth ground together as she huffed at him.

That only added to his smug appearance. "You know the rules for fighting in the tournament. No women."

At her side, Chloe and Grace had stiffened. Even without seeing their faces, Elora could tell they were eager to leave. To hide. Maybe her years of sword training had taught her to be braver than she should have been. Whatever the reason, Elora was more determined than ever to win this argument. If she had to get married, nothing would stop her from fighting in a tournament.

Turning to the most heart-wrenching argument she had, Elora tilted her head to the side with a demure frown. "But we need the money."

Bastien let out a puffy laugh and slapped the front of his leg. "Don't you have a husband waiting for you in another village? What do you need money for?"

Heat burned through her neck as anger threaded through her fingers. Not even her father could have stopped the next words that left her lips. She gestured toward the panting competitors with a wrinkling nose. "I'm better than them, and you know it. I should be allowed to fight."

The last bits of decorum vanished from the man's face in an instant. He stepped toward her again, apparently eager to use his height as an advantage. "Years ago, your father made me promise to be gentle with you if you ever tried to join a tournament. I'm afraid this is as gentle as I get."

Her eyebrows raised as a spark of hope flashed through her. "What if I use another sword? Then how would you recognize me?" Using another sword was out of the question, not that Bastien needed to know that. But maybe she could figure out a way to disguise the symbol on the pommel of her sword.

The man's face had contorted, removing all trace of kindness. When he spoke, spit shot from his mouth. "The rules allow me to kill any woman who tries to fight in a tournament. Don't think I wouldn't do it."

Elora had found her sword hilt. Without even thinking, her hand had gripped tight around the leather covering the hilt. Scores of people may have been surrounding them, but something much bigger than that would have to convince her to not draw her sword. Heat dripped down from her head to her toes as she prepared to pull out her sword.

Something buzzed in the air, which made the hairs on her neck stand straight. Someone was definitely watching her.

The brief silence between them offered just enough time for Chloe to step forward. Her blonde hair nearly glowed in the dimming sunlight. She gave a delicate pat to Bastien's arm, which brought at least some of the bite out of his face. After another pat, calm had almost overtaken his features.

Even before she started speaking, the expression on Chloe's face foretold her words would come out in a charming lilt. "How unfortunate for you, Bastien."

He lifted his chin a little higher at the words.

Chloe gave his arm one last pat before dropping her hand away. "It's truly pitiful that you are so intimidated by my sister's sword skill that you have to threaten her life to feel better. Tell me, do you wake up feeling inadequate, or does it get worse when you remember how easily my sister could beat you?"

In all her life, Elora's eyes had never stretched so wide. She grabbed both her sisters by the arms and yanked them away from Bastien. The faster they left, the better. As incredible as the words were, young women—especially fifteen-year-old young women—were not supposed to say things like that to an elder.

As Elora pulled her sisters away, Grace looked over her shoulder with a haughty air. "You have the ugliest shoes I have ever seen." She turned up her nose at Bastien before allowing herself to be pulled away.

Smothering the grin on her face was more difficult than Elora expected. She pulled her sisters into a crowd of spectators before donning the most serious face she could muster. "What were you thinking? Both of you." She shook her head just before a roar went through the crowd. Someone had just been named champion of the tournament. Ignoring it, she continued to pull her sisters deeper into the crowd. "You cannot say things like that to such a respected man."

Chloe let out a scoff as she rolled her eyes. "Bastien's just upset that Father didn't even consider him as a potential husband for you."

Elora's feet jolted to a stop. "What?" A cringe jerked through her body. "But he's as old as Father. How could he even want—" The cringe returned, but she shook her head to clear it away. "It doesn't matter. You shouldn't have said that."

A smirk passed over Chloe's face that held no trace of guilt. "What is he going to do, challenge Father to a duel? We all know how that would end."

Grace's reddish-brown bun bounced with her nod. "Father would win in three strikes or fewer."

The crowd began to disperse around them, which made it easier to disappear among the people. After they had moved closer to the path that led to their cottage, Elora finally let go of her sisters' hands. Her serious face made another appearance. "I do not condone anything you said." It really wasn't her fault that a smirk emerged. Chloe's accusations flitted across Elora's mind, which only made the smirk grow. She glanced at her sister. "But thank you."

Both Chloe and Grace erupted into giggles.

Their delight lifted Elora's spirits but not enough to forget the crushing truth she had just discovered. Joining a tournament in her own village was out of the question. Bastien would be looking for her.

But other villages had tournaments too. She just needed an excuse to leave town for a few days. Her parents wouldn't fall for a bad lie, but surely she'd be able to come up with something.

Despite the setback, she had never been more determined to win a tournament. She might have to disguise herself and her sword; she might even have to leave town. But nothing could stop her now.

CHAPTER

4

The sky turned dusky as Elora and her sisters continued down the path that led to their cottage.

Shouts and clambering filled the air while tournament spectators filled their carts and leather bags before continuing home. Elora breathed in the scents of sweet rolls, freshly turned earth, and even sweat. Tournament smells always made her happy, even the unpleasant ones.

Spectators from other villages must have set up camps nearby because crackling embers and thick smoke billowed above the trees.

Getting into a tournament would be harder than she ever imagined, but that only made her more determined. While walking down the path, details of a new plan zipped through Elora's mind. Her sisters trailed behind with their heads together. They were giggling again. And talking about dryads.

About halfway down the path, Chloe caught up to her oldest sister and lifted one eyebrow. "Mother said Mr. Mercer has his very own library. Won't that be a nice way to spend your days? You love learning about new places."

Coming up on Elora's other side, Grace bobbed her head up and down. It made her eyes look big and young all at the same time. "And he has loads of money. That's good, right?"

It was always fun to watch Grace attempt a grown-up conversation while saying things in a not-quite-polite way. Though even that couldn't untwist the knot that had gathered in Elora's stomach. Here they were consoling her again. Because marriage was awful.

When she only grimaced in response, her sisters looked at each other. A gleam appeared in Chloe's eyes right as she wrinkled her nose. "But he's not very handsome, is he?"

Elora shot her sister a scolding look, which didn't seem to affect her at all.

"Well, he's not." Chloe shrugged. "But I suppose it would be romantic if you managed to fall in love with him despite that."

A gentle wind floated around them, bringing with it even stronger smells of smoke. Why would the villagers make camp this far from the tournament grounds?

Chloe skipped up to her oldest sister and hooked an arm around hers. "If there are any handsome young men in Mr. Mercer's village, you have to write and tell me about every one."

Elora yanked her arm away, glancing ahead for the source of all that smoke. She raised an eyebrow at her sister. "Oh, so *you* can marry a handsome young man, but I have to be stuck with someone who is merely rich?"

Though Chloe most certainly detected the malice in her sister's tone, she clearly chose to ignore it. "I just want to be in love. *True* love." She let out a sigh. "But don't you think it would be wonderful if the man I loved could be handsome too?"

"Where is that smoke coming from?" When Grace pointed at the clouds of ash ahead, the air seemed to still around them.

No chill or breeze of any kind gave feeling to the air. And yet, all of them felt something at that same moment.

Color drained from Grace's face as the smoke rose above their heads. Chloe's eyes watered from keeping them open for too long.

When dread painted all their features, they looked to Elora. The oldest. She was supposed to watch over them and set right their exaggerated fears.

The lump in Elora's throat had grown too massive to swallow over. Even breathing became a challenge.

How could she calm her sisters when the thoughts in their heads were the same as the thoughts in hers?

The smoke came from the exact same direction as their cottage.

She took in a steady breath while the hair on her skin raised. "I'm sure it's fine."

Her sisters nodded obediently, but clearly, neither of them believed the words. She didn't either. But what else could be said? Her feet seemed to move of their own accord closer to the cottage. Closer to the smoke.

The giggling had stopped.

The talking too.

With each step, they moved faster than before. Walking turned to jogging. Then running.

It was *not* the cottage. *Not* the forge.

Saying the words in her head did nothing because each step forward only seemed to confirm her worst fears.

The trees in the woods were so dry. The tiniest spark could have set the trees on fire.

It *had* to be the woods.

A spark from the forge probably landed on a pile of leaves. *But*—.

Her father would have noticed. He would have gotten a thick blanket to put it out.

Terror crept up Elora's fingers and into her arms. Her chest. Her legs.

Her father was the great Theobald, greatest sword fighter and sword maker in all the land. He could win any duel, silence any threat. He could protect them from anything.

The smoke continued to billow above the trees. The crackling wood popped so loudly she couldn't even hear her feet hit the path.

Grace had started crying.

Elora tried to swallow.

She refused to look back at her sisters. Her feet flew down the path, eager to disprove the horrifying thoughts that filled her.

The cottage *wasn't* on fire. It *wasn't* the forge.

And it definitely *wasn't* her parents.

Her feet froze in place as the source of the smoke came into view. Her heart hammered, but it didn't matter because she had forgotten how to feel.

Everything moved around her, but she had disconnected from it all.

It had to be a dream. Things like this didn't happen in real life.

Chloe sobbed into a handkerchief, holding their youngest sister tight.

A spark from the fire landed on the back of Elora's hand. It burned. With a snap of the wrist, she flicked the ember away. But the pain had forced her to admit the truth she could only barely accept.

This wasn't a dream.

Elora's knees slammed into the dry ground while a hard sob shuddered through her. The cottage's shutters sat in a pile, too blackened to hint at their once-bright blue. The fire must have started inside because the rest of the cottage had been reduced to soot and burnt planks.

The forge had been built of stone instead of wood, but even so it suffered great damage. Her father's trunk with his old clothes had been so badly burned she could only barely make out the metal closure that had once been nailed to the front. The clothes were gone.

The silver of her father's hammer was poking out from a heap of blackened timber. Its handle had been devoured by flames.

She focused on the tools just so she could ignore the bodies.

But even if she didn't look, she could still *feel* them. In truth, she had seen them before she even noticed the shutters or the loose harp strings or anything.

Bone was visible where flesh had melted away. Her father shielded her mother with half his body. But it hadn't saved either of them. They were nothing but corpses now.

And then it sank in.

A wail burst from her lips as pain ripped through her chest. She couldn't even breathe between sobs. Her knees drug through the dirt as she crawled over to her sisters.

They held each other in a heap. Each tear that fell could have come from any one of them.

At least the fire had died down. No one else in the village would be in danger.

But did it even matter when her parents were dead?

Their possessions, their home, everything they had… gone.

As Elora clutched her sisters, she could only think one thing. She was the oldest. Their father couldn't protect them anymore. It was *her* job to watch over them now.

From beneath her corset, the letter from Mr. Mercer seemed to burn against her skin.

Only one thing could save them.

CHAPTER 5

O ther villagers arrived not long after Elora and her sisters. They pulled them apart and offered fresh handkerchiefs. Mrs. Rolfe helped Elora brush the dust away from her skirt. Everyone offered words of comfort.

None of them said it to her face, but Elora heard more than a few people remark how lucky she was to already have her marriage arranged. As if she and her sisters would have died too if not for Mr. Mercer.

When evening fell, Mrs. Rolfe ushered the orphaned sisters into a spare room in her home. She wished them all pleasant dreams, which was completely useless. Surely they wouldn't be able to sleep at all that night. Or possibly ever again.

An ache squeezed through Elora's chest as she brushed the tangles from Grace's hair. Maybe it was just the light, but her hair seemed darker. The red hues that usually ran through it were—duller, almost.

Chloe sat on a corner of the bed taking the same sock off and on again while her eyes gazed at nothing.

After clearing her throat, Elora attempted to speak. Her voice felt strange coming out. It was clipped and stiff and not quite right. "Didn't you say you found a note in the rubble, Chloe? What did it say?"

A flinch shook through Chloe before she gave the barest shrug. "That was nothing. It said some nonsense about the fire being revenge for the death of a troll. It must have come from one of the poems in my collection." At the mention of her poems, she flinched even harder than before.

Those poems were gone now. Nothing but ash. Just like Elora's book of drawings from the castle. She didn't even have the drawing of the knight she'd admired. Not even her father's old clothes.

Everything was gone.

Grace tucked her knees up to her chest and flashed a tentative glance toward her oldest sister. "I shouldn't be sad that my harp is gone, right? We lost Father and Mother." Her chin quivered as she forced the rest of her words out. "The harp shouldn't matter."

It was Chloe who burst into tears first. She curled herself into a ball at the corner of the bed and held a piece of her blonde hair tight in a fist. "I want my poems." Her weeping shook the bed. "It took me years to gather that collection, and…" Her eyes widened as she eyed each of her sisters. Her lips pursed in exactly the same way their mother's had just earlier that day. Chloe buried her face in a blanket, so her muffled words were only barely audible. "I even wrote a few poems of my own. Father always encouraged it, especially my poems about Faerie. I never read them to anyone because they weren't very good, but now they're gone. And I never even showed them to anyone."

Elora ushered her youngest sister onto the bed before sitting down at a small desk. She smoothed out the fresh piece of parchment Mrs. Rolfe had gotten for her. Like she had by the cottage, Elora felt disconnected from the world. The tragedy had seemed to strip away her emotions, so she could look at everything without them. It made her mind clearer than ever.

It took no effort to speak in an even tone. "You aren't wrong for missing your poems."

"I miss Mother and Father more." Chloe sat up straight, tears streaming down her cheeks in steady drips.

With a nod, Elora said, "I know." She stared at the blank page before her, swallowing down any sense of regret. "And Grace, you have every right to miss your harp. Once I get married, I will save every bit of money my husband gives me until I can buy you a new one."

"But who's going to teach me?" Grace's voice came out softer than a squeak.

Elora's jaw clenched as she stared at the empty page. It should have been easy to write the letter. She just had to pick a wedding date. The sooner the better.

Instead, she climbed onto the bed and pulled her sisters into her arms. Maybe they didn't have their parents anymore, but they still had each other.

She squeezed them tighter than necessary, but they didn't seem to mind. In fact, it seemed to help them drift off to sleep. Soon, their steady breathing filled the air. Only light from the moon lit the room, but it shone a beam onto the blank page on the desk.

The marriage to Dietrich Mercer was more crucial than ever before. Elora knew that, no matter how loath she was to admit it. With no home, no father, and only a single pouch of coins, it wouldn't be long before they had nothing left at all. Only Mr. Mercer could save them now.

But that didn't mean she had to give up on winning a tournament. Once married, she could ask her husband for money to buy tournament clothes. She'd just tell him they were standard outfits for sword training. Hopefully, he wouldn't ask too many questions.

Then, she'd just have to wait for him to leave their home on merchant business. Once he was gone, she could disguise herself and sneak into a nearby tournament. He'd never have to know a thing.

Buying chainmail would be difficult. The other things she could buy without too much suspicion, especially because she could tell shopkeepers the clothing was for her husband. But no one would believe Mr. Mercer had any use for chainmail, and Mr. Mercer would know Elora had no use for it in simple training.

Then again, chainmail was made to survive. Though many things had been lost in the fire, perhaps there was a small chance her father's chainmail had survived.

Soft sunrays streamed in through the little window and onto the bed in the Rolfes' spare bedroom. Elora had been awake for a while, but the sun meant others would soon arise. It had been a week since the fire.

Mrs. Rolfe had kindly promised to let Elora and her sisters stay in the spare bedroom until Elora's wedding.

Whatever feelings she'd been having about her parents, she carefully tucked deep inside. They had no place in her today. Right now, she just had to get out of the house before anyone caught her. If her sisters found out what she planned to do, they might insist on coming with her. Solitude was the only way to sneak away her father's old chainmail without anyone knowing.

When Elora opened the door to leave the room, Chloe curled herself into a tighter ball on the bed. Grace let out a soft grunt and squeezed her eyes shut. Holding her breath, Elora watched for any signs that her sisters were waking.

They didn't. A moment later, they had both snuggled deep into their pillows with chests rising and falling at rhythmic intervals.

With a steady hand, Elora silently shut the door behind her. She tiptoed down the hall and into the kitchen. Before leaving the room, she had written a quick note explaining how she intended to spend the day going through the remains of their home. Just in case anything had survived the fire. With any luck, she would have enough time to find out if the chainmail had survived and hide it before her sisters tried to join her. She already decided to hide the chainmail in a bag she kept tied up in the tree she had recently climbed.

Pangs of hunger coiled through her gut when she tiptoed into the kitchen. Holding her breath, she lifted the lid from a wooden barrel. The potatoes that had filled it a week ago were nearly gone now. Only two left. It was probably best to leave those. She lifted the linen cloth that covered the breadbasket next. Her stomach growled when she found it empty.

"I'm so sorry."

Elora jumped at the sound of Mrs. Rolfe's voice. After whirling around, Elora noticed the woman sitting in a rocking chair at the edge of the room. Even in the dim light, a rim of bright red was obvious around the woman's eyes. She dabbed at her face with a handkerchief as she sniffed.

"With so many people staying here, our food has disappeared more quickly than I anticipated." Mrs. Rolfe twisted the handkerchief between her hands, staring at the ground.

Elora's thoughts immediately turned to the leather pouch of coins her father had given her the day of the fire. It was tucked under her corset now. She'd counted the coins at least twice a day in the last week. Those few coins were all they had left.

"I wanted to help you. Everyone knows you deserve it after what happened to your parents." The woman sniffled as her shoulders shook. "I didn't think it would be hard, since your wedding is so close." Her nose twitched before she put the handkerchief up to it again. "But I haven't heard from my oldest son for a while and—"

"Do not worry, Mrs. Rolfe." Elora had been thinking about that pouch of coins. She had already used some of them to buy a few necessities. Even being careful, the money would barely last until the wedding was supposed to take place. But they couldn't very well go with no food. For the first time, she was grateful that she had put off choosing a date for the wedding. She'd just have to choose a date sooner than she wanted.

Elora took a few steps closer to the woman. "Your kindness has helped us more than you know. I will do anything I can to help with the food." Her fingers curled tentatively as she tilted her head ever so slightly to the side. "That is, if we can continue living here until my wedding?"

"Of course!" The rocking chair let out a loud creak as the woman jumped up from it.

Mrs. Rolfe took her by the hands and squeezed them gently. "Thank you, my dear."

Giving a nod, Elora moved to the door. As she started down the dusty path outside, the sound of clanking pots filled the air. It only took a few paces to find the Bakers' front door open wide.

"Good morning, Elora," Mrs. Baker called from inside her shop.

"Morning," Mr. Baker mumbled as he kneaded a ball of dough.

Reaching for the leather pouch under her corset, Elora strode into the shop. "I would like to order a meat pie."

The Bakers gave hurried nods and asked a few questions. After talking for a bit, they had the specifications worked out. They seemed mightily pleased for her business, but it didn't stop Mr. Baker from grumbling about how he couldn't gather enough apples for an upcoming order. Elora dropped a few coins into Mrs. Baker's hand, and the woman promised to bring the meat pie over to the Rolfes' residence right at midday.

The cottage was still in shambles. The village had come together to dig simple graves for her parents, but everything else lay undisturbed. Elora's stomach roiled as she took careful steps over the burnt remains. The pounding in her heart was almost too much by the time she reached the charred wood that had once been a trunk.

After finding the chainmail, she lifted it into the air and shook out the debris covering it. Nausea twisted through her. Tucking the chainmail under her arm, she bolted out of the burnt forge and toward the woods.

A lightness filled her chest the farther she got from the cottage. The smell of sap and brittle leaves drowned out the decay that had filled her nose only moments earlier. With each step closer to her special, knotty tree, her heart settled into a steadier pulse.

Dark leaves clung to the trees in the woods around her. Normally, the leaves would have fallen by this time of year. The winds that usually contributed to the fall were not around. As it had for several weeks, the air hung stagnant. It felt heavy without a breeze or wind to move through it. The days were growing colder, which made the thick air more oppressive.

Still, being in the woods had always brought her peace. When she reached the base of the gnarled, knotty tree, she grabbed the low branches and hoisted herself up. The chainmail got one more shake before she tucked it into the bag she had hidden in the tree. Not much remained inside except a coil of rope, a few pressed wildflowers, and now the chainmail.

Instead of returning to the cottage, she headed straight for the village. Seeing the burnt remains again was more than she could handle. The chainmail would need some cleaning, but it would work. Her dream of winning a tournament was one step closer.

But now she had to do something she had been avoiding for too long. She couldn't put off writing the letter to Mr. Mercer any longer.

It was time to choose a wedding date.

CHAPTER 6

The letter had been signed and sealed. Holding it gave Elora the desire to burn it.

A flinch rocked through her. No, not burn. If she saw another fire in her entire life it would be too soon. With winter coming, it wasn't reasonable to fear flames. But she couldn't help it.

Not when smoke and crackling embers brought forth images she couldn't bear to recall.

Pinching the folded parchment between her fingers, she forced herself to focus on the present moment. These days, it was all too easy to let the past swallow her up. The blue wax seal on the letter had just finished hardening.

Mrs. Rolfe had sealed it since Elora refused to be anywhere near the candlelight required to melt the sealing wax.

The woman had recently returned to her bookstore, which left the home empty. And dark. The sun had nearly dipped beneath the horizon. Crickets chirped outside the windows, their pulses slow and soft.

Frigid air crept in through the cracks and crevices in the house, but the air continued to float with no breeze at all. Shadows flickered across the dusty floorboards of the house.

Left to their own devices, Elora's feet would have led her back to the room where she and her sisters had been staying. She would have thrust open the door and thrown herself onto the bed. Sobs would have burst out instantly if she had let them.

But only a child would believe tears could save her now.

Just like the letter, her fate had been sealed.

Daylight faded fast. She had to hire a messenger as soon as possible. But no matter how she told her feet to move, they wouldn't.

When her sisters entered the home through the front door, neither wore any semblance of a smile.

Chloe's eyes flicked to the letter in her older sister's hand. She must have known how much it hurt because she immediately decided to fill the air with chatter. "I helped arrange books in the bookstore today. I had to decide which would be most interesting and find a way to display them more prominently."

A sinking feeling nibbled at Elora's stomach. Though her sister chattered at the same speed as usual, the words held none of the vivaciousness they usually did. Elora attempted a smile. "I'm sure you did it very well." The words tasted cold in her mouth. Before the fire, she probably would have made a sarcastic comment or given a friendly tease. These days, she couldn't bear to do anything but say kind things to her sisters.

It wasn't the same as truly being kind. They all knew it. But how could she do anything else when her sisters were all she had left?

Grace tucked a strand of hair behind her ear. It looked duller than it ever had. She licked her lips as her eyes wandered over to the kitchen. "I cleaned the windows in the bookshop." Her arms folded over her stomach right when a little noise came from it. She winced and turned away from the kitchen, staring off into nothing instead. "Do you remember when we used to have someone who cleaned our house for us? And someone else to cook our meals?"

Elora locked eyes with Chloe for the briefest moment. After a hard swallow, Chloe wrapped an arm around their youngest sister's shoulders and guided her toward the back of the house.

"Come on, Grace. Let's get ready for bed. Then I can read you the latest lines of the poem I'm writing."

Craning her head toward her younger sisters, Elora opened her eyes wide. "I didn't know you were writing a new poem."

If possible, Chloe's face fell even more than its perpetual dejected look. She continued to lead their youngest sister toward the back room. While looking over her shoulder, she mouthed, "It's terrible."

Chloe's eyes fell as she pointed with her chin toward the door. "I saw a messenger talking to Mr. Cooper. You better hurry if you want to catch him."

The letter in Elora's hand seemed to burn hot. The imagined fire sent crackling pain through her fingers. She couldn't acknowledge her sister since Chloe had already disappeared around a corner. Ignoring the imagined pain, Elora marched toward the front door.

Moving quickly didn't help the letter seem less frightening. It had been difficult to write for many reasons. Not only did she have to choose a wedding date, but she also had to inform Mr. Mercer of her parents' deaths. That part probably came off more abrupt than it should have. She didn't even make a request. She just informed him that her sisters would also live at his home after the wedding. Maybe he wouldn't like it, but they were betrothed. Her sisters were his family now too.

If she had to accept that a tournament might be the most exciting thing that would ever happen to her, it was only fair that he should have to sacrifice too.

"Oh, I almost forgot." Chloe bounded back into the room with a bright red ribbon clutched in her fist. She grabbed her older sister's hand and gently wrapped the silk ribbon around Elora's wrist.

"What is that for?"

The ghost of a smile appeared on Chloe's lips. "Red is for courage. Having a piece of it around your wrist or ankle is supposed to give you strength to overcome any challenge." She glanced at the letter before tying off the ribbon in a beautiful bow. A mischievous smirk overtook her face. "Plus, a red ribbon like this can act as a ward against fae enchantments."

A snort sputtered from Elora's mouth before she could stop it. For the briefest moment, she had forgotten her grief and remembered to tease her sister instead. The look that passed between them proved they both had felt it. That simple snort had made things feel normal again. It vanished too soon.

Elora raised an eyebrow as she moved toward the door. "Thank you, Chloe, but Faerie isn't real."

When Chloe shrugged and dashed off toward the back room again, it lacked the energy she usually exhibited. Everything about their lives had become subdued.

Elora glanced at the shiny red ribbon around her wrist as she pushed open the door. Chloe might have been the one to talk about Faerie all the time, but no one in the world could have wished for it to be real more than Elora.

Even a tournament would be mundane in a land as thrilling as Faerie.

Her head hung as she trudged down the path toward the Coopers' home. Even with her head down, she still managed to catch sight of the messenger preparing to mount his horse. Normally, she would have run toward him or walked faster at least. Instead, her feet dragged across the cracked dirt at a sluggish pace.

The messenger jogged toward her instead.

After giving him instructions to deliver the letter to Mr. Mercer, he held out a hand for payment. She dropped a greater number of coins into his hand than she'd used for any other purchase since the fire.

As the messenger rode off on his horse, she stood rooted in place. The leather pouch of coins sat in her hand. She stared inside it. Only one third of the coins remained from the full bag her father had originally given her.

It had been foolish to offer money for food when so little money remained. It had been even more foolish to set her wedding date so far away. She could have chosen any date. Instead of being reasonable, she chose the furthest possible date. Three weeks.

Knots squeezed in her chest as she closed the leather pouch up tight. The money wouldn't last that long. If other villagers heard of their plight, they might be willing to help. But many of the villagers were in the same state as Mrs. Rolfe. The dry spell in their land had meant fewer crops that year. Fewer crops meant less food to go around.

The throbbing in Elora's chest only grew when the sun dipped beneath the horizon. Shadows covered the street in misty darkness. The cold, stale air was uninviting.

Mr. and Mrs. Baker stood outside their shop arguing with one another. Something about the apples they needed to fill an order.

"We have plenty of apples," Mr. Baker said, wiping a handkerchief across his brow. "But they're all stuck in that blasted tree no one can climb."

Mrs. Baker wiped her flour-covered fingers on a stained linen apron. "Why can't you use the ladder?"

A sigh escaped Mr. Baker as he covered his face with one hand. "I told you. It broke last time I used it. I have to build another one, but we don't have money for the supplies."

"Can't you climb the tree then?" Mrs. Baker's voice had gone shrill. "If we don't fill this order, our shop will be ruined."

Mr. Baker gave a long glance at his belly before his eyelids fell. "No." His voice was barely a whisper.

"I can do it."

They both started at the sound of Elora's voice.

Mrs. Baker put a hand to her heart, but Mr. Baker was the one to reply. "That is kind of you to offer, dear, but I'm afraid it's impossible. We stripped the bark away from tree as a sort of experiment, but that failed miserably. The trunk is too slippery to climb, and even the lowest branches are too high to reach. No one can climb that tree."

With a nod, Mrs. Baker added, "We've gotten apples from our other trees just fine, but this one has been difficult. Usually the wind helps the apples fall when they're ripe." She shrugged. "But there hasn't been much wind this year." Her lips perked up. "Besides, we could never ask you to do something for us without giving anything in return."

Elora pursed her lips, hoping she didn't look too pathetic. "My sisters and I have no food."

Flour sat under the fingernails that Mrs. Baker touched to her lips. "Oh dear." She glanced at her husband, and they shared a look that caused Mr. Baker's eyes to narrow.

Since they were clearly in their own predicament, Elora couldn't blame them for being less than eager to help. But she wasn't about to give up either. A quick breath might help her get through the words. She gave the briefest glance toward her wrist. Maybe the ribbon truly would give her courage. "If I gather the apples for you, will you give us bread until my wedding in three weeks? And maybe a meat pie when you can spare it?"

The Bakers shared a look again, but the pleading in Mrs. Baker's eyes was unmistakable now. She leaned closer to her husband with her eyebrows tilting up just so. He let out a sigh and waved his hand toward the barrel behind him.

"Very well. If you fill that barrel with apples, we can give you bread until your wedding." He raised one finger and flashed her with a pointed stare. "But we need them by midday tomorrow or we won't be able to fill our order."

Elora bounced her head with quick nods.

Leaning back, Mr. Baker folded his arms. "Very good. You remember where our apple trees are, don't you?"

"I do." Elora glanced around their shop to look into the woods behind it. "I'll head out early tomorrow morning and bring you those apples in no time."

Her heart thumped as she said goodbye. How strange that a task as simple as gathering apples could fill her with excitement. She couldn't explain it, but the air seemed to buzz around her. Again.

Maybe the morning would bring a surprise to distract her from her impending doom.

CHAPTER 7

The sky was still dark when Elora rose the next morning. She climbed into her skirt and fastened her corset without bothering to put on the linen underslip she hated. The leather pouch of coins got tucked under her corset just before she buckled on the belt with her sheath and sword.

The red ribbon from Chloe had come undone during the night. Elora plucked it from the ground and slid a finger over its silky surface. If her sisters had been awake, she could have asked one of them to tie it around her wrist. Instead, she hoisted her foot onto the desk and tied the ribbon around her ankle.

She didn't need courage, exactly, since she was just gathering apples. But having something from her sisters seemed nice.

If things went according to plan, she would be back before the rest of the village awoke.

Her belt hung heavy on her hips with the sword in its sheath. Holding the hilt with one hand, she crept out the door. Chloe and Grace didn't even fidget in their sleep as the door creaked open.

Elora gave one last glance at the mess of blonde tresses and the soft reddish waves of hair on their pillows. Their faces held the most peaceful expressions they had managed since the fire. For a moment, Elora almost smiled.

Leaving her sisters was much easier knowing she wouldn't have to face the cottage again. And this time her efforts would provide them with food.

Shadows enveloped the street when she left the Rolfe's house. The crisp morning air bit into her bare arms now, but it would be perfect weather once she started climbing. Not even the softest breeze rustled as she headed toward the woods.

Still, something hummed around her. It prickled the hairs on the back of her neck. The strange sensation caused her to glance up at the dark sky above. Stars were already disappearing as a soft gray edged up the black horizon. The moon stole her attention more than anything.

A bright red hue shined on the surface of the full moon. Its normally yellow color was washed away in black and an orangey-red.

Blood moon.

Her parents had told her about the phenomenon before. They said it was an extremely rare occurrence and always signaled change. She huffed at the moon with a scowl, as if that would make any difference.

"You're too late," she muttered under her breath. That moon should have appeared the day of the fire. Her life couldn't possibly change more than it had then.

Her boots stomped over the dry ground, causing little clouds of dust to follow her every direction. By the time she reached the apple tree, her sour mood had only thickened. Her palm slid over the smooth surface of the stripped trunk, trying and failing to find a knot or bump for her shoes to grip.

Nothing.

The lowest branches loomed high overhead. She jumped and reached for them anyway. Luckily, no one was around to watch because the failure had been complete.

After rubbing her hands on her woolen skirt, she wrapped her arms around the tree and attempted to use her arms and boots to scoot up the trunk. The bare trunk was even more slippery than she imagined.

When she slid to the bottom of the trunk, she stepped back and brushed herself off. Lifting the hem of her skirt, she tied it in a knot at her thigh. She hadn't done such a thing since the fire, mostly because her mother would have fainted at the sight. It felt wrong to go against her wishes now that she was gone.

But this was desperate now. Elora's soft skirt only worked in unison with the trunk's slippery surface. The leather trousers she wore under the skirt would have a much better chance at gripping the stripped wood.

Preparing for a second attempt, she held the trunk with her legs instead of her feet. The new method failed as quickly as the old one had.

All those years of sword training had taught her to grunt at inopportune moments. Fortunately, no one stood near enough to hear the unseemly noise.

In desperation, she drew her sword. Doing so always made her feel better, no matter the occasion. The blade shined in the shadowy light. With one hand on the hilt, she moved the sword perpendicular to her body and on the opposite side of the tree. With her other hand, she gripped the pointed end of the sword. She had to arrange her hand just right so her fingers and thumb held tight to the blunt sides but not so tight that the sharp edge of the blade cut into her palm.

Next, she hoisted her boots up against the trunk, trying to use the sword as leverage. Already, the cold air wasn't cool enough. Sweat dripped down her hairline as, somehow, her muscles already ached from her sad attempts. The blade sank into the trunk, but her frail grip on the pointed end of her sword wasn't enough. She collapsed to the ground after only a few moments.

A loud grunt erupted from her lips as she swung her sword at the tree. With perfect form, she cut slices into the trunk. The rational side of her mind claimed that the cuts might make notches for her boots to grip. But deep down, she just wanted to take out her anger on the tree.

The sword swung through the air in arcs and jabs. Even though her opponent was no more than an unmoving tree, she wouldn't stop using perfect technique.

If the tree had been a breathing creature, it would have had several fatal wounds through it now. Her arms shook as she sliced a deep gash across the slippery trunk. Just as she did, a twig snapped behind her.

Her eyes widened as she whirled around. The sword pitched forward in attack. More sweat beaded across her forehead and neck, but this time it wasn't just from exertion. Fear tightened her grip on the hilt even as her years of training loosened it.

But nothing could stop her heart from pounding against her chest like a hammer.

A man stood before her.

The wicked smile on his face paired perfectly with his shoulder-length black hair. He wore a necklace that rested against his neck. Four strands of long, white beads lay one on top of the other. Dark red beads separated the long white ones. Fitted suede trousers covered his legs. He wore a tan coat made from leather that looked too soft to be leather. When he shifted, she could just make out a white feather tied inside the silky black strands of his hair.

The clothes weren't what made her stare. She had never seen someone dressed in such a way, but she was almost too distracted to even notice the clothes at all. Even his skin color barely registered in her mind. The light brown skin had copper undertones that shone even in the dark.

But none of those things had stolen her breath away. It was simply the way his features formed the most perfect face she had ever seen. No, not just the face. His strength, his stance, his eyes...

All of it perfect.

She lifted her jaw and shook her head a little. How cruel of fate to bring her face to face with the most beautiful man she'd ever meet, but only *after* she had gotten betrothed to another.

He quirked up an eyebrow, and her heart skipped in her chest. There was that dangerous smile again. "Your sword skill is most impressive."

Of course. Even his voice had to be perfect too. Low and strong with just the right amount of grind.

After a hard swallow, she tried to remember how to breathe. Her feet stumbled over the flat ground as she attempted to turn. Maybe talking would be easier when she couldn't see his chiseled features anymore.

"I know." Her words came out too fast while tingles spread up her arms. The sword went back in its sheath. Shaking her head again helped focus her attention back on the present moment. Only slightly, but she'd take it.

His voice rippled through the air from behind her. "I attempted to see you in action, but that sadly failed. Fortunately, I have it on good authority that your skill is great."

Not a single word came to her mind to respond. At least she was breathing normally again.

He took a step forward, leaning to the side to catch her eye. "Could you teach me how to sword fight like that?"

"Yes." The word slipped out before she could stop it.

The tree. *Focus on the tree.*

She swallowed again and stared at the notches she had cut in the trunk. Maybe her boots could grip onto those.

"Could you teach me right now?"

He did that leaning trick again, but she studiously turned away and pressed a finger inside one of the notches. It probably wasn't deep enough. Still, she wouldn't know until she tried.

The man cleared his throat.

"No." Her voice came out slightly higher pitched than she intended. She swallowed again. "Just because I *can* teach you doesn't mean I will. I am busy at the moment."

Wrapping her arms around the tree trunk, she dug her boot into one of the notches. It didn't seem sturdy enough, but maybe if she moved fast it could work. With a quick hoist, she attempted to use the notch while her other foot dug into another spot on the trunk.

The attempt ended with her landing hard on the ground. She let out a grunt and punched the tree with the edge of her hand.

A laugh jittered from the man's lips. "You act as if climbing this tree is a matter of life and death."

She whirled around to face him, which was a terrible idea because it sent her stomach flipping. Her eyebrows lowered as she attempted to glare at him. "It is." Her mouth pinched into a knot as she shot him with another glare. "If I don't gather these apples, my sisters and I will starve."

One side of his mouth twitched upward. "You only eat apples?"

"No." Another huff escaped her when she folded her arms over her chest. "I have an agreement with Mr. Baker. If I gather a barrel of apples, he'll…" She shook her head and turned back to the tree. "You know what? You don't need to know. I shouldn't bother to explain."

In a rare moment of clarity, she scanned the landscape around them. It didn't have much besides crusty dirt and brittle leaves, but there *was* a large rock nearby. Maybe it would help her reach the lowest branches.

As she began shoving it toward the tree, the man glanced from her to the rock and back again. He wore an infuriating smirk as she worked.

That attempt was probably the least effective at all.

The man seemed to finally understand that she was trying to gather apples from the tree. A strange calm settled over his face. "I can help you."

She glanced at him through the side of her eye before giving a quick nod. "That's a good idea." She clasped her hands together, forming a little table with them. "Hold your hands like this. I'll step on your hand, and you can hoist me up."

He raised a single eyebrow. "That might get you up the tree, but then how will you get down? Especially since, I assume," his eyes flicked over to the wooden barrel that sat near the tree, "you will be carrying apples on your way down."

A sigh escaped before she could stop it. Of course, he was right.

"Fear not." The man held out one hand, as if that might solve every problem the world had ever faced. "I have another way to help you."

But she wasn't listening anymore because the barrel had given her an idea. Why didn't she just turn it over and use *it* to reach the low branches? Yes, it would be difficult to carry the apples down with her, but she had a whole skirt to help with that. Then she could make a pile of apples on the ground until she had enough to fill the barrel.

She had already turned the barrel over by the time the man spoke again.

He cleared his throat, perhaps unhappy about how she wasn't giving him undivided attention. "The truth is, I am a fae prince."

She let out a long groan just as she got the barrel into the right spot. "I hear enough about Faerie as it is. I do not need a delusional fool in my life." After waving a flippant hand through the air, she said, "Just go back where you came from."

He raised that one eyebrow again and her stomach decided to flip flop inside her. She didn't even know her heart could beat so fast.

The man leaned toward her, his face looking more attractive with each moment that passed. "You do not fear me?"

Hopefully he could hear the indifference in her laugh. She gestured to her side. "Do you see this sword? I know how to use it well enough to defend myself. So no, I'm not afraid of you."

The barrel teetered as she climbed on top of it, but she still managed. With her arms reaching high, the lowest branches were still *just* out of reach. Her hands fell to her sides like weights.

"I could give you wings." The man didn't even flinch, even though he had just said the most preposterous thing she had ever heard.

"Excuse me?" Her hands landed on her hips.

Again, his face gave no hint of a tease. He almost seemed passive. He flapped his hands a few times and said, "Wings. You know, like on a butterfly or a pixie." He tilted his head to the side. "Do you have pixies?"

She hopped off the barrel and turned her back on him. "Stop talking nonsense."

After eyeing the tree again, another thought filled her mind. If only she had some rope. She could throw it over one of the low branches, then grab the two ends and use them to climb up the slippery trunk.

Luckily, she knew exactly where to find just such a rope. It sat at the bottom of the bag hidden in her special, knotty tree. It wouldn't take her long to retrieve it.

Somehow, she knew the man would follow behind her when she tromped deeper into the woods. What did come as a surprise was her reluctance to stop him. She glanced back, noticing the gentle way his long hair moved with each of his steps.

She chuckled to herself as she continued onward. He might have been crazy, but what harm could he really do? She might as well let him follow.

CHAPTER 8

The hidden tree didn't take long to find. Elora knew its knotty and gnarled trunk almost as well as she knew the woods.

From behind her, the man's feet moved quietly across the dry ground. It didn't bother her until a twig snapped nearby. The sound came from behind her but not directly behind her. Someone or some*thing* was in the woods with them.

She whirled around to identify it but came face to face with the man instead. For a moment, his eyes caught hold of hers, mesmerizing her until every part of her had gone still. They were beautiful, almost too magical. But then he blinked, and the moment was gone. His eyes dulled to a rich brown that lacked dimension.

"Would you like to have a pair of wings? You could easily gather those apples without any difficulty." His eyebrow bounced as he spoke.

Remembering the twig snap, she glanced to the side where the noise had originated. Nothing was there but trees and brush and cracked, dusty earth.

She frowned and turned back to her special tree. "Why would you help me? And don't say it's out of the kindness of your heart."

He let out a chuckle that held more contempt than she expected. "I promise, there is no kindness in my heart." After stepping up beside her, he placed a hand on her forearm. "I need your help."

His proximity did not help with the tension inside her. She wriggled out of his grasp and twisted up her mouth. "*My* help?"

With an indifferent nod, he brushed a bit of dirt from his soft leather coat. "Yes, I need you to teach me how to use a sword. Everyone expects me to use magic in an upcoming…" He trailed off as his head tilted to the side. Then he gave a short nod. "*Tournament* of sorts."

When her eyes widened, her arms dropped to her sides purely of their own accord. "A tournament?"

He leaned one shoulder against the tree trunk, coming far too close to her own shoulder. The subtle smirk that graced his lips brought a thrill through her. "I assure you it is much better than any mortal tournament could be."

Nothing could have controlled the skittering of her heart. Her eyes stared into his as she brought a hand against her heart. "Can I participate in it?"

"No."

Just like that, the spell was broken. Her heart dropped as she let out a sigh. Apparently, not even made-up Faerie tournaments would allow a woman to fight.

Running a finger over the bark of the tree, the man continued. "Only select fae are allowed to participate."

His leather coat brushed across her bare arm, which caused her to take in a sharp breath. It was *much* softer than it looked. She moved away from the tree. "What's the prize?"

He glanced at his nails, but his indifferent mask couldn't fool her. Whatever he was about to say clearly meant something to him. Glancing up, he said, "A throne."

Skepticism took hold again as she shook her head. "But I thought you said you were a prince already." Her head cocked to the side. "Do you have to fight your brothers for the throne?"

The man gave a hurried shake of the hand. "No, I am already the ruler for my court." He moved his hand in a little flourish before giving a short bow with his head. "I am Prince Brannick from the Court of Bitter Thorn. This testing is a chance for me to become High King, the ruler over all six courts in Faerie."

He hadn't even finished before she grabbed a low branch and hoisted herself up the tree. Maybe his name was Brannick, but that was probably the only true thing he had said. While climbing, she rolled her eyes. "Is this how leaders are always chosen in Faerie?"

Brannick remained at the base of the tree, apparently unconcerned by her decision to climb it. "No, but the high king is dying. His son poisoned him and then the high king found out and executed him. Now the high king has no heir, and the poison will soon kill him."

After opening her hidden bag, she dug through the chainmail for her rope. "Forgive me, but Faerie doesn't sound like a very nice place. A prince poisoned his own father?"

The rope landed in a heap at the man's feet. He looked at it for a moment before giving a small shrug. "Faerie is not nice, but it is enchanting." When she dropped to the ground, he flashed her a hopeful look. "Will you help me?"

She raised an eyebrow at him that hopefully conveyed every ounce of the skepticism inside her.

"If I give you wings?" he amended.

After picking the rope off the ground, Elora wound it around her arm. "Wings don't seem very practical for a *mortal* like me. How will they fit around my clothes? What if they frighten other mortals?"

With a finger tapping his chin, the man gave a thoughtful look off into the distance. Then his eyebrows shot up his forehead. "What if I make them retractable? You can bring them out or put them away at your discretion. They will be ready when you need them and easily hidden when you don't."

It took a fair amount of effort to stop a snicker from escaping her lips. She hoisted the rope onto her shoulder and began walking toward the apple tree. With a sideways glance at the man, she asked, "Can I choose what color wings I get?"

He took several quick steps to catch up to her. "Sadly, no. I will create the wings using the essence inside you. In a way, the color has already been chosen." He gestured his hand outward with a smile. "The color is already inside of you."

A long sigh puffed out of her mouth.

His eyebrows bounced up as he looked her in the eye. "Think of all the ways you could use wings. You could get those apples. You could reach the top of any tree." A grin tilted his mouth upward with a rebellious sort of air that her heart recognized. "You could fly higher than a bird."

Her chest rose as she took in a deep breath. An involuntary wistfulness filled every part of her body. What if she could really fly? It seemed ridiculous, but it also seemed more incredible than she could possibly imagine. A tournament was one thing, but all she really dreamed about was adventure. *Anything* to escape her upcoming marriage.

"I propose a bargain." Brannick smiled, but a flash of greed glinted in his eye. "I will give you wings that you may use or hide at your discretion. In return, you must travel with me to Faerie and help me become High King."

It didn't matter how silly the conversation was anymore. The idea of wings that could take her far away from her betrothed was enough to make her play along. Maybe they could even take her to a place where a woman would be allowed to fight. She drew her eyebrows together as they walked, as if thinking very carefully about his proposition.

"I don't like these terms. How long would I stay in Faerie? I can't stay there forever; my sisters need me. And I don't like the promise I have to make. I have to help you become High King? That's too vague. If you need me to teach you sword fighting, then you should specify that in your bargain."

Was that a hint of admiration in the man's eye? A smirk appeared on his lips for the briefest moment before it disappeared. "Very well, mortal. I will give you wings that you may use or hide at your discretion. In return, you will come to Faerie and train me in sword skill until I become High King."

She raised an eyebrow at him while folding her arms over his chest.

He seemed to understand her question even without it being spoken. He nodded and added, "Or until the high king deems me unfit to take his place."

The apple tree came into view, and she lowered the rope from off her shoulder. Letting out a chuckle, she shrugged. "Fine."

A wild excitement filled his eyes. "You agree?"

With another shrug, she prepared to throw the rope over the lowest branch. "Why not?" With wings, she could find her own adventures. Tournaments would pale in comparison to the excitement she could have. Though it was all pretend, the dream of it still thrilled her.

The man smirked. At that exact moment, a rush of wind blew all around her. Dust lifted in a thick cloud, and several leaves dropped away from their branches. Her skirt rustled against her leather-covered legs.

With the rope in her hands, she turned slowly to look at the man more carefully. The air had been so still that season, which made the wind seem magical.

Just then, another twig snapped. It sounded like it came from directly next to the man. When she went to look in that direction, Brannick tilted his head and caught her eye.

He raised his hands in front of his chest, his fingers straight and twisting in the air. "Interesting," he said as his eyes narrowed. "You have fae blood in you."

She let out a scoff and shook her head at him.

Her reaction didn't stop his fingers nor the strange look in his eye. "Not much. It comes from at least three generations back. It is not uncommon for mortals to have fae blood." His head tilted. "Do not get your hopes up; you are still fully mortal. But it does make the wings easier for me to create."

Blinking seemed like the only response to such a declaration. She wanted to glare, but even that seemed impossible.

After a few moments, the slightest smile appeared on his lips. "I think you will be pleased with the color. They are more beautiful than I expected."

His eyes shifted, changing in that subtle way they had earlier. Everything about him seemed more incredible than before. Brighter. More beautiful. Enchanting.

She shook her head to force her thoughts to clear. When she looked again, he was as handsome as ever but not otherwordly.

She let out a sigh and rolled her eyes. "Are you done?"

He offered a mischievous smirk in return. "I am. Would you like to see?"

Without any warning at all, her heart thumped hard enough to tighten her chest. Why did the words seem so terrifying? This man was clearly nothing more than a fool.

But then a flutter from the corner of her eye caused her stomach to leap into her throat. She clutched Brannick's arm with the strength of steel. The flutter shifted and the edge of a wing came into view.

A *wing*.

Her vision seemed to close in from the sides as a woozy feeling took over. But the moment passed when the edge of a wing appeared on her other side.

It had a translucent white sheen that glittered even in the dark morning. It looked purple until the light caught it and then it looked blue. But a moment later, the purple hue was back again. Silvery veins ran through the wings. The edges were curved and twirly in all the right places.

The look of it alone was enough to steal her breath away, but her heart was ready to give out too because she couldn't just see the wings. She could *feel* them. She could *move* them. They were like a limb she had always had but never quite been able to control. Now they eagerly bent to her will.

Two thoughts struck her at the same moment, both gripping her with a thrilling fear.

First, what if these wings and this prince were actually real? And even more terrifying, what if they weren't?

CHAPTER 9

Gripping her sword hilt did nothing for Elora's sanity. Even closing her eyes didn't help. She could still feel the wings on her back. The *wings*.

After taking three of the deepest breaths of her life, she whispered, "I don't believe in Faerie."

Brannick rested one shoulder against a nearby tree with a curious gaze toward the sky. "Your moon is red."

Both hands went over her eyes as she tried to shake some semblance of reality back into herself. But now, the blood moon itself seemed to be staring at the very real pair of wings on her back. "It's not usually like that."

"I know." The man—who may have been fae after all— moved away from the tree. "Are you finished with your meltdown yet? I thought gathering these apples was a matter of life and death."

"It is." She whirled around to face him. As soon as she spat the words from her lips, a weight seemed to press down on her shoulders. "But..." Her eyes narrowed as she took a closer look at the man. "How do I know if this is real or not?"

Now he was the one shaking his head. "You said you had some arrangement pertaining to the apples, correct?"

Her last grip on reality allowed her to nod in answer to his question. But a shudder went through her when she tensed her muscles and the wings flapped in response.

Brannick massaged his temples as he let out a long sigh. "Fae never interfere with arrangements or bargains, so you can collect the apples. But could you please *use* the wings? The creation magic inside them will make it easy to control them, but that will wear off soon."

Was he still speaking? She had stopped paying attention and could only focus on the short, stiff breaths that escaped her mouth much faster than they should have.

With a scoff, he shook his head again. "Oh, never mind."

It took two steps for him to reach the apple tree. He gripped the slippery tree trunk with no effort at all. His feet flew up the tree as if he was climbing a ladder. After another breath, he stood on one of the lower branches and stuffed apples into his pockets. No barrel. No rope. Not even a sheen of sweat graced his forehead, and yet, he had climbed the tree.

Her jaw hung slack when he jumped to the ground in a single, graceful bound. The apples in his arms and pockets went neatly into the barrel.

His eyes flicked to hers as he set the last of his apples inside. "We are going to Faerie as soon as these are gathered."

And then he was up the tree again for another armful of apples.

The impossibility of the situation still rocked through her but seeing him climb the tree with so little effort sent a spark through her chest. She liked being the best, and she definitely didn't like being told what to do. Both of those qualities may have had something to do with her decision to learn sword fighting.

They also gave her the urge to gather apples faster than he could. How strange that a little competition was all it took to get her to focus. With her eyes on the tree, she attempted to flap her wings enough to raise her into the air.

Easy. Her feet lifted off the ground and into the dry leaves of the tree with only a few internal commands. After untying the knot in her skirt, she gathered apples into its woolen fabric.

The command to flutter back to the ground came instinctually, barely requiring more than a thought. Brannick had taken a few trips up and down the tree, but the apples in her skirt far outnumbered those he had gathered. Already, the barrel had been filled more than halfway.

A second rise into the branches sent her heart soaring. The fear and anxiety in her stomach settled. They were soon replaced by a pure, unadulterated delight unlike anything she had ever experienced.

On her third rise into the tree branches, Brannick jumped down to the ground. He glanced up at her with mild interest. At almost the same moment, her wing flaps suddenly required more effort. The muscles in her back strained against their movements.

While dropping apples into her skirt, the wings jerked, dropping her slightly closer to the ground. Her heart leapt into her throat. "What's happening?"

The unconcerned voice of Brannick drifted up to her. "My magic inside your wings is wearing off. They are becoming fully yours, and you haven't learned to fly. You will have to practice the skill once we get to Faerie."

She fluttered to the ground with another skirt-full of apples. A strange tightness thickened her throat as she placed the apples inside the barrel. She glanced at the fae, only somewhat fearful of how he would take her words. When she placed the last apple inside the now-full barrel, she nodded to herself. It didn't actually matter if he liked it or not.

"I'm not going with you to Faerie." She folded her arms over her chest as she said it.

Apparently, her attempt at looking determined had done a less than perfect job. He chuckled at her words and didn't even bother to respond.

Her eyebrows lowered as she folded her arms tighter. "I only made that promise because I thought you were a fool. I have to take care of my sisters. I can't leave." The words probably hurt her more than they could possibly bother him. He'd never know how much she dreamed of going anywhere but to the village with her betrothed.

But that didn't matter. Without the wedding, her sisters were doomed to poverty and starvation. Whatever throne Brannick wanted to win, Elora still had to take care of her sisters.

Annoyingly, her words had no effect on him at all. Far too much amusement lingered in his smirk. "Is there a place you are supposed to deliver these apples, or can we leave them here?"

This fight wasn't over yet, but for now, she'd accept the distraction. If only so it could give her a moment to think of a more persuasive argument. "I must bring them to the Bakers' home." She gestured at the path she had taken to get there. "It's in the village."

Brannick tapped his chin as he stared off to the side for a moment. When he looked back at her, he seemed surer than before. "Their house will smell like bread, correct?"

"Yes?" Her eyes narrowed as she tried to determine why he would ask such a question.

With a nod, he lifted the barrel of apples with even less effort than he used to climb the tree. "I will deliver the apples. As part of our bargain, you must stay here until I return."

A snort erupted from her mouth. He couldn't find the Bakers' home just because it smelled like bread. And anyway, it didn't seem like a great idea to let him roam the village on his own.

Even as she decided to follow him, he disappeared down the path with truly impossible speed. Her eyes widened as a subtle realization dawned on her. Brannick *was* fae. The wings should have confirmed it, but she'd been too busy grappling with the fact that she had actual wings—the man himself had escaped her scrutiny. Did that mean he was truly a prince as well?

Her jaw tightened in a clench as she glared down the path. That only meant going with him would be even more fascinating than she originally imagined.

The slightest hint of regret passed through her. Why did she have to be the oldest?

Lifting her chin, she accepted her fate as best she could. She *wouldn't* abandon her sisters. No matter what Brannick was, she wouldn't let him take her to Faerie. She'd just have to hide from him until he left her alone.

Deciding to run deeper into the woods, she tried to lift a foot. But it didn't move. After a little head shake, she tried to lift the other foot. It remained rooted to the ground. Perhaps she just needed momentum.

78

She rocked her shoulders forward and back until she had enough power to swing herself forward.

Her feet did not move.

Dust puffed out around the palms of her hands as they slapped the cracked dirt of the ground. With a huff, she pushed herself to an upright position once again. Feeling her wings at her back, she decided to try another method.

Maybe the wings wouldn't work well without practice, but they might still move her. She willed the wings to flap, but they stayed as still as her feet. After several desperate attempts to use them, she ordered them to hide in her back. Though they obeyed with hardly any effort, it did nothing to change her predicament.

A loud grunt came out of her next. Normally, she didn't even notice, but now, she desperately wanted to do more than just grunt.

Her eyes glanced up at the red-hued moon in the dark sky. It looked brighter than it had before, almost as if mocking her. Was this her punishment for believing the fire was the biggest change she'd have in life?

Taking a deep breath, she exerted every part of her body in an attempt to move her feet.

Nothing changed.

Just as scream bubbled at the back of her throat, Brannick dashed through the trees to her side. He ran with incredible speed but moved as if taking a leisurely stroll.

"I'm not coming with you." She shot him an extra hateful glare to be certain he understood.

His lips pressed together. "You do not have a choice. You entered the bargain. Now you are bound by it."

With a wave of his hand, a spinning tunnel appeared directly in front of her. The tunnel seemed to be made of green, brown, and black whirls, but she closed her eyes tight before her curiosity could be too entranced by it. The sound of fluttering leaves and the crisp scent of rain drifted toward her. Was that a hint of wild berries in the air?

Before she could peek through one eyelid, she slammed her eyes shut even tighter. "I am *not* going."

He let out an exasperated sigh, but then went a little too silent. Despite her better judgement, she opened her eyes just enough to manage a quick glance.

A sly smile played on his lips. "Let me make it easier for you." He gave a gentle wave of the hand, as if beckoning.

A sweet scent filled the air. Her arms drooped in response. Her eyelids felt heavy and scratchy against her eyes. Just when her consciousness seemed ready to slip away, her eyes snapped open again. She shook the strange sleepy sensation out of her head and limbs.

Brannick's dark brown eyebrows lowered. "How did you do that?"

"Do what?" It seemed like a good moment for another glare.

His nose twitched as he sniffed the air around her. When he reached for a lock of her hair, she couldn't lean away fast enough to stop him from smelling it. But it didn't seem to answer his question. Soon, he bent at the waist and lifted the hem of her leather trousers.

If her feet hadn't been stuck to the ground, he would have gotten a swift kick to the nose. He raised an eyebrow at her as he stood upright again. "You do not believe in Faerie, yet you wear a ward to protect yourself against fae enchantments?"

"What?" But then she remembered the red silk from Chloe that she had tied around her ankle. "You mean the ribbon?"

He narrowed his eyes, glancing up and down her body. She's seen a similar look in the eyes of tournament opponents. Brannick was trying to determine how big of a threat she was.

Good. He deserved to stew a little.

Now *he* folded his arms over his chest. "It won't protect you from the bargain. You made it willingly."

She held her hands out, begging him to understand. "But I thought it was a game. Pretend." She gulped as she glanced toward the village. "My sisters need me." She shook her head while attempting to rip her feet from off the ground. "And I have a wedding coming up. I can't leave the village."

A sneer passed over his face as he leaned in close to her. "I am going to regret this bargain; I can already tell."

Her fists tightened at her sides. She looked him straight in the eye. "I'm not going to Faerie."

"Yes, mortal. You are."

With the flick of his hand, a root snapped through the crusty ground and hit hard against the back of her knees. She stumbled forward, straight toward the tunnel filled with green, black, and brown swirls. Apparently, her feet *could* move but only if she moved in the direction Brannick wanted.

It took every ounce of willpower to stop her feet from stumbling. They landed less than a step away from the swirling tunnel that was filled with the smells of a damp forest.

The tree root snapped again, slamming even harder against the back of her knees. Balance betrayed her as her feet moved off the cracked dirt of her woods and into the tunnel filled with black briars and smudges of brilliant color.

Despite her insistence to stay, Faerie hurtled forward to greet her.

CHAPTER 10

Elora's palms landed heavy on moist soil. Bright green blades of grass pushed through the damp surface, tickling her fingers.

Birds chirped above her, but their song was accompanied by other small noises that were difficult to decipher. It sounded like the twinkling laughter of miniscule creatures.

Smells slammed into her from every angle, but none could be described as unpleasant. Wet tree trunks and fresh moss overpowered the air. The subtle scent of wildflowers and plump berries laced through, providing a depth of smell she had never experienced before.

Out of necessity, she closed her eyes before she could be entranced by any of the sights Faerie had to offer. It didn't matter if this was the most magical place she'd ever seen. She still had to get home.

Swift footsteps sounded behind her, heralding the appearance of Brannick. From behind, a whoosh of air blew her hair into her face. Her eyes remained closed, but she guessed the wind meant that the swirling tunnel they'd entered through had now disappeared.

Her arms shook with a combination of terror and excitement so feral, she could barely keep herself breathing.

I must not like it here. She took in a deep breath, attempting to calm her racing heart. *I must go home to my sisters.*

With that internal scolding, she finally decided to open her eyes.

A wolf stared back at her. Kindness glinted in his eyes, but that didn't take away the razor-sharp fangs in his mouth. It didn't matter how soft and beautiful his black fur seemed. The creature probably could have ripped out her throat in a single bite.

With a yelp, she jumped off the soil and bounded toward the nearest tree. "Where did that thing come from?" Her voice wavered as she clumsily tripped over stones and moss to get away.

One thing wolves couldn't do was climb trees. She hoped.

"Calm down, mortal." Brannick sounded bored. "Blaz has always been with me, even in the mortal realm. He will not hurt you."

His words offered little comfort. Elora reached out for the nearest tree. The dark brown trunk had brilliant green moss growing over it. The moss was so brilliant, it almost looked emerald.

"Not that one!" Brannick grabbed her shoulder from behind and forced her away from the tree. He let out a scoff. "Have you no respect?"

She had turned away from him when he pulled her, but she could still see him from the corner of her eye while she sucked in a breath.

The wolf—Blaz apparently—sat on his haunches next to the fae. He looked at her curiously, but that didn't make any sense because he was a wolf. How could a wolf be curious?

Even though she had accepted the reality of Faerie, a part of her still hoped she had hit her head too hard or that she was having the most vivid dream of her life.

Brannick began speaking to the tree. The *tree*.

At least that seemed to be what he was doing. Not that it made any sense.

"I told you it was bold to assume a mortal would cooperate. Even if her skills are as great as you claim, she will be trouble. I can already tell."

When he turned toward Elora, she snapped her head away, refusing to let him have proper eye contact.

She lifted her chin into the air. "Excuse me for being combative after you tricked me into a bargain."

Braving a glance at the fae, her eyes were quickly distracted by a pair of eyes blinking inside the tree. Her heart fluttered as she tried to make sense of what she was seeing. The tree was blinking. The. *Tree*.

But then a woman with dark brown skin stepped straight out of the tree trunk.

Elora sucked in a gasp. Her body tilted at a strange angle after the unexpected sight. The soft soil caught her boots as she tripped backward, trying to catch her balance.

She tumbled right into Brannick, who caught her by the shoulders with his surprisingly strong arms. After wrenching herself from his grasp, she whirled around to face him. Another gasp went through her at the sight of him. "What happened to your face?" Of its own accord, her fingers reached out to touch his cheek.

He had been handsome before, strikingly so, but it was nothing to how he looked now. His light brown skin radiated with a copper glow. The black hair falling just past his shoulders looked glossy and soft. His ears poked through the black strands, coming up to delicate points.

And his eyes…

She had forgotten how to breathe. She could only soak in his frightfully perfect appearance. Perfect.

It didn't even bother her when his lips raised in an arrogant smirk. "This is my true form. I used a glamour in the mortal realm to appear more human."

"A glamour? What is a glamour?" It took every bit of willpower she had not to brush a finger across his lips. Why had she been so eager to escape his arms?

A chuckle from the fae's lips broke her from her trance. After shaking her head, she pushed him away. It must have been another fae trick. Why else would the sight of him affect her so?

As she stomped away, she took great care to keep her eyes on the ground. Faerie had already fascinated her too much for her own good. This wasn't the time to be swept away by it.

"I demand to be taken back to my home." Home. The word escaped her before she had even realized she was going to say it. Her thoughts flitted to her blue-shuttered cottage. And then they rounded almost as fast to billowing smoke and crackling embers.

Her eyes slammed shut, and she grabbed her head with both hands. *Now* was not the time to remember that fire.

"Hush, child. You must calm down."

Elora jumped. She had forgotten about the woman who had come out of the tree. Something about the woman's voice sent an inexplicable calm through her. Elora turned to get a better look.

The woman's dark brown skin looked just as dark as the tree she had come out of. Emerald hair even more brilliant than the moss fell down in soft waves past the woman's waist. She had the same pointed ears as Brannick. Her eyes seemed to hold the wisdom of many years, but her skin looked soft and young.

"You're a dryad." Elora swallowed. For a moment, she almost felt guilty for seeing such a creature when Chloe had been the one to believe in them.

The dryad nodded. Her gauzy light brown dress fluttered lightly in the wind. "Yes, child." Her eyes twinkled, and she suddenly looked very pleased with herself. "I assume that you've heard about creatures like me in your mortal poems?"

Elora could only blink in response. How could the woman have known?

The dryad touched Elora on the arm. The gesture could only be described as motherly, but the woman still looked as young as Elora.

Something told her the dryad was actually much older.

"I am Kaia." The dryad turned to Brannick. "She will cooperate. We must let her get settled. I will give her a room in the castle."

Tingles went through Elora's arms. A castle? She tried to breathe indifference into herself, but her limbs didn't seem eager to comply. Instead, her heart pattered in her chest, and a trill of excitement shot through her. She had always dreamed of visiting a castle.

The thoughts came laced with guilt as she remembered her sisters. Her fingers stiffened while she tried to damper her excitement. She had important things to do in the mortal realm. She would not allow herself to be seduced by the magic of Faerie.

"Fine," Brannick said, touching a hand to his forehead. "Just make sure her room is far away from mine." He grimaced as his hand fell to his side. "I still think we should have found someone in Faerie to teach me sword fighting."

Kaia raised a delicate eyebrow, still looking impossibly old and impossibly young all at the same time. "If someone in Faerie taught you sword fighting, then everyone would know you planned to use the skill during the testing. You would lose the element of surprise."

The bone-bead necklace around Brannick's throat shifted when he gave a hard swallow. "But why did the most skilled sword fighter have to be this stubborn," his nose twitched as he looked Elora's way, "fool."

Her hands clenched, ready to teach him how accomplished she was at punching too. But his next words stopped her in her tracks.

"I wanted to learn from Theobald, the greatest sword fighter and sword maker in the mortal realm." He frowned. "But, as you predicted, I could not arrive at the right place."

Kaia shrugged, gesturing toward Elora. "This mortal will do just as well."

The words only halfway registered in Elora's mind. Everything inside her had stilled. She could have been made of stone for how little she moved. The words jangled inside, but they wouldn't stick. They wouldn't settle.

"Mortal?" The man fae poked her in the arm. "Has it fallen asleep?"

"Theobald is my father," she whispered.

Brannick's eyebrows rose before his eyes flicked to the pommel of her sword. He brushed a thumb over the raised shield mark on top of it. His eyes lingered over the star inside the shield.

"That explains this mark." Brannick tapped the symbol once more before pulling his hand away.

Leaning forward, her voice darkened. "How do you know about my father?"

The fae shrugged. "His skills are known throughout Faerie. He made a bargain with a fae named Ansel. If he beat the fae in a duel, he was promised strength against his enemies and protection from all fae until after he had lived a happy life."

At Brannick's side, the dryad nodded with a knowing glimmer in her eye. "That is probably why you could not arrive at the right place. The magic of the bargain must have kept you from finding him."

"He's dead." The words tasted bitter in Elora's mouth. "My mother too." She whipped around just so she wouldn't have to face them. A tight pain went through her chest as she tried to swallow. "You have to take me back to the mortal realm. I'll find someone else to train you with a sword."

A sound erupted from Brannick's mouth that was halfway between a snort and a grunt. "It is too late now. The bargain has been made."

She spun on her heel and slammed her hands to her hips. "But my sisters need me. And I have a wedding coming up."

"Your sisters will be fine." He touched a hand to his forehead as he turned to walk away. "And you won't miss your wedding. In the morning, you must meet me in the training room, and we will begin. Kaia, take her to her room." He glanced over his shoulder at the dryad. "And lock her inside."

A lump grew in Elora's throat at the words, but it hardened to stone when the dryad nodded without question.

"Come, child."

Not seeing any alternative, Elora stomped after the emerald-haired dryad. The excitement of finally getting to see a real-life castle was already thrumming through her. She did her best to ignore it by keeping her eyes on the damp soil just ahead of her feet.

Moss, grass, and black briars filled the small amount of the forest that she allowed herself to see. Even though the moss was spongy and fresh, she tried to focus on the sharp thorns of the briars.

The last thing she needed was to fall in love with her prison.

When climbing a lush set of moss-covered stone steps, she focused on the black, decayed bits of moss. After entering the castle of black walls and high-reaching spires, she pretended the black came from mold.

She refused to admire the many windows and gentle breeze blowing through the open halls. The vines, and even trees, growing *inside* the castle walls managed to flip her stomach in delight. But she squashed the feeling down almost as fast. Pinching herself helped to keep the scowl on her face.

People and creatures wandered through the halls, but she wouldn't look closely at any of them.

Even inside the castle, forest sounds abounded. Rustling leaves seemed to flutter down every hallway. When boots stepped over the stone floor, it sounded just like gravel crunching. Black thorns and briars wove through many of the halls, twisting and creaking in the whispering wind.

By the time Kaia stopped in front of a wooden door, Elora almost wished she had paid more attention to the path they'd taken. How could she escape the castle if she couldn't remember how to get out?

But that thought was replaced by another unwanted shot of thrill. Now she'd just have to explore the castle. She tempered the excitement by reminding herself of her sisters all alone at the Rolfes' home.

"Enjoy," Kaia said as she gestured inside the room.

A wide-open window filled the wall opposite from where Elora stood. She couldn't help but smile. "How does Brannick expect me to stay in here?"

"*Prince* Brannick." A slight twitch appeared across Kaia's forehead.

Elora refused to make the correction the dryad suggested. She just smirked and stepped into the room. "Even if you lock the door, I can just climb out the window."

The playful look in Kaia's eye quickly turned devious. "Without fae magic, you cannot open a door to the mortal realm." A smirk played across her face, making her appear even more frightening than before. "And I won't be using that kind of a lock."

The dryad disappeared into the hall before shutting the door. A shimmer of gold light burst from the door and quivered out through the rest of the room. It continued to shimmer as it rested alongside the edges of the room. In a flash, the gold sparkled in a brilliant light before it disappeared.

A weight dropped in Elora's stomach.

The shimmer of gold had lined the room perfectly. Almost like a barrier.

CHAPTER

11

Sunlight stroked Elora's eyes the next morning, waking her from a peaceful sleep.

For a brief moment before consciousness took hold, she snuggled into the softness of her bed. A tightly woven wool blanket covered her from her shoulders to past her toes. The white wool fringe on the blanket's edge tickled her neck and chin. Green, brown, and black designs were woven into the blanket. Most prominent was the black diamond in the center. It had large, brown triangles on top and below it. Small, lighter brown triangles surrounded it.

After making several failed attempts at escaping the room the night before, Elora had spent most of the evening running her fingers over the impossibly soft geometric designs of the blanket.

Now, she jerked herself to a sitting position. *Escape.* The word rang through her mind. The last of the fuzziness in her eyes disappeared when she rubbed them.

The stone ground felt surprisingly warm beneath her feet. A cool wind blew in from the large open window. Even with a window taller than her, the bed still felt closed off from the rest of the room. It sat behind a mossy stone partition, which ran directly behind a tree.

A *tree.*

Inside a room in the castle. Its reddish-brown roots stretched over the stone floor, as if the castle itself could provide more nutrients than soil. The sound of chirping birds and trickling streams, combined with the large tree and cool breeze, made it feel as if her room sat outside in the forest.

In fact, it was even better than the forest. No bugs flew around and not a trace of dew could be found. Soft, green lights floated near the ceiling. Despite the early morning hour, the room also seemed to maintain a perfectly pleasant temperature.

Elora dug the heels of her hands into her eyes before shaking her head hard. This was *not* the time to admire her surroundings. As she had done many times the night before, she rubbed a finger across the silk ribbon around her ankle.

Her sisters' faces appeared in her mind while guilt thrashed through her. How could she enjoy this adventure when her sisters needed her so badly?

Sliding off the bed, she moved across the room. A large stone basin sat behind a wooden wardrobe and a wall of hanging vines. The evening before, she had wondered what purpose the stone basin served. The fact that the wardrobe and vines provided privacy from the doorway gave her a bit of a clue. Now, steaming hot water filled it. A little table made of wicker stood next to it, black briars woven throughout. Sitting

92

on top was a smooth wooden tray covered in clay pots of various sizes.

Her muscles ached just looking at the bath. Even though she refused to enjoy anything the castle had to offer, she took a few steps forward. The oils and soaps inside the clay pots smelled like crisp rain and fresh wildflowers.

She looked down at the dirt smudges covering her bare arms. The Rolfes had been good to bring Elora and her sisters into their home, but they only had small washing basins with which to clean. Elora hadn't had a proper bath since well before the fire.

Maybe she didn't need to feel guilty about it though. Maybe she could enjoy a Faerie bath but still hate Faerie. That was all the justification she needed to slip inside.

After removing the red ribbon from her ankle, she made a note to herself to put it on before any of her clothes. The ward had already protected her from a fae enchantment. She wasn't about to go anywhere in Faerie without it. Except inside the bath.

When she massaged the scented oils and soaps into her body, a contented sigh escaped her lips. It didn't matter how rich Dietrich Mercer was. He couldn't possibly find items as fine as these. Nothing so exquisite existed in the mortal realm.

Afterward, she used a smaller wool blanket that hung over a wooden frame to dry off. A soft smile remained on her lips as she ran a hand over her perfectly moisturized skin. It almost gave her the urge to look inside the wooden wardrobe. Would there be clothes inside?

Dropping the blanket, she shook the thought away. Her sturdy purple skirt would do just fine. The thin wool fabric seemed far scratchier than she had ever noticed before. Still, she wouldn't let such a simple thing dissuade her from wearing her mortal clothes. After all, the skirt and corset were the only things she had left from her mother. Next, she put on her belt and slid her sword into the sheath. The blanket remained on the ground near the stone basin.

Taking in the room around her sent a flush through her, which she simply couldn't suppress. Maybe being in Faerie wasn't *so* bad. She still had three weeks until her wedding. Thanks to her apple gathering, her sisters would have food until then. Perhaps being bound by this bargain didn't have to be so terrible. As long as she didn't stay in Faerie for too long.

A knock sounded at the door, making her nearly jump out of the boots she was just tying up. She leapt for the door, feeling like she had left something behind, but she couldn't think of what.

The wooden door was weathered. It looked soft, with cracks and moss growing through it. Around the doorframe, black vines with sharp thorns wound in and through the wood. Before she could reach the leather strap that worked like a doorknob, the door swung toward her.

With a tiny gasp, her feet toppled backward. Just as she caught her balance, a stocky creature appeared in the doorway. He had puffy round cheeks, a thick mustache, and a white pointed beard that fell down to his chest. He wore a long green shirt with a tan leather belt wrapped around his belly. Suede pants and soft leather boots completed the look.

Without the pointed brown hat sitting on his head, he stood no higher than her waist. His eyes were all black, just like a bug's. He held a wooden spear with feathers and leather strings tied to it at different heights. The sharp tip had been carved from stone, but that didn't make it any less lethal.

His fair skin and pointed ears turned red when he let out a grunt. "Prince Brannick asked me to escort you to the training room." His voice was gruff, his eyes deadly.

Her first instinct was to argue. But the words died in her throat when the creature began grumbling under his breath.

"A captain of the guard like me shouldn't be sent on such menial tasks." He flashed a glare at her before turning back to the hallway. In a flash, gold shimmered all around the edges of her room before it vanished again.

Biting her bottom lip, Elora stepped one toe out of the room. The dryad's barrier enchantment must have worn off because unlike the evening before, she could move out of the room.

Sucking in a gleeful breath, she reached for her sword hilt. Fighting such a short creature wouldn't be too difficult.

While she was still lifting her blade, the creature slammed the handle of his spear against her chest with surprising strength. He pinned her against the wall and narrowed his all-black eyes. "Do not think you can catch a gnome like me off guard." He rattled his weapon against her. "I am good with a spear, and I am even better with my fists."

He shot her a final sneer before pulling back his spear and gesturing down the hallway. Under his breath, he grumbled again. "The prince said she would be trouble, but still. It is my sacred duty to protect this castle and its court, yet, I am left to deal with a weak *mortal*."

A lump formed in Elora's mouth as she sauntered after the gnome. She was used to being looked down upon for being a woman, but now she was going to be looked down upon for simply being mortal?

It wasn't like she had a choice in the matter. But the strange anger made her remember the gnome was angry too. Maybe there was some way to use that to her advantage.

She sidled up to the bearded creature and held her hands behind her back in the demure way her mother had taught her. "You're the captain of the guard, are you?"

"I can smell you scheming, mortal." The gnome responded without even glancing her way. "Do not bother. I am too busy protecting Bitter Thorn to be tricked or beguiled by you."

She was struck with the urge to stick her tongue out at him.

A moment later, a creature just larger than a rabbit scurried past them. It had brown skin with a bulbous chin and long spindly fingers. Its big eyes and flappy ears looked strange paired with its short, squat nose. It wore a brown leather coat and green pants.

Her feet had stopped at the sight of the creature. Inexplicably, she had touched one hand to her chest as she sucked in breath.

The gnome let out a gravelly chuckle. "That is just Fifer. He is the brownie for this wing of the castle."

"A what?" Now probably wasn't a good time to notice the glowing lights that lazily floated above their heads. They moved like living creatures. Their lights glowed brighter than a fire but with a green hue.

When the gnome gave her a sidelong glance, it made her stomach squirm. "Faerie has many creatures. The high fae like Prince Brannick look most like you mortals, but we have low fae too. Brownies, gnomes, sprites. Even dangerous creatures like ogres or trolls."

A knot twisted in her stomach at the mention of trolls, though she couldn't begin to imagine why.

The gnome continued on, apparently unaware of her hesitation. "Gnomes are protectors, but brownies prefer household tasks like cooking and cleaning. Fifer tidies the rooms and prepares food for those residing in this wing."

He raised an eyebrow at her. Even though his spear hadn't moved, she could feel the threat in his fully black eyes. "If you are not nice to him, Fifer will make your stay here very unpleasant." He gave a short nod and continued down the hall. "He likes flowers, berries, and occasionally nuts. Be sure to leave him an offering every night before you sleep."

If rules like this kept popping up, Elora would have to start taking notes on them. As her stomach grumbled, she decided it would be important to treat the creature well who provided her meals.

With an abrupt stomp, the gnome halted in front of a wooden door covered in crumbling black paint. He pushed it open and gestured inside. "Prince Brannick will be here soon. You may not leave." He turned away but cast a quick glance over his shoulder. "Do not try anything funny."

She rolled her eyes as the gnome shut the door. It didn't matter what the prince said, she only intended to stay in that room long enough for the gnome to be out of sight of her escape.

No sooner did she reach for the leather door handle, than Brannick himself entered through the door. He swept forward with an air of grace that only made him look stronger. The black-furred wolf from the day before trailed behind him. The creature rubbed his snout against Elora's leg before joining the prince on the other side of the room.

Brannick flicked an invisible speck of dirt off his soft coat before removing it. His muscles rippled as he stretched out his arms. "It seems Soren managed to deliver you here without incident." His eyes narrowed. "Why did you not change your clothes? I stocked your wardrobe with all sorts of things."

Jerking her head away from the sight of Brannick's bare chest did not calm her racing heart. The speed of it caused her to let out a defiant huff. "I didn't want to," she said while pointing her nose in the air. "When is the tournament? My wedding is in three weeks, and I need to be back home before then."

Behind her, a scrape seemed to indicate a blade being lifted from the stone floor. "*When?*" The prince let out a scoff. "There is no time in Faerie. The testing will begin when High King Romany requests our presence."

The prince appeared at her side, his wolf not a step behind. He gripped the hilt of an oddly made sword. His nose twitched as he stared at her. "Lift your hem."

An all-new sensation swept through her. She took a step back as her heart leapt into her throat. "Excuse me?" Hopefully Brannick didn't hear the croak in her voice.

He raised an eyebrow and tapped the point of his sword on the floor near her. "I made myself perfectly clear. Lift your hem."

She took a hurried step backward, her palms sweating as she reached for her sword. "I'm not lifting my hem. I don't know what you're after, but if you try to touch—"

Her back neared a moss-covered wall. The wolf bounded toward her, nudging his nose against her leg in a strangely comforting gesture.

A small twitch appeared in Brannick's eye at the sight of his wolf's reaction. Next, he rubbed a hand over his forehead and let out a sigh. "Your ankle. That is all I want to see. And trust me, I have no desire to touch anything."

The words untied a knot that had twisted in her chest. She heaved a sigh of relief. The wolf nuzzled into her leg again, which brought a smile to her lips. Maybe she wouldn't have been so frightened of him if she had known he was so friendly. She gave him a soft pat on the head, which he seemed to like very much.

Now her eyes flicked back to the prince. He raised his eyebrows with an expectant air. If necessary, she would have used her sword against him. But she much preferred it to not be necessary. Too relieved to question further, she lifted her skirt just enough to show off her ankle.

This caused a half smile on Brannick's lips. "And the other?"

She turned to the other side and quickly showed her other ankle.

Rubbing his hands together, Brannick lifted his chin at the wolf. The creature padded across the floor to stand at his master's side. "It seems the bath did the trick, Blaz. She removed the ward."

The knot in Elora's chest tightened right back up again. She held a fist over her heart, suddenly feeling naked. Chloe's ribbon. The ward against fae enchantments. It was back in the room by the stone basin, probably under the blanket where she hadn't seen it.

Elora pressed her back into the mossy wall.

"Calm down, mortal." The prince pinched the bridge of his nose. "I will not hurt you. I need you, remember? I am merely going to put an enchantment on you. No one but Kaia, Soren, and Blaz know that I plan to learn sword fighting. I need to keep it that way."

A shudder swept through her as she sucked in a breath. Her heels backed into the stone wall behind her. With a hard swallow, she accepted a dreadful truth. She had nowhere to go.

CHAPTER 12

Elora's heart wouldn't stop racing as the prince reached for a vine growing along the stone wall at her side. After a gentle tug, the stone wall opened up into a larger, octagonal room.

An armory.

Spears lined three of the walls. Some had tips carved from black stone, others gray stone. Leather had been wrapped around the wooden handles with leather strings and feathers hanging at different heights. Even the spears were different heights, probably for the various sizes of creatures who would use them.

On three of the other walls, wooden bows hung. Underneath them, tall clay pots held bundles of arrows. Black leather armor sat in neat piles in front of the wall across from her. Next to the stacks sat suede bags decorated with black beads and feathers.

Vines and moss hung throughout the room. Black briars and even more vines wound around the wooden rafters above.

When Brannick reached for a thick vine, Elora paid careful attention to which one it was. His gentle tug slid the stone wall closed behind her. Every other part of the castle felt open, airy, like the castle rooms were part of the forest itself.

Not this room.

It had no window. The octagonal shape seemed to close in on her. It didn't have the crisp scent of forest or rain. It smelled like old leather and rotting wood.

Even with the moss, vines, and briars, it felt nothing like a forest. It felt like a prison.

Brannick moved toward her with predatory eyes. She swallowed as she backed into a new wall. Her shoulder bumped into a spear hanging from a leather loop that had been nailed into the wall.

How could a tiny piece of ribbon cost her so much?

Breaths skittered through her nose, refusing to flow properly. Her limbs shook a little harder each time the prince stepped closer. Her hand gripped the hilt of her sword so hard it made her fingers burn. But what good would it do her now? She couldn't use a sword to defend herself against words.

In a burst of fear, the overwhelming urge to escape came over her. Fly.

Her wings snapped out behind her back, getting caught between her shoulders and the wall.

She had almost forgotten about her wings. Relief shot through her for a briefest moment. Perhaps the wings could save her.

But her back was too close to the wall. The wings could barely flutter before smacking against the stone wall. More attuned to them than ever before, she could feel how the stone battered against the delicate veins of her wings.

Brannick stepped even closer still. His bare chest rose and fell in steady and irritatingly calm breaths. He leaned closer, which suddenly made him feel so much taller than her. The top of her head barely reached his chin.

But his chin was tucked down, and he was staring into her eyes.

Had her heart stopped beating? Or was it beating so fast she could no longer feel individual beats?

His eyes seemed more extraordinary than ever. They changed colors faster than anything she'd ever seen. Dark hues filled them, but then they immediately turned light. They pulsed and glowed and looked so magical she could barely breathe.

The wings behind her folded neatly into her back, hiding once again. But she hadn't told them to do that. Had she?

The prince blinked and a shimmer went over his eyes, making them appear as if they had no color at all. But the next moment, they looked like every color, even ones she hadn't seen before.

"Stop." The word came out barely louder than a breath. She gulped and forced herself to use a more commanding voice. "Stop doing that with your eyes."

His light brown skin gave off a copper glow that could have been her imagination, but she'd never know. A smirk curled one side of his mouth upward. She simultaneously adored and detested how perfect it made his face. "I am not enchanting you with my eyes. I just happen to have amazing eyes."

She shifted from one foot to the other, needing to swallow again before she could speak. "Get away from me, then. Why do you have to stand so close?"

With narrowing eyes, he leaned close enough to warm her brow with his breath. "My greatest magic is in essence. By studying your essence, I know what enchantments to put over you."

Her chest rose with tiny breaths, but she couldn't focus enough for longer ones. "Can't you study my essence from over there?" Even her hand seemed unwilling to raise itself too high when she tried to point.

"No."

He offered no other explanation. Everything in her body moved in sharp bursts. When he breathed in, she breathed in. And then her heart and mind and soul would stop until he breathed out. Then, she'd do the same.

She had to push him away.

Her arms twitched at her side, but it was so *hard* to lift them. The thought of touching his bare chest certainly contributed to her hesitance. But after another sharp breath, she was ready to take action.

Before she could speak, Brannick lifted his hand and traced a finger over her forehead. The touch sent a shiver through her. "You will not speak, write, or attempt to communicate in any way about your true purpose in Faerie."

The words prompted a tingling sensation over her whole body, but not the good kind. Around her, the entire room shimmered with the same strange colorless color as the prince's magical eyes. A metallic taste slid over her tongue while a quiet buzz filled her ears. The smell of iron shackles drifted in through her nose.

And then, it all went away. The room went back to normal, but *she* didn't feel the same. The words seemed to steal away a piece from inside her.

With another soft brush of his finger over her forehead, Brannick spoke again. "You will not speak, write, or attempt to communicate in any way about our bargain."

The strange sensations returned. Even knowing what to expect, they still assaulted her, leaving her heart a tangled mess.

Another brush. "You will not speak, write, or attempt to communicate in any way about your sword skill."

It didn't end there. He continued the enchantments, carefully closing any loophole almost as soon as she conceived of one. With each of his words, another piece of herself seemed to be stolen away. Each enchantment made her weaker. Emptier.

The will and determination that had always gotten her into such trouble had been subdued from a rolling boil to a gentle simmer.

"That should do it." The prince gave his wolf a pat on the head as he spoke. The wolf looked up, but something about his expression seemed displeased.

She shook the thought away. That didn't make any sense. Wolves couldn't look displeased. Elora let anger rise in her chest.

Heat spread through her arms, prompting them to action. Some of her determination had been sucked away, but seething hatred replaced it. Luckily, the hate seemed capable of spurring action just as well as her determination had.

With tight fists, she slammed her hands against Brannick's chest, forcing him to step backward. Air huffed hard from her nostrils as she marched to the opposite end of the octagonal room.

She felt weak. Used.

But what could she do when fae could rip away her will with the brush of a finger?

"I will never forgive you for this." Hot air escaped through her clenched teeth. Her glare could have set a block of ice on fire.

Brannick's attention had been stolen by the wolf. The creature's black fur ruffled around his pointed ears. He sat back on his haunches, but he looked even more distressed than before.

With eyebrows pinched together, the prince tried to run a hand over the wolf. Blaz wouldn't allow it. In a distracted voice, Brannick said, "The enchantments protect me, but they also protect you. Now you can roam the castle and castle grounds freely. I know you will not divulge my secret. Think of the enchantment as your freedom."

Elora huffed as she turned away. The more she tended it, the more rage seemed a perfect substitute for determination. "Isn't restriction the opposite of freedom?"

The wolf lowered his nose, covering it with one paw.

Brannick blinked in response. He got down on his knees and tried to rub a hand over the wolf's fur. "What is it, Blaz?"

The wolf lowered himself even more, resting his head on the stone floor.

Now the prince's eyebrows had pinched even closer together. Was that a hint of guilt in his eyes? He didn't glance toward Elora as he answered her question. He only offered the slimmest portion of his attention. "They do not have to be opposites. You can think of it as protection instead. Now you are safe because no one knows how valuable you are to me."

Her sword sang as she slid it from its sheath. Her anger needed an outlet immediately, and sword fighting had always worked best for that sort of thing. Clenching her jaw, she glared at the prince. "You won't change my mind, so stop trying. Just get your sword, and let's begin training."

With one last glance at his wolf, Brannick stood from the ground. He grabbed the sword he'd been holding earlier and stood across from her.

She glanced toward his blade with a grimace. "First, you need a better weapon."

"Why?" He looked at the sword in his hand, but his attention was clearly still on Blaz.

Using the tip of her sword, she tapped against the blade of his. "This one is terrible. The balance is off. Where are the other swords?"

With each exchange, Brannick seemed more focused on her. He gestured around the room with a huffy laugh. "There are no others. We only use spears and bows and arrows in Bitter Thorn. That's why I chose a sword master to train me for the testing. No one will ever suspect that I learned how to sword fight."

Heat still thrummed through her body, but at least she had something productive to focus on now. "I can't teach you with that sword. It will throw you off balance as you fight. Your body will overcorrect, which will cause you to learn incorrect form. You must have a proper sword."

The corner of his eye twitched. "Then I will use yours."

With her own eyes widening, she took a step back. "No."

"How else will I learn? You made the bargain. You have to teach me." He took an unforgiving step forward.

Panic seized her every muscle as she clutched the hilt tighter. Her thumb brushed over the raised shield symbol on the pommel. "Can you get another sword? A better one?"

He took another step forward, which sent knots all through her chest. "Yes, but I will not get it for a while."

Just like that, the knots loosened, and she could breathe again. "Fine, then I'll start by teaching you correct stances. You don't need a good sword for that."

She launched into an explanation and demonstration just in case the prince had any ideas about pushing the issue. Fortunately, he went along without any persuasion. In fact, he seemed more than eager to learn everything he could from her. He seemed desperate.

But anger still fueled most of her actions. She might have made the lesson more boring and drawn out than it needed to be. Even though the skills she taught were fundamental and essential, she wanted him to *feel* like he was learning nothing.

After droning on for a particularly long time about a stance, the prince threw his sword on the ground. "We are done for the day, mortal. I have *productive* things to do."

It took a great deal of energy to walk past him without a visible smirk.

"Wait."

The prince stopped her when she was mere footsteps away from the sliding wall that doubled as a door. She still remembered which vine to tug to open it.

Brannick looked down at his wolf. Blaz's mood had improved about as much as Elora's had. Something about his black eyes and pointed ears still seemed tense. But he looked up at his master and seemed to nod.

That caused the prince to nod in return, his long black hair glistened in the light at the movement. He turned to her with darkened eyes. "If others see your sword, they might guess my secret."

"How unfortunate." She turned away and reached for the vine.

With her back turned, she didn't see what Brannick was doing, but she did hear a strange scraping of stone that urged her to turn around.

A narrow, hidden compartment had opened up in the stone wall across from her. The prince set his sword inside it. He spoke again with his back to her. "Both our swords must be hidden, so no one suspects my plan. Put your sword and sheath in here."

The death grip she used to hold her hilt could have crushed an apple. "No."

He turned toward her with a calculating stare. "You will not like the consequences if you try to defy me."

Hard lumps lined her throat when she tried to swallow. In her weakest voice yet, she said, "This sword is the last thing I have from my father. You *can't* take it away."

Before she could blink, Brannick had bounded to her side. He touched her forehead with one finger.

Shoving him away before he could perform another enchantment, she tromped toward the hidden compartment. "Don't you dare try that again."

Her fingers tensed as she gripped her sword hilt. Soreness lined her throat a little more with each step. A single tear slid down her cheek. She crossed the room.

"How can you call this protection?" Her voice cracked as the words came out. "How am I supposed to defend myself without my sword?"

Like a coward, the prince didn't respond.

She jerked her head toward him to slice him with glare. The tears hovering in her lashes seemed to have a greater effect. Still, he stood without a word.

When her hands dropped the sword and sheath into the compartment, it closed up immediately. In response, she slammed her boot against the stone wall.

"What more can you take away from me?" She pounded her fists against the stone, which didn't improve her mood in the slightest.

After one last huff, she stormed out of the room, not bothering to spare a glance at the prince as she left.

It didn't matter if she was allowed to roam the castle now. She only had one destination in mind. With heavy stomps, she marched toward her room. Once there, she would tie the red ribbon around her ankle and never take it off again.

Now she knew: the consequences would be dire if she went anywhere without the ward.

CHAPTER 13

Elora sprinted back to her room.

The moment she arrived, she tied the red ribbon from Chloe around her ankle. Her hands fumbled with the silky fabric while trying to tie it properly. No bow this time. She tied a tight knot instead, determined to never remove it, possibly for the rest of her life.

Tears pooled in her eyes as she rocked her body back and forth. Tightness filled her muscles from the strain, but that only made her grab her legs tighter. The floating green lights near her ceiling pulsed as tiny hums passed over her head.

Brannick had said she could go anywhere inside the castle or on the castle grounds now.

She didn't.

Fear had never gripped her more than when the handsome fae prince waved a hand and took away her free will. Even with the ribbon around her ankle, terror throttled her and wouldn't let go. Hadn't Brannick told her it would be like this? He said Faerie wasn't nice. Just enchanting.

The beautiful sights and glorious smells *had* enchanted her. And now she was stuck in a cruel world with no escape. If she didn't return to the mortal realm in time for her wedding her sisters wouldn't survive. They had no one to protect them now. No one to keep them from being thrown out on the streets.

She buried her face in the scratchy wool of her skirt. That wouldn't happen. No matter what, she'd find a way to return before then.

The entire day passed in the same manner. Elora switched between pacing, wallowing, and practicing her stances. In her better moments, she waved her arm around as if swinging a sword. Throughout the years, she had always imagined a faceless enemy when practicing alone. Now, it was easy to imagine Brannick as the victim whose chest she pierced. If only that could become a reality.

When a chilled breeze and dark shadows danced around her room, she considered crawling under the green wool blanket on her bed. Her stomach grumbled after having gone an entire day without food. According to the gnome, Soren, that was because she had failed to leave an offering for her brownie.

Wracking her brain, she tried to remember the acceptable offerings. Berries or nuts? And wildflowers? Nodding to herself, she took in a breath. Yes, wildflowers, berries, and sometimes nuts. With the forest just outside her window, it wouldn't take too long to find something.

After slipping on her leather trousers, Elora knotted her skirt at the thigh. Going through the castle was probably more practical, but she had no desire to face any more fae. Instead, she climbed out her open window, finding jutted rocks and ledges in the black castle walls for her feet. The ground below wasn't far.

The forest stretched out around the castle in lush green beauty. Moss and bright grass dotted the damp brown soil. Huge trees reached into the clouds, each with varying shades of trunks from reddish-brown to light brown to some so dark they almost looked black.

A cool mist seemed to hang in the air, but it didn't feel cold. Just pleasant. Those same glowing green lights floated above her even outside. They helped provide light with the sky turning a dusky gray.

Following a little stream, Elora hunted around for some berries.

With such focus, she nearly tripped over a woman laying on her belly next to the stream. The woman splashed in the water with her hand, her dark brown skin providing a beautiful contrast to the bright blue dress she wore. A large green and white pattern wove through the floaty blue fabric. Dark blue lace wrapped around her arms from her shoulders to her mid-upper arms.

The dress was cut straight with no flounce or curves. It was made of a soft cotton that looked impossibly floaty and svelte.

"Oh, a mortal." Silver bursts sparkled in the woman's light brown eyes. Her pointed ears were more delicate than the others Elora had seen.

The woman nodded and went back to splashing water in the little stream. "I heard rumors, but I did not believe them. Prince Brannick has never kept a mortal before."

The word *kept* didn't sit well with Elora, but fear stopped her from voicing any concern. At least the red ribbon around her ankle was knotted tight. "Who are you?" She didn't even care that her words sounded tight.

"Lyren." The woman's black curls bounced as she nodded her head. At the same moment, a twinkling song filled the air.

But Elora knew better now. She wouldn't be enchanted just because something seemed nice. She took a hardened stance. "What are you doing?"

Lyren's chin tilted up as she glanced at the glowing lights above them. "Listening to the sprites."

The bright green lights floated and spun in unison with the song in the air. Were those lights living creatures? *Sprites?*

Elora stepped away, refusing to be impressed with the woman's radiant brown skin or how her eyes seemed to know more than they should have. "Do you live at the castle?"

With one finger, Lyren traced a swirling pattern in the stream. "Yes, but I am not from Bitter Thorn. I come from the court of Swiftsea. We are the only court who allies with Bitter Thorn."

A large rock covered in moss stood nearby. It seemed like a nice enough place to sit to keep an eye on the fae while they talked. "How long have you been here?" Elora asked.

Lyren stuck both her hands into the water. Moving them into a cup, she scooped water above the stream only to let it trickle through her fingers back into the stream again. Tilting her head to the side, her eyes stared off in the distance. "I have learned a new skill since coming to this court. Also, my perspective has changed slightly."

Elora raised an eyebrow. "No, I mean how *long* have you been here? How many days? A month? A year?"

This earned her a glance and a soft chuckle. Lyren scooped more water into her hands once again. "We do not number days in Faerie."

Even after several stunned blinks, the words didn't register inside Elora. The fae didn't *number* their days? Then how did they keep track of events or age? Was that why they all looked so young? She shook the thought out of her head. If the fae was willing to speak, they had more important things to discuss. "Why are you here? In Bitter Thorn?"

With a small stretch, Lyren pushed herself up off her belly and moved to a sitting position. She had a white sea flower tucked behind one ear. It paired perfectly with her subtle smile. "I am here to help Prince Brannick become the next High King. I provide him insight on words."

Lowering herself onto the soft moss covering the rock, Elora eyed the fae carefully. "You trust him then? Brannick?"

Lyren raised a single eyebrow, staring back with a watchful eye. "Trust is not something fae give often. The queen of my court is not interested in the position, so I cannot help her win it. I believe *Prince* Brannick is the next best choice." She touched a delicate hand to a dark silver chain hanging from her neck. "Though some in my court believe he is the rightful High King anyway."

The fae's hand trailed down the silver chain until it reached the shimmery seashell hanging at the end. A single blue pearl was fastened inside the shell.

With a jerk, Elora forced herself to sit up straight. She hadn't even noticed leaning forward to look at the necklace. Everything in this magical world made it difficult for her to act disinterested. She glanced at the seashell one last time. "Does everyone in your court wear those?"

A glistening laugh spilled from the fae's mouth. "Oh no. Only the accomplished receive a necklace like this. Only Queen Noelani of Swiftsea can award them." She touched a hand to the necklace again. "I earned this one for my mastery of words, but I hope to earn another for bravery. It is part of why I am here. The testing might give me an opportunity to be brave. But there are other necklaces I hope to earn too."

Elora adjusted herself on the mossy stone just as a black briar creaked in the wind. The movement caused thorns to leave small scratches on her arms. Scowling, she scooted to the other side of the rock. "Why are there so many thorns everywhere? Who decided that would make the court better?"

A gleeful delight filled Lyren's eyes as she folded her legs crisscross in front of her body. "We love telling stories in my court. How lucky of me to relate the most important story of Faerie to someone who has never heard it before."

Again, Elora leaned forward. How could she help it when the fae made it sound so important? Her eyes opened wide, her ears pricked and ready to drink up the words.

In a deliberate and expressive voice, Lyren began the tale. "Bitter Thorn is a cursed court. It used to be the High Court ruled by High Queen Winola. Now it is disgraced, and the ruler can only be called prince or princess but never king or queen."

In response to her words, the glowing lights above stopped their directionless flying. Now they moved in twirls and loops around and above Lyren's head.

She continued. "The first fae was an enormous being called Nouvel. He grew out of the magic of the land. The mortals called him a monster. When fear overtook their minds, they attacked him in great numbers. Knowing he would die, Nouvel split the world into two realms that were connected by essence but separated physically. Upon his death, he broke into tiny seeds which grew into fae."

Lyren gestured toward different parts of her body as she continued. "From his toes came the brownies who help wherever they go. From his arms grew the redcaps who fight

115

until their last breaths. From his head grew the high fae who resemble mortals but have more intelligence and cunning than they. From his bright eyes grew the sprites who light the realm with their glow."

The fae stood now, giving her voice more volume. "As the fae grew, they created a world free from conscience or emotion. Every fae took care of himself, and no one ever faulted him for his desires." Her eyes turned down. "But without the emotions of mortals, fae also lacked music, art, and all forms of creativity. We could sense these things from the mortal realm, but we could not experience them. One fae found this lack unacceptable."

Lyren gestured toward the black walls of the nearby castle. "High Queen Winola forged a portal between the realms and stole away into mortal lands. When she returned, she brought with her musicians, artists, sculptors, and storytellers. The fae devoured these new experiences, never to be satiated. They wanted more creativity, more emotion. What they had was never enough."

A strange twist went through Elora's chest. Folding her arms, she glanced toward the black briars at her side. "You *stole* music and art from mortals?"

With a playful shrug, Lyren said, "Yes, but we made them better."

Twigs snapped behind Elora. She wasn't even surprised when Brannick appeared wearing a deep scowl directed straight at her. "Your capricious talents had unintended consequences," he said continuing the story. "We fae soon began to experience human emotions and conscience. It was despicable. Our minds have been tainted by your sickening ways."

116

He rubbed a hand over his wolf's neck. Did that creature follow him everywhere? Brannick spoke again through clenched teeth. "We seek to distance ourselves from your vile ways. We have vows and bargains to satisfy our consciences, but we do not tie our consciences to emotion."

Pricking his thumb on a nearby briar, his eyebrows lowered even more. "The thorns represent the mistake my mother made. All of Faerie has suffered from her actions."

Elora swallowed hard. It didn't matter how cursed the prince's court was, she would never feel pity for him. He had tricked her into a bargain and forced an unwanted enchantment over her. He deserved none of her pity.

His eyes snapped toward hers, looking more perfect than ever. "Get back to your room, mortal. I want you well rested for tomorrow."

Before stalking off, he waved a hand at the soil. A patch of small purple wildflowers appeared at Elora's feet. Now she had an offering for her brownie. And a host of reasons to hate her captor even more.

CHAPTER 14

When Elora woke the next morning, a steaming plate of food sat on a wooden tray next to her bed. A fluffy golden scone sat in the middle with raspberries and blackberries sprinkled on top. Tangy, sweet berry syrup had been drizzled across the food. A sprig of mint leaves decorated the edge of the plate.

Apparently, her brownie had found her offering acceptable. She settled the tray onto her lap and enjoyed the delicious scone with a pillow at her back.

After eating, Elora went to the stone basin hidden behind the hanging wall of vines. As it had been the day before, it was filled with steaming hot water. Her mouth pinched to a knot as she huffed at the water. She had allowed herself to be taken with Faerie and had dearly paid the price.

With a sharp glare at the bath, she chose to wash herself with a rag and a little soap instead. A sour stench filled her nose as she pulled on her skirt. Maybe that evening she would have to use the bath water to clean her skirt and corset.

By the time she finished dressing, a heavy knock sounded at the door. This time, she expected the stocky gnome who stood in front of her with puffy cheeks and black, bug-like eyes. A stone-faced growl hid behind his white mustache and beard.

The gnome, Soren, didn't say a word to her as he turned and tromped down the hallway. The grumbling under his breath started almost immediately. "I am a captain of the guard. I should not have to play guardian to a mere mortal." A puff of air shot from his nose. "I will speak to the prince about this, so I can focus on more important tasks."

The words didn't hurt Elora as much as they had before. Now, every bit of her anger and frustration focused on the prince who had decided to remove some of her freedom. On instinct, she reached for the sword hilt at her hip.

It wasn't there.

Tension ripped through her body with each step. The cool breeze and moss-covered walls could do nothing to improve her mood. The black briars and thorns were a much better reflection of the emotions storming inside her.

Without her sword she felt naked. Vulnerable. Fearful in a way she had never experienced before.

When Soren led her into a large hall, she refused to be impressed by the small forest that grew inside it. A dozen trees with bright green leaves and rich, rough trunks flanked a long wooden table.

On one end of the table, a large tree had been merged with a stone-carved chair. The branches of the tree grew around the stone so fluidly, it looked as though the stone had grown straight from the tree itself. Black vines with sharp thorns twisted around the branches and stone. The armrests had more thorns wrapped around them than anything else in the room.

As the grandest chair at the table, Elora guessed it was a throne. Though, the thorns must have made it uncomfortable for using.

The other chairs at the table were built from light wood. Simple tree designs had been carved into their backs. Soren gestured toward the chair to the right side of the throne. Once Elora sat in it, he settled into the chair across the table from her.

The dryad entered the room next, her emerald hair flowing behind her. She wore a light brown dress with a soft belt around the middle. It fell to her mid-calf with fringe along the hem. Her dark brown skin glistened in the sprite's glowing light that shone down on them.

"Kaia." The gnome spoke in a gruff voice, but he gave a nod that indicated respect.

With a light smile, Kaia nodded back. Taking the chair next to Elora, she said, "You seem in good mood compared to earlier. Did the prince approve your request for more soldiers?"

The exchange left Elora with eyebrows pinched together. *This* was a good mood for Soren?

Another man entered the room. Elora had never seen him before. His light brown skin was a shade lighter than Brannick's, the copper undertones in it more subdued. He had a long, straight nose. His black hair was cut short and swept over with a part on one side.

"Welcome, Quintus." Kaia offered a nod in the man's direction as he took the seat next to Soren. "We are so grateful to have a craftsman with your skill here."

The fae Elora had met the night before, Lyren, entered next. She wore another bright blue dress with a large print. The seashell necklace hung past her chest. A bright white flower was tucked neatly behind her brown skin and luscious curls.

Before Kaia could greet the fae, a chorus of laughter sounded from the doorway. Brannick stood in the doorway with another man.

The man appeared to be the prince's friend. He had fair skin like Elora's. His brown curls were short and tumbled neatly over his forehead. He wore a simple leather coat.

Brannick shook his head at the man. "You have the best adventures, Vesper. I cannot believe you have visited so many places."

With a chuckle, Vesper ran his fingers through his hair. It revealed his pointed ears just as he took a seat.

Brannick stood at the head of the table looking as perfect as ever. His black hair drifted against his shoulders as he spoke. "Welcome everyone. We are all here to prepare for High King Romany's testing. The winner will inherit his throne and become the next High King or High Queen. You all have an important role to play here."

With a sweeping hand, he gestured toward everyone at the table individually. "Soren is my captain of the guard. Quintus is a master craftsman. Vesper is my longest friend and has explored each court in Faerie. Lyren is a master of words, and Kaia is my wisest advisor."

At the end of speaking, Brannick lowered himself into the stone throne. His hands automatically went to the backs of the armrests. With a sharp flick, he pushed his thumbs through the thorny vines that wrapped around the stone. The vines snapped apart and fell in a little pile at the bottom of the throne.

His movements looked so practiced, it seemed like something he did every time he sat down. Did that mean the thorns grew back, even after being snapped away? They sat in a sad heap, broken but still as sharp as ever.

They looked about the same as Elora felt.

She glared at the prince, hoping it might remind him of her existence. As she glared, the black wolf that followed the prince everywhere settled onto the ground between her and his master. The creature looked up at her with bright eyes. For a moment, she could almost forget he was a wolf with razor-sharp teeth.

When Brannick opened his mouth again, another voice cut him off before he could begin.

"Who is the mortal?" The voice belonged to the prince's friend who had traveled through Faerie. Vesper.

Refusing to acknowledge such a ridiculous question, she kept her head facing forward. But she couldn't quite help taking a quick glance toward the throne.

The prince's eyes looked more brilliant than ever, but he too seemed to be avoiding eye contact. "Ignore her." The words were accompanied by a flippant hand wave. One of his eyebrows quirked up for half a moment, as if he had just had an idea. "She is my pet."

Elora's eyes widened as she jerked her head toward him. "What did you just say?" The question had as much spit as it had bite.

The prince continued to look at every person in the room except her. "She is outspoken for a mortal. And stubborn. You need not listen to a thing she says."

Wool fabric curled in her fists as she clenched them in her lap. Her eyebrows had dipped low enough to cause tension between them. "I will not be ignored."

He looked at her then, his eyes shimmering between light and dark. "Hush, mortal."

Her chair toppled to the ground as she sprang to her feet. "Elora." It felt good to look down on him for a change.

One eyebrow raised high on his forehead. "What?"

She folded her arms over her chest. "My name is Elora. Stop calling me mortal." She let out a huff. "Since coming here, I've had to learn countless things. I've learned all *your* names." She gestured around the table. "I've had to learn about dryads, sprites, bargains, wards. I was brought into this world, expected to learn your ways, yet not one of you has bothered to even ask my name."

Her blood boiled as she glared at each of the fae at the table. Her eyes lingered on Soren and Kaia a little longer than the others, but Brannick got the longest and sharpest glare of all. The fae shifted in their seats, eyes turned down at the wooden table before them. One of them cleared their throat at one point, but it only seemed to add to the tension in the air.

When Elora plucked her chair off the ground and shrank back into her seat, Lyren stood. She pinched one of her curls as she spoke. "I vow to give you a shell from my court that can make any water taste as sweet as honey."

Confusion trickled through Elora as she looked back at the dark-skinned fae.

Kaia stood next. "I vow to watch over you while you are in Bitter Thorn."

Shaking both hands in front of herself, Elora glanced at the dryad. "I don't want these vows. I just want you to apologize."

The room stilled into complete silence.

One puff from the prince's nose indicated the depth of his anger. Heat emanated off him as he slammed a fist onto the table. The wood shook, sending a clattering noise to bounce against the walls. His jaw was clenched tight when he spoke again. "We do *not* apologize in Faerie. We clear our consciences using vows and bargains. How dare you infect us with your mortal guilt?"

Squirming in her seat, Elora lost the ability to look anyone in the eye.

He gestured toward the others. "You will allow them to offer vows. And when they complete their tasks, you will free them from their guilt."

Soren vowed to bring her a feather that would protect her from any accidental danger. Not expecting a vow from Vesper or Quintus, since they hadn't known her before, she now turned to Brannick.

He stared straight across the room as he spoke. "I vow to give you a ward necklace. The magic inside it will last even after you remove it, but only for a day, a night, and a day."

His offer may have seemed impressive to the others, but he knew she already had a ward tied around her ankle. How much help could another one be? "That's not good enough. I don't even want your ward necklace."

Jerking his head toward her, his eyes locked with hers. "What else then? What would you have me do?"

His words from earlier prickled through her. But how could she help the seething hatred inside her when he had done so much to deserve it? Clasping her fingers on top of the table, she leaned toward him. "If you call me *pet* ever again, I will claw your eyes out with my bare hands."

"Fine." He looked away. "I agree to your terms. Now, sit back and listen, so we can discuss the testing."

CHAPTER 15

Silence reigned in the hall for several pulses. Elora folded her hands in her lap but kept her head held high. The others already looked eager to leave. Everyone except Brannick.

The prince lounged over his throne with one arm resting on one of the tree branches that fused with the stone. Oddly, he looked more regal than ever, despite the casual posture. "The testing consists of three phases. The vow, the speech, and the tournament. Lyren will help with the speech and with wording of the vow. Since High King Romany is dying and cares only for his legacy, my vow to him will be that everyone will remember him. I will erect a statue in his honor. Quintus will design and create the statue. For a dying man, stroking the high king's pride is the best we can do. Vesper will help flatter the high king throughout the testing period."

Twisting a few strands of his hair between his finger and thumb, Brannick continued. "King Huron of Dustdune and Queen Alessandra of Fairfrost are the only true competitors for the throne. Queen Noelani from Swiftsea will not participate in the testing. King Jackory from Mistmount will, but everyone knows he does not truly care to win." The prince leaned forward in his seat, eyes growing mischievous. "For now, we will focus on removing King Huron from the testing. Mostly because we aren't stupid enough to mess with Queen Alessandra." The slightest jerk went through the prince's shoulders at the mention of that last name.

Everyone nodded at his words. Everyone but Elora. Her blood wasn't finished boiling yet.

"What about the tournament?" Vesper touched a hand to his chin.

Brannick grinned. Elora fought the urge to smack him.

Apparently, the *prince* was allowed to tell anyone he wanted about his plan to sword fight. Yet she couldn't tell anyone? According to the enchantments, she couldn't utter a word about her sword skill or their training lessons or anything about their bargain.

But when Brannick spoke, he didn't say what she expected. His smirk grew with each word. "You know how skilled I am with magic." He waved a hand through the air and wind began blowing through the trees that grew alongside the table. Small purple flowers bloomed from the branches in a burst of bright light. "The tournament will be the easiest of the three phases."

Narrowing his eyes in Elora's direction, Vesper slid a hand through his brown curls. "So, why *is* the mortal here?"

A warning in Elora's gut told her to give an answer before the prince could. Maybe he had promised to not use the word *pet* again, but she feared he would still imply it.

"I begged him to take me here."

She could feel how Brannick's eyes glanced her way, but it didn't stop her. "I hate the mortal realm. I wanted to escape my betrothed."

That last part came out so unexpectedly, she had to stop herself from clapping a hand over her mouth. Guilt crept through her when she realized how much truth laced her words.

She had a duty to her sisters, which she fully intended to fulfill. But now that she'd said it, she had to admit, a part of her *did* hate the mortal realm. And she'd been trying to escape her betrothed since before she even met him. Sucking in a sharp breath, she hoped no one noticed her discomfort.

At the other end of the table, Vesper raised one eyebrow. "Fae do not give favors to mortals. What did you offer in return for being brought here?"

Panic rose in her chest. Brannick's enchantment prevented her from speaking about the bargain. She couldn't explain her true purpose. But now she had dug herself into a hole with her lies. The only choice was to commit to them.

"I offered to play the harp for him." With eyebrows lowered, she shot a nasty glare in Brannick's direction. "But he still hasn't given me one to play."

Before the prince could respond, Lyren clapped her hands together. It nearly made the sea flower fall away from her ear. "That is perfect. High King Romany loves music. You can play the harp during the revels. It will put Prince Brannick even more in the high king's favor."

"Exactly," the prince said. But his knuckles had turned white as he gripped his stone armrests. Blaz stood up to his paws and moved closer to the prince. After flexing his jaw, Brannick quickly changed the subject back to the testing.

The meeting continued through the entire day. Everyone mostly ignored Elora. So much for making the prince promise to not call her *pet*. It clearly hadn't changed anything.

At one point, tiny brownies with floppy ears came in bearing trays of food. Too much irritation ran through her to enjoy the meal. She was vaguely aware that her thick soup contained squash, beans, and corn, but she didn't register much else.

Dark shadows filled the room when the meeting finally ended. Not bothering to look at the others, Elora stomped off as soon as she could. It took her some time to find her way through the winding halls of the castle. High fae and low fae filled the halls, often not even acknowledging her presence. Eventually, she pushed through heavy wooden doors that stood in the front of the castle and stepped out into the cool forest.

Briars and thorns snapped under foot as she stomped around to find an offering for her brownie. She tried to remember his name as she worked. It seemed important after her sudden outburst earlier in the day. It definitely started with an *f*. Frederick? No, it was sillier than that. Fido? No, it had a musical sort of sound.

Rounding a corner on the path, a bush filled with plump blackberries appeared. Moss and little blades of grass covered the damp soil around the bush. But like everything in the cursed court, black thorns twisted in and through the bush.

Obtaining the berries without scratching herself would require finesse. As she began plucking, twigs snapped behind her. She turned, fully expecting to see Brannick preparing to spout off some Faerie rule she had broken.

Instead, the soft eyes and brown coat of Vesper stood before her. He nodded. "I did not think anyone would be out here." Almost as an afterthought, he added, "Elora."

The sound of her name was even more magical than the glowing green sprites above.

Setting her berries into a neat pile, she stood to face him fully. "You seem more reasonable than the others. Can I ask you a question?"

He gave her a sidelong glance before his eyes scanned the forest around them. "It depends on what the question is."

That seemed like as much approval as she'd get, so the question came out. "How long is this testing going to take?"

Whatever Vesper was searching for seemed to be able to wait. He turned his full attention on her now, glancing over her with a curious eye. "I have met many mortals in my travels and all of them are strangely obsessed with time. Why are you so attached to it?"

Her fingers curled into her wool skirt. "Will you please just answer the question?"

He gave a thoughtful nod, tapping a finger on his chin. "In your mortal terms, I believe it will take a few," he paused as his eyes narrowed, "months."

A lurch went through her stomach. "Months?" She reached for a lock of her light brown hair, as if it could act as a lifeline. "But I thought the high king was poisoned. How can he live so long when he is dying?"

Vesper shrugged. "Time does not exist in Faerie. If uninjured, fae live forever. When the high king has a task to complete before his death, the land delays his death until it is done."

"What if someone cut out his heart?" Elora raised both eyebrows. "Or chopped off his head? Would he continue to live even then?"

The fae began looking off into the forest again. "No, death would come instantly in those cases."

A frightening thought went through her mind, one just vile enough for Faerie. "What if someone poisoned the high king just so he would live long enough to do this testing? Then the poisoner would have a chance to win the throne."

With eyes on the forest, Vesper gave a vague nod. "It does seem a likely possibility."

After a moment, his eyes flicked to hers. They shared a look that seemed to communicate more than words. Were they both thinking of Brannick? Was the prince so determined to earn back his rightful title that he would poison a high king?

Vesper turned abruptly. "Excuse me."

He disappeared into the trees without another word.

Elora bent to retrieve the blackberries she had gathered earlier. Weight settled into her shoulders, a weight that pressed in on all sides. She didn't have time to wait for the testing to end. Hoping for another way out, she focused on recalling the exact words of her bargain.

Originally, Brannick had said she would have to help *until* he became High King. After a sharp look from her, he had added to that.

Or until the high king deems me unfit to take his place.

A spark lit in her chest as she remembered the words. She *didn't* have to wait until Brannick won the throne. She only had to train him in sword fighting until she could figure out a way to sabotage his chance in the testing.

But how?

The question seemed to be answered for her as she wandered deeper into the woods. A nervous-looking Vesper stood in an empty clearing, glancing over his shoulder. She ducked behind a tree just before he could see her standing there. Apparently convinced he was alone, Vesper faced forward again.

He waved his hand, and a swirling tunnel appeared in front of him—a *door* as Kaia had called it. The tunnel looked nothing like the green and brown leafy door Brannick had opened to bring her to the Faerie realm.

Vesper's tunnel was filled with fog and mist. Red roses popped out from the edges while flashes of flashes of green, orange, blue, and gray pulsed throughout. It smelled like adventure.

When Vesper stepped into the door, she recalled his face when she had suggested a fae might have poisoned the high king for a chance to win the throne. And why had Vesper been so nervous and careful to check that no one followed him? If anyone could help her sabotage Brannick's chance at the crown, she was certain to find him at the other end of that door.

Her feet began moving before she had even consciously made the decision. Without knowing what lay on the other side, Elora stepped into the mist.

CHAPTER 16

A blast of warm air blew Elora's hair back when she stepped onto the other side of the Faerie door. Dry heat filled the air even though night had fallen. In a single breath, sand clung to her nose and throat.

All around her, large sand dunes rolled over the landscape. On first glance, they looked orange. Upon closer inspection, dozens of other colors stretched through them. Striations of brown, pink, orange, yellow, white, and red moved through the sandy terrain. Their natural curves and dips brought a sense of motion even when she stood still.

A dusky gray sky towered overhead, the same as it did in Bitter Thorn in the evenings. The glowing green lights of sprites floated and pranced in the air above. Best of all, a magical energy buzzed all around her.

It still felt like Faerie, but it certainly wasn't Bitter Thorn. Maybe if she had paid more attention in the meeting earlier that day, she might have guessed which court she stood in now.

This court was probably just as populated as Bitter Thorn, but Vesper must have brought them to a secluded area. Only the whispering wind and dancing sprites seemed to accompany them.

Ahead of her, Vesper ducked around the edge of tall sand dune wall. If he had noticed her presence, he gave no indication of it. Her tiptoeing preserved the quiet of the night all around.

Just as she neared the sand dune wall, a voice stopped her feet in their tracks.

"Ah, my favorite spy. You're a little late, but I'm sure you have plenty of information to make it worth my while."

The voice didn't belong to Vesper. Such knowledge kept her feet frozen in place. She had already guessed Vesper might be capable of betrayal but knowing it for sure sent a flood of terror through her insides.

Simple things like breathing and swallowing felt like impossible chores. Maybe the light coating of sand in her nose and throat were the only cause, but maybe being steps away from a traitor had something to do with it too.

Elora had every intention to betray Prince Brannick herself, but the prince didn't call *her* a friend. How would Brannick react if he found out about Vesper?

Considering the prince had enchanted Elora and tricked her into a bargain, guilt clearly wouldn't keep Brannick from acting out. There probably wasn't much he *wouldn't* do to a traitor. Would the prince punish Vesper? Kill him?

Her thoughts continued to spin and grow because the voices around the corner were hushed now. She couldn't make out any of their conversation.

Sand tickled her throat as she tried to swallow. A horrible truth became utterly clear. If Brannick found out *she* had betrayed him in any way, he might kill her too. And he wouldn't have any remorse.

It probably should have scared her. Maybe it did, but rage immediately washed out any fear. If someone could kill without any remorse—even a fae—he deserved to be betrayed.

Besides, hadn't she wanted adventure? A tournament had always been her dream, but perhaps betraying a prince could be even more thrilling. Hadn't she wished for *anything* more exciting than getting married to a stranger?

If she didn't return to the mortal realm soon, her sisters would starve. Chloe might be forced to marry someone even worse than Mr. Mercer. They needed someone to protect them, and only Elora could do it. Returning to her mundane existence in the mortal realm would be difficult after knowing the magic of Faerie. But maybe it would be a little more bearable knowing she had once betrayed and defeated an evil prince.

With that thought, she touched a hand to the sand dune. The wall warmed her fingers as she peered around it.

Vesper was gone.

She had been so deep in her thoughts she hadn't even noticed when the voices stopped speaking. She hadn't heard the gentle whoosh that came with an open Faerie door. But the owner of the other voice was still there.

He looked back at Elora with surprised delight. Just like every other fae she'd met, he looked nearly the same age as her. But he also didn't. His eyes seemed to exhibit experience and wisdom. He carried himself with the same weight as someone who had lived for many years. Yet, his physical appearance still seemed young and vibrant.

"Hello." The man's voice didn't sound dry like their surroundings. It came out low and strong but with a whimsical lilt that put her at ease.

A long-sleeved tunic hung down to the fae's knees. The shimmering silk fabric was a dark coppery orange. A golden sash went from one shoulder and across his chest until it wrapped around his waist. Crystals and gems in the same varied colors as the sand dunes adorned the tunic's collar and down the chest.

His crown wasn't like any she had ever seen. A silk turban in an even richer orange than his tunic wrapped over his head. Glittering jewels were stitched to the front in a swirling circular pattern. A wispy white feather flared out at the very top, floatier and more exotic than any feathers she'd seen in Bitter Thorn.

"I know who you are." The words were her way of putting herself in power, however little it might be. Many details from the meeting earlier had already slipped through her mind, but one thing she remembered well enough. She hadn't forgotten the name of the king that Brannick sought to sabotage. And she remembered the name of the court now too. "You are King Huron of Dustdune."

He gave a nod, confirming her guess. "And what brings you to my court, mortal?"

Now was her chance to speak her intention out loud, but it suddenly seemed too grand and horrifying.

The king didn't seem bothered at all. Bursts of gold and amber sparkled in his brown eyes. His brown skin was radiant. The mustache above his lip seemed silkier than his tunic and turban. More importantly, he seemed happy to deal with Elora's sudden silence.

"You came through the door with Vesper, did you not?"

She nodded. Sand continued to scratch her throat as she tried to swallow.

The king raised a knowing eyebrow. "But Vesper did not know you entered with him, am I right?"

Again, she nodded.

King Huron steepled his fingers and held them close to his mouth. "I see." Now he tilted his head forward and looked deeper into her eyes. "And what do *you* want?"

Her time in Faerie had taught her one lesson a little too well. No one in Faerie could be trusted. She knew she couldn't trust this king. Still, no one in the Court of Bitter Thorn had bothered to ask what she wanted. Was it really wrong to think of herself for once?

"I want to return to the mortal realm."

The king tapped his fingers over his mouth as he nodded. "What is stopping you?"

She tried to answer. Her mouth opened, but the explanation about her bargain seized in her mouth before it came anywhere near her lips. When she tried to speak, tightness closed off her throat. Only a sharp cough allowed her to breathe again.

A dark brown eyebrow rose into the king's silk turban. "An enchantment. Interesting." He tilted his head to one side. "Perhaps we should try a different approach. Is there anything I can do to help you return to the mortal realm?"

This time, an answer came without incident. "You can win the testing or just get Prince Brannick kicked out. But you need to do it soon. I can't wait."

"How convenient." King Huron's smile caused nausea and excitement all at once. "It seems our goals are aligned. If you tell me what Prince Brannick has planned, it will be easier for me to defeat him. Do you know any of his secrets regarding the testing?"

Her throat constricted until she found the proper words. "Yes, but I can't tell you."

That didn't seem to bother the king in the slightest. "I understand. What *can* you tell me?"

Hesitation caught inside her, clutching tight to the information the king wanted before it could spill out. Did she really want to do this? Betray the prince?

The hesitation didn't last long. Memories of Brannick enchanting her and taking away her sword made her stomach writhe. When she remembered how he had called her his *pet*, she couldn't spit the words out fast enough.

"He has a master of words to help him with his speech and with the exact wording of his vow. For his vow, he has a master craftsman who is going to design a statue of the high king. He plans to stroke the high king's pride since the high king is dying and legacy is all he has left."

A small chuckle erupted from King Huron's mouth as he looked off to the side. "A statue. I am disappointed I did not think of that myself." He pinched one end of his mustache between his thumb and forefinger. "This is very helpful, but it is not enough."

With a patter, her heart raced to a heavy thump. She had already done so much to betray Brannick, why would she stop now? "What do you need? I have to return to the mortal realm *soon.*"

The smirk that passed over the king's face had a dangerous tilt. "Can you find out the exact words of Prince Brannick's vow? I can use them to my advantage if I know what to expect."

A cord of guilt braided through the twisting in her stomach. Before heeding it, she let rage burn it to dust. "I can probably find out." She drummed her fingers against her thigh. "But how will I give you the information if I find it?"

He gestured toward the glowing green lights above them. "Sprites deliver all messages in Faerie. They require an offering from the message giver and the message receiver. When you have the information, do this to signal a sprite."

He clicked his tongue three times and held his palm flat and high above his head. In an instant, the glowing lights above stopped in place until one floated to his hand in a twirl. "Sprites require an offering of something with a personal connection. It can be anything that means something to you. A berry will work if it is your favorite berry or even if it is a berry you hate. A rock you found that you liked the look of, a thread from your clothing, you get the idea. Anything that has a connection to you."

The king pulled a chunk of orange sandstone from a hidden pocket in his tunic and held it out to the glowing creature. The sprite stood no taller than the king's thumb. Its body was small, but its limbs looked strong. Four bright green wings flapped on the sprite's back.

Though the sandstone piece was twice as large as the sprite's head, the creature easily held it aloft to examine it. The sprite's body, wings, and even its floaty green dress glowed when it gave a nod. Reaching for a pocket that hadn't been visible before, it stuffed the chunk of sandstone inside its dress. Despite the chunk being twice as big as the sprite's head, no part of it could be seen once it disappeared inside the magical pocket.

"If the sprite accepts your offering, you then relay the message." He cleared his throat. "I, King Huron of the Court of Dustdune, have information about Prince Brannick that you will be pleased to hear." He glanced toward her. "Then clearly state the name and court of the message receiver." He turned back to the sprite. "Deliver to Queen Alessandra of the Court of Fairfrost."

With a gentle lift, the sprite darted upward before zooming off at frighteningly fast speed.

The sight nearly caused Elora's jaw to drop, but the king didn't even glance at it. He looked at her instead. "When I receive a message from you, I will open a door, and you can step through it to meet with me." His eyebrows drew together as he leaned forward. "Do not forget the offering. You must have one ready both to send and to receive."

The information bombarded her in a swarm. What if she forgot something important?

King Huron didn't seem to notice her discomfort. He waved a hand and a swirling tunnel appeared to his side. Orange, red, and copper lights swirled through the door. Heat emanated from it even warmer than the air around them. It smelled like gold, sand, and dusty clouds. "That door will return you to the castle grounds in Bitter Thorn. I assume you know where to go from there."

She nodded, but he wasn't looking at her anymore. Just as well. A crippling weight had settled into her stomach, and it didn't seem eager to leave.

After returning to Bitter Thorn, she rushed through the forest without allowing herself to think. She grabbed a handful of the first berries she saw and quickly climbed the black castle walls up to her room.

She ignored the fresh scent and pleasant forest sounds that filled the air around her. When she glanced at the tree growing in the middle of her room, she ignored that too. Prince

Brannick may have ruled a magnificent Faerie court, but that didn't make him magnificent.

The little guilt lingering inside her vaporized as soon as she remembered her sword hidden in that stone compartment in the armory. Brannick had taken everything away from her.

Crawling under her covers, she had only one thought on her mind.

Tomorrow, she'd find out about that vow.

CHAPTER 17

The next morning, Elora stared at a leaf sitting on her hand. The greenery looked as bright and as fresh as when she'd first plucked it. But it shouldn't have.

Fear simmered in her belly as she recounted the events after picking the leaf. She'd gone to bed. Only moments after crawling under the covers, she threw them off and picked a leaf from the tree growing inside her room. Knowing no one else would keep track, she'd used her thumbnail to scratch three distinct lines on the surface of the leaf. Three lines to represent the three days she had been in Faerie.

But none of the lines remained.

Somehow, the leaf had healed the lines away. But how? The question didn't stay long because her mind clung to an even more important thought. *Had* it been three days? That number seemed right, but it also seemed wrong. Had it been four days? A week?

How many days had it been since meeting with King Huron?

It had just been the day before. *Hadn't it?* But with the fresh, unmarked leaf in her hand, nothing seemed certain anymore. She let out a sigh and swept a hand over her skirt to loosen the wrinkles. It would be harder than she thought to keep track of her days in Faerie. No wonder the fae didn't number them.

Her eyes wandered to the empty wooden tray on her bed.

The brownie had brought her another delicious breakfast that morning. This time, it was a corn hash seasoned with rosemary and sage. After reaching for her sword that wasn't there, she let out a grunt. Perhaps the brownie had replaced the marked leaf with an unmarked one.

Running a hand over her hair to check that everything was in place, she exited her room. That had to be it. She'd just have to find another leaf and hide it from the brownie before falling asleep.

The hall outside her room stood empty, which meant she had gotten out of her room before Soren would arrive to escort her to the armory. Just as she had planned. Training with the prince could wait. She had more important things to worry about now.

She had to find out about that vow.

Acting quickly was essential. Especially if it became more difficult to keep track of the days.

Glowing green lights moved in twirls and curlicues near the stone ceiling of the halls. They had just looked like magical Faerie lights at first. How incredible that they were actually tiny fae who delivered messages all across Faerie.

Rounding a corner, Elora nearly toppled over a fae walking down the hall. Kaia's brown cheeks looked warm in the glowing green light. Her emerald hair had been parted down the middle and hung in two long braids.

The dryad brushed her suede beaded dress before glancing up. "It is good to see you, child. You seem to be adjusting well to the castle now. Yes?"

In this wing of the castle, various fae bustled around, always busy and walking fast. High fae and low fae moved at impossible speeds, whirring over the stone almost too quickly to watch. Elora's wing of the castle was much more secluded. Hardly any fae roamed those halls except her and the sprites. She had seen a few high and low fae in her hallways, but never like in this wing.

There must have been hundreds of fae living in the castle.

It had been difficult to ignore the beauty and magic all around her, but Elora had a mission now. She had a way to get back to her sisters. She wasn't about to lose sight of it just because so many fae moved about.

"Have you seen Lyren?" Elora asked.

The dryad's motherly air made her seem more approachable. Though even Kaia was probably just as capable of treachery as all other fae.

The dryad blinked with an almost-smile tugging at her lips. "How wonderful that you and Lyren are becoming friends. I have not seen her, but Prince Brannick is looking for you. He is in the armory. He said you would know where that is."

Elora nodded as she trailed down the stone corridor. Black briars coiled in a rush of wind along the stone walls. If she didn't step carefully, the thorns might pierce her skin. Sometimes, it seemed as if they jumped out at her.

She didn't go to the armory.

The prince could wait.

Remembering how Lyren had been splashing in a stream when they first met, Elora pushed through crowds until she moved onto the castle grounds. The smell of wet tree bark seemed stronger today. A pleasant breeze cooled the warm air to a perfect temperature. Birds chirped above. Briars and thorns writhed in response.

It didn't take long to find the curly-headed fae. Lyren wore a white dress with a grand blue flower print woven into it. Like always, a fresh sea flower had been tucked behind her ear where it stood out against her tight, black curls and glowing brown skin. With her dress held up to her knees, the fae kicked and splashed her bare feet in a stream. A sweeping, mournful song hummed out from her lips.

Above her, the sprites dove and twirled in the air to the rhythm of her song. After a moment, they joined but with high, twinkling voices.

"I didn't know those creatures could sing." Elora glanced up at the sprites as she moved closer to the stream. She had heard their voices before, but she hadn't known it came from them.

Lyren responded with a smile before splashing another toe in the water. "Oh yes, they are quite loud in Swiftsea. But they have very specific rules for speaking to other fae. Usually, they only speak with each other."

Lifting her dress a little higher, the fae crawled onto a rock with moss growing on one side. She kept one foot in the water as she turned to face Elora.

Finding her own mossy rock, Elora settled down with only one question on her mind. But how could she bring it up without making the fae suspicious? "How did you become a master of words? Are there many like you in Swiftsea?"

With a scoop of one hand, Lyren sprinkled water over both her arms. "You asked me enough questions before. Now it is your turn for questions. Most mortals I have met lead boring lives compared to fae. Do you have any great skills or accomplishments? What is the most interesting thing about you? Is it your harp playing?"

The words dug into Elora's skin like a thick splinter. They twisted and gnarled inside. Anger bubbled up, but only because the words were true. Once she returned to the mortal realm, Elora was going to marry an old merchant. The most exciting part of her life would be practicing her sword skill in a meadow, *if* he allowed it.

Brannick's enchantments prevented her from saying anything about her sword skill. Still, she couldn't bear to admit that playing the harp was the most exciting thing about herself. It just seemed like an incredibly cruel truth.

Another thought entered her mind, one that might save her from embarrassment. With a grin, she popped out her wings for the fae to admire.

Lyren's eyes opened wide as she touched a hand to her seashell necklace. "Magnificent." Her voice came out breathless. The stream had been forgotten as the fae reached toward the glittery wings. "I have rarely seen such exquisite wings, even in Faerie."

Her fingers hovered over the edges, just shy of touching them. "Did Prince Brannick give you these?"

"Yes."

Lyren's hand dropped to her side. One eye narrowed as she examined Elora carefully. "Why?"

Getting used to the enchantments would take some time. Without thinking, Elora tried to explain how the prince promised them in exchange for her help. But the words caught in her throat, bulging until she couldn't breathe. It took several hard coughs to open her airway again. Apparently, talking about the wings was too close to mentioning her bargain.

With a knowing look, Lyren tucked a tight curl behind her ear. "I cannot speak about the prince's vow either."

It probably should have brought comfort to hear those words. It confirmed Brannick had enchanted others, not just Elora. Instead, it made her heart burn. To live with the truth that he had violated her was one thing. To know he had violated others? It curled her fingers into fists. Though oddly, Lyren didn't seem distressed about her own enchantment.

Even worse, now Elora had no way to get the information King Huron wanted. She couldn't very well ask Brannick about the vow. He'd probably just put a new enchantment on her.

With the unfortunate truth settling in on her, Elora tried to decide how to make a non-suspicious exit.

"I almost forgot." Lyren tucked a hand into a pocket that definitely hadn't been there a moment ago. Brannick had a similar pocket in his own clothes. So did King Huron and even that little sprite. Did all fae have them? After a moment, the fae held out a hand. "Here is your shell."

A white shell about the size of a thumb sat on Lyren's palm. It spiraled down, almost in the shape of a cone. Though white, it gave off a blue shimmer. Textured white ridges grew over the twists, each getting closer together and thinner as it neared the small point at the bottom.

"Stick it at least halfway down in any water, and it will make it taste as sweet as honey. It cleans the water too in case it is poisoned or spoiled or anything."

These were the moments that made Elora forget home. Her fingers tingled as she reached for the shell. How could something so magical be real? Running a thumb over the textured ridges, she said, "Thank you."

The smile that stretched onto Lyren's face looked almost as devious as one of Brannick's. "You should not have said *thank you*. Those words imply you received a gift. Now you owe me one in return."

"But…I…" Elora stammered, but no excuse seemed strong enough to counteract Faerie rules. It wasn't fair. Lyren could have told her about saying *thank you* before she offered the shell. It was almost like she expected Elora to say it. And now she'd taken advantage of Elora's mortal nature too. Just like Brannick.

The devious smirk on Lyren's face continued to grow. "Do not worry. I will ask for something simple in return. But first, you must absolve me from guilt for not learning your name."

Would Lyren find another way to take advantage if Elora tried to fight the rule? She cleared her throat. "I absolve you from guilt." Now one eyebrow quirked up her forehead. "But I may infect you with guilt again depending on what you ask of me."

A delighted chuckled erupted from Lyren's mouth as she settled back onto her mossy rock. One foot went straight into the stream. "I like you, Elora." With gentle strokes, she smoothed the glistening fabric of her dress. "This is my request. I want a story from your realm, a true story. In Swiftsea, stories are valuable. But all the stories I know take place in the Faerie realm. I want something new."

Even with careful concentration, Elora's breath of relief was nearly audible. A story. That really *was* simple. She turned the request over in her mind but couldn't think of a way the fae could use a story against her. After tucking the shell under her corset, she shared the first story that came to mind.

"Both of my parents used to work in a castle in the mortal realm. They served the king of our small kingdom. My mother played her harp for the king, and my father forged his weapons." She chose to leave out her father's skill with the sword since her enchantments might have interfered with that part.

"They both had great skill and could have lived in the castle for all their days." Now came the depressing part, but Elora tried to tell the story the way her mother always did. As if it was the most romantic and wonderful thing in the world.

"After meeting each other, they fell deeply in love. Because of their great love, they sacrificed their jobs in the castle and decided to move to the country. There, they would raise their three children away from the dangers and politics of the castle."

At the end of the story, Lyren closed her eyes and breathed in deeply from her nose. Her body remained completely still as she breathed, as if soaking the story into her soul.

Bursts of silver sparkled in her light brown eyes when she opened them. "Are all mortal stories so," her eyes narrowed as she looked to the side, "emotional?"

With a shrug, Elora jumped off her mossy rock. "I guess so."

Lyren seemed eager to continue pondering the story, which offered the perfect moment to leave without looking suspicious. The curly-headed fae didn't even acknowledge Elora's departure. *Perfect.*

Now Elora just had to decide where to call on a sprite to send a message to King Huron. Just when she found a secluded spot in the forest, a large group of fae exited the black castle right in her view.

Lowering her hand, she frowned. It would probably be safer to wait until she was in her room before calling on a sprite.

Once she was inside the castle, Soren appeared from nowhere. Even being half her size, he still managed to wave an intimidating hand in front of her face. A long, white feather tickled her nose as he moved his hand back and forth. "I have your feather as I vowed."

She blinked in response.

He let out a sigh and spoke in an even gruffer tone than before. "I vowed I would give it to you. It will protect you from any accidental danger."

"Right." Her nods came a little too fast to look casual. "Of course."

The gnome mumbled a few incomprehensible words before using one hand to gesture at the ground. "Get on your knees. I'll attach it to your hair."

The entire experience had taken her so off guard, she could do nothing but comply. Her knees met the hard stone at once. Soren used a long piece of black string and wound the feather to a chunk of her hair.

When finished, the feather hung just behind her neck, off to one side. This time she knew better than to say *thank you*. As quickly as possible, she absolved the gnome from guilt and continued to her room.

Once in her secluded wing of the castle, she expected to be alone. Unfortunately, Brannick appeared around one corner holding a long sword and wearing a grimace. She could only hope the hammering in her heart wasn't loud enough for him to hear. Things would have been much easier if he didn't make her stomach jolt every time she saw him.

His arm reached out with a jerk. "Does this sword work?"

At least he didn't want to exchange pleasantries.

She took the sword from him, ignoring how his skin brushed against hers as she grabbed it. "Where are you getting all these swords from?"

Leaning against the wall with one shoulder, an arrogant chuckle left his lips. Her heart skipped in response. His voice came out regal and much too confident for his own good. "Never you mind. A prince has his ways."

Now was definitely a good time to look *away* from him and examine the sword instead. After holding it for only a moment, she pushed it back into his hands. "The blade is thicker on one side than it is on the other. It's better, but no, it's not good enough."

When she glanced up, she caught him staring at her hair. Sucking in a sharp breath, he jerked his head away. He made no eye contact as he ripped the sword from her hand. Without another word, he sauntered off down the hall.

Hot anger trickled through her limbs, but it mixed with another emotion she absolutely refused to acknowledge. It didn't stop her head from spinning as she marched into her room. Slamming the door closed behind her, she slid to the floor with her back pressed against one wall. Her room looked the same as it always did. Foresty and open. Empty.

With a grin, she glanced up at the green lights floating near the ceiling.

Time to deliver a message.

CHAPTER 18

A soon as Elora lifted her palm into the air, the glowing green lights above her slowed. She clicked three times with her tongue, and the sprites hovered, as if frozen in the air. One breath later, a green light with a sparkle of pink zoomed toward her palm.

The sprite landed on her palm with a soft pad. Elora brought her hand close to her face to examine the tiny creature. It looked much smaller than the sprite she had seen in King Huron's court. The frail legs barely seemed strong enough to hold the sprite's little body upright.

Now that Elora could examine it up close, she noticed so many more details than before. Furry green wings spread out from the sprite's back. They glowed with green light even brighter than the light of the sprite's body. It had fair skin like hers, but even the skin gave off a green glow.

Long pointed ears grew on each side of its head. Instead of hair, it had velvety grass-like strands that had been twisted up to several points all around the head. It wore a sparkly pink dress tied with a green, velvety belt. The dress landed just above the tiny creature's knees.

If Chloe could have seen the sprite, she would have squealed. Even Elora had a difficult time keeping a straight face. In her entire life, she had never seen anything that looked so cute.

"Hello."

At the sound of Elora's voice, the sprite cocked her head to the side.

Maybe a smile would help. And a gentle voice. "What's your name?"

Soft green eyebrows lowered over the creature's pink and green eyes. She blinked at Elora without any response. After a moment, the sprite held out a hand expectantly.

"Oh." Keeping her hand steady, Elora retrieved the offering she had already decided on: the leaf she had tried to keep track of the days on. When she pulled it out from under her corset, doubt crept in.

The little sprite was only half the size of a thumb and the leaf was as big as Elora's palm. The sprite's knees buckled under the weight of it. When Elora tried to help, the sprite shot a glare filled with daggers. The frail fingers of the sprite traced over the leaf as it narrowed its eyes. After a little nod, the sprite stuffed the leaf into a magical pocket on one side of her pink dress.

Setting her soft pink shoes shoulder width apart, the sprite placed both hands on her hips and looked up expectantly.

"Do you have a name?" Elora asked.

Again, the creature blinked. Her little face screwed up in thought, which made her cuter than ever. Still, she didn't speak.

Letting out a silent sigh, Elora decided to just get on with it. Apparently, the sprite had no interest in communicating with her. "I have a message for King Huron of Dustdune Court. Here is the message: I tried to obtain information about the vow, but the fae I spoke to was enchanted. I don't know how else to get the information."

The furry green wings began flapping the instant Elora finished. The sprite zoomed off in a flash of light. Its green glow gave off a faint pink sparkle as it disappeared.

Elora let out a sigh before falling onto her bed. Now to wait. The sour stench of her skirt and corset hit again. Unfortunately, the large stone basin at the edge of her room sat empty.

Instead, she decided to examine her gifts. Pulling the shell from under her corset, she ran a finger over the ridges. The shimmer looked even more blue in the shadows of her room. Next, she reached for the white feather hanging in her hair. Nothing about it seemed remarkable, but maybe it really was as special as Soren claimed.

A frown overtook her face. Even if it was, how much good could it do to be protected from accidental danger?

Tucking one hand under her pillow, Elora pulled out the pouch of coins hidden there. *Why* had she taken them with her to gather the apples? Now her sisters had been alone in the mortal realm for days, and they didn't even have any money. And the Bakers had only promised to give them bread, not enough food for every meal.

Her fingers found the ribbon around her ankle next. She stroked the silky fabric with images of her sisters filling her mind. They were starving and wore tattered clothes on the edge of the street.

Elora's heart quickened at the thought. Maybe she couldn't find out about the vow from Lyren, but there had to be another way to get Brannick out of the testing.

With one last stroke over the ribbon, she tightened the knot that secured it to her ankle. Just in case.

As she finished, a whirring noise sounded behind her. The air grew warmer as she glanced over her shoulder.

A door.

It had the same orange, red, and copper lights swirling through it as King Huron's door. But how did he know the exact spot in the castle she'd be? The sprite must have told him.

With that thought, the king's rich voice floated toward her from the other side of the door. "Come."

A little twist went through her gut, but she went through the door anyway. King Huron stood at the other end wearing another silk tunic, this time red with shimmering orange thread running through it in a swirling pattern. He wore the same crown with his jewels and crystals encrusted on the silk turban.

The scenery surrounding them was similar to her first visit to Dustdune, but it was not exactly the same place. They stood in a cove inside a large, colorful sand dune. Voices could be heard on the other side of the sand dune along with carts and the bustling sound of a city.

With a slight frown, King Huron stroked his mustache. "I will admit, I expected more from you."

"What?" The question came out as a gut reaction, but his statement offended her more the longer she thought about it.

He lifted the corner of one eyebrow. "You held yourself with such height. Such determination. I did not think you would give up so easily."

Twitches went through her fingers, getting closer to curling them into fists every moment. "I didn't give up."

"No?" He stared back at her with a straight face.

In a single breath, she willed the muscles in her arms to relax. "I can still help you, but I don't know what to do next."

The king nodded, giving the slightest eye roll with it. "And you need someone to tell you what to do?"

Pressure tightened between her eyebrows as she drew them together. "No."

He looked off to the side. Everything in his demeanor indicated this conversation was no longer worth his while. "Then, what do *you* think you should do?"

A huff escaped her as she reached for her sword. It wasn't there. And then she let out a grunt because years of sword training had taught her to grunt when frustrated. "I don't know." She stared at the ground while her foot tapped at an increasing speed. "I'm new to Faerie. I don't know what to do. I don't know all the rules."

King Huron let out a sigh as he pinched the bridge of his nose. "I see."

Now her fingers curled of their own accord. "What is it?" The words came out sharp, but they still didn't seem angry enough.

"You are weak." He didn't even say the words as if they were an insult. He said them like they were an obvious fact that everyone should know. "You will do what others tell you to do, but you cannot make your own decisions."

The instinct to grab her sword came swift enough to tangle her gut. With it gone, shaking a fist at him seemed like the only reasonable thing to do. "That's not true."

"No?" The king stared at his fingernails, pushing back a few cuticles. "Then tell me, why are you here? Did you ask to be brought to Faerie? Are you here because of your own choice?"

Just like that, weight pressed down on her. The lump in her throat didn't just make swallowing difficult, it made breathing difficult too. Anger lined her body, boiling with a stinging heat. But deep inside? An even stronger rage burned as she recognized the truth in his words.

His fingernails still held the king's attention. "See? You will always be a piece in someone else's game, but you will never play your own."

Her jaw flexed tight. "That is not who I am." It only took one breath to regain her cool. The rage still burned but with an entirely different focus now. Lifting her chin, she said, "I *will* find out what's in the prince's vow."

King Huron gave a quick glance her way, still verging on rolling his eyes. "I admire your resolve, but I need more than a promise. From a mortal like you, it means nothing."

Her leather sole slammed into the orange sandstone beneath her feet. "Then, I *vow* it."

A hearty laugh bubbled out of his mouth. "No, that will not suffice either. I need a bargain. You must tell me the exact words that Prince Brannick plans to use in his vow." The king's eyes narrowed with a devious smirk.

She almost let out a sigh at the sight of it. Did everyone in Faerie have devious intentions? Probably.

The smirk twitched on his lips. "If you tell me the exact words, then I will find a way to remove Prince Brannick from the testing."

Against her ankle, the red ribbon seemed to give off a tingling energy. Was it from the heat in the air? Surely, it had to be something like that. Still, the strange sensation made her pause.

"Unsure now?" The king brushed invisible dirt from his silk sleeves. "Do not tell me you have decided you would rather stay in Faerie?"

She rolled her shoulders back, remembering to make the terms specific. "Will you make sure I return to the mortal realm in time for my wedding?"

"Of course."

"Then I agree to the bargain." It came out in a rush. Maybe she just wanted to prove him wrong, but even more than that, she wanted to be in control for once. She didn't want her fate decided by the arrangement of others. She wanted to play her *own* game.

"I thought you might." The king waved a hand, and a swirling Faerie door appeared at her side. "Next time I get a message from you, I want it to say you know the exact words in the prince's vow."

Each step through the door felt like a kick to her gut. By the time she reached her room, her knees shook in anger. Not just at the mysterious Prince Brannick anymore. No. The anger turned in on herself. But it gave fuel to a new fire.

She *had* let herself be a piece in someone else's game. She had played the prince's games, agreed to his bargain. She had taught him sword fighting stances and dutifully ignored all the wonders Faerie had to offer. Her hand curled into a fist. It wouldn't continue.

Not anymore.

On the other side, her foresty room greeted her. She was in *Faerie*. There was a tree growing in her *room*. Ever since her arrival, she had suppressed her curious side. For what? All she'd ever dreamed of was adventure.

And now when she'd stepped right into one, she wasn't allowed to enjoy it?

157

She would still leave Faerie eventually, and she'd still marry Dietrich Mercer as she must. But no one could stop her from enjoying an adventure even greater than a tournament first. And when she did return to the mortal realm, her head would be filled with amazing memories to get her through the rest of her boring, mortal existence.

Even more importantly, she would start to play by her own rules.

The prince would soon regret making a bargain with her.

CHAPTER 19

Everything looked different when Elora woke up the next morning. Brighter. Crisper. For the first time since her bargain, she allowed herself to enjoy the thrill inside.

Faerie was *real*.

From the comfort of her soft bed, she took in a deep breath. The fringe from her green and black woolen blanket tickled her nose. She grinned in delight at the feel of it. Her hand swept over the geometric pattern on the soft wool. Nothing in the mortal realm felt so satisfying to touch.

Swinging her feet over the side of the bed, she remembered too late to watch out for her breakfast. But her feet hit the textured stone. No wooden tray sat nearby.

Before she could recall if she had set out an offering, the door to her room blew open as quiet as a whisper. A little brownie appeared through the opening, its long pointy ears flapping as it walked. The creature's light brown skin looked nearly the same color as Brannick's. It even wore a light green coat today with brown suede pants.

The creature's bulbous chin bounced as he nodded at her. "You are awake earlier than usual." His voice came out high, but it didn't carry the squeak she expected. Instead, the voice had a feathery quality to it.

"Is it earlier than usual?"

The brownie's big eyes blinked above his short, squat nose. With long spindly fingers, he set the tray into her lap. "I liked the offering last night. Black berries are always delicious, but the purple berries are my favorite."

Once he said the words, she remembered how she had snuck out her window and into the forest to gather a handful of black berries. Maybe one of these nights, she would have to explore a little more to find some purple ones.

"Eat, mort…" The brownie slammed his eyes closed and stomped a hairy bare foot. "*Elora* is what I meant. Prince Brannick said we should call you by your name."

The prince had said *what?* When had he decided to do something even remotely humane for her?

Fear seemed to shimmer in the brownie's brown and blue eyes as he gulped. "Is that wrong? Should I call you something else?"

"No." A tentative smile curled her lips. "I like it. But I can't seem to remember your name? Is it Finfer?"

A snicker made the brownie's bulbous neck jiggle. "It is Fifer. Now eat your breakfast. It has delicious meat mixed with scrambled firebird eggs."

That didn't sound especially promising.

"And it has a ground chicory and dandelion root gravy over it. You will love it."

It *still* didn't sound promising, but she didn't want to offend the little creature either. After one bite, she was convinced. The flavors married in a delightful burst that tasted like magic in her mouth.

While she ate, the brownie tidied her room and replaced the oils and soaps by her bath with new ones. A moment later, steaming hot water filled the large, stone basin. Apparently, the brownie could make water appear by magic.

All the scurrying suddenly made her worried. "Fifer, do you get paid to do this work?"

The brownie's bare feet squeaked over the stone floor as he skidded to a stop. With such large eyes to begin with, it looked positively strange when he opened them even wider. He didn't seem to be offended, just utterly confused. "We do not use…" His squat nose wrinkled in thought. "Money. That is the mortal word, is it not?"

Now it was her turn to be utterly confused.

"You don't use *money?* Really?"

With a shrug, Fifer went back to wiping dirt off the window ledge. "A brownie does not have to cook and clean, but most of us do it because it is the work we like best. We can leave the castle at any time. We can live anywhere we want. Most brownies prefer to live with high fae because it has advantages we could never have on our own. Prince Brannick is good to the brownies who live here. I hope one day to serve him personally. He offers us protection and luxurious rooms. The offerings I get here are some of the best in all of Faerie."

"So, offerings are like money?"

Fifer responded with a noncommittal shrug.

Elora bit her bottom lip as she pinched a piece of skirt between her fingers. "Could you do something for me then?"

The brownie looked her way, but he didn't respond.

"Could you wash my clothes for me?"

A grimace overtook his features as he glanced at her skirt. "That fabric is hideous and poorly made. Can you not destroy it and wear one of the dresses in your wardrobe? They are more stunning than anything in the mortal realm."

Tightening a fist around the purple fabric, she sucked in a breath. "My mother gave this to me."

The brownie responded by looking off to the side, as if working hard to make sense of her words. "Did you make a vow to keep the skirt?"

"No, it's just. My mother is dead now. It reminds me of her."

This only brought more wrinkles across the brownie's forehead.

Letting out a sigh, Elora shook her head. "It's a mortal thing. Never mind, I can clean it myself."

A sharp gasp erupted from the brownie's mouth. His eyes were wider than ever. "I can certainly clean it. How dare you suggest otherwise?"

"Oh, I didn't mean to offend—"

"Go on, get behind the hanging wall of vines. Toss the clothes around once you've removed them. I will have them back to you when day dawns. They will be cleaner than they have ever been."

Elora barely held in the snicker that sat at the back of her throat. It didn't seem possible for a creature slightly bigger than a rabbit to boss her around, but then again, this was Faerie.

"What type of dress would you like to wear?" Fabric rustled as the brownie dug into the wardrobe she had yet to open. "And jewelry? There is plenty to choose from."

Unbuckling her corset, her nose wrinkled. "Just set out the simplest dress you can find. I will only wear it this one day."

A heavy noise came from the other side of the hanging vines, one that sounded very much like a suppressed snort. The wardrobe doors closed a moment later. "I have laid a dress out for you. Your clothes will be cleaned by the time day dawns."

"I'll try to find purple berries for your offering tonight," she called out as she tossed her clothes around the wall of vines.

Fifer let out a squeak of delight before he scurried out of her room.

Lowering herself into the steaming hot water, she let out another sigh. Trying to hate Faerie and everything in it had taken so much energy. But loving it and being awed by it took almost no effort at all. The oils and soaps that day smelled like moss, berries, and vanilla.

After her bath, she put on the tan suede dress Fifer had set out. The fringe along the hem went down to her ankles. A bright green belt went around her waist. Despite the thickness of the fabric, she had never worn anything so soft and breathable. Maybe fae magic helped the fabric feel so supple.

Once ready, she left her room with the intention of finding some paper and pencils. The book of drawings from her father had been burned in the fire, and she had barely allowed herself to think of it. The pages had been filled with clothing the courtiers and gentlemen wore, the gardens and plants, and even the architecture of the castle. Of course, her favorite part had been the drawings of the knights and their weapons.

But now she herself lived in a castle. If she had to go back and marry a merchant, the least she could do was create a new book of drawings to remember all the wondrous things Faerie had to offer. After she found paper and pencils, *then* she'd find out about the vow.

Her wing of the castle seemed as empty as usual. The halls near the castle entrance weren't busy either. When she moved into the entrance hall, ready to exit the castle, Lyren stepped out in front of her.

The fae's light brown eyes glittered with silver as she clapped her hands together. "Here she is. We have something for you."

The words sounded nice, but a warning sparked in Elora's stomach. She considered Lyren a friend to some extent. Yet, the energy around the fae spoke of nothing but scheming.

Even as Elora swallowed over the sudden lump in her throat, thrill buzzed inside her. A scheme could be frightening, but how could she refuse any sort of excitement?

"Look! You must see what we have." The delight in Lyren's voice drew both high and low fae with every word. Soon, the entrance hall had scores of feet pattering nearer.

Now the thrill in Elora's stomach seemed more like a pit. Luckily, it didn't last long. Once she glanced at the corner Lyren indicated, calm took over.

Sitting in the corner—with the craftsman standing next to it—was a tall harp. Its wooden pillar had trees and briars carved into the wood.

Right then, Brannick entered the room wearing a scowl. The wolf at his side bared his teeth at anyone who got too close. "What is this?" the prince asked.

Lyren clapped her hands together again, her smile growing wide. "Since you still haven't gotten a harp for Elora, Quintus decided to make one instead."

Every muscle in the prince's body seemed to freeze for a moment. His wolf's nose twitched as he stared at Lyren.

In only a few steps, Brannick leapt to Elora's side. He set a hand against her back, trying to lead her away. "I have business with her. She cannot play the harp now."

Elora tried to step away from him, but Blaz stood on her other side with his teeth still bared and his nose twitching. It probably would have frightened her if the wolf's wrath had been directed at her. Yet strangely, the wolf seemed eager to intimidate anyone *but* her.

A pout overtook Lyren's face. "Why not? I have been dying to hear her play." A flash went through her eyes, which made her scheming more obvious than ever.

The craftsman, Quintus, slid a hand over the harp's pillar as he glanced toward Lyren. They only exchanged a brief glance, but it was enough to make dread trickle through the air.

"I built the harp just so I could hear Elora play." Quintus gave his own pout. "Could she not just play one song?"

Brannick still had his hand at Elora's back. Tension seemed to run through it as he nudged her a little closer to himself. At the same moment, the wolf moved closer to her as well.

Were they trying to *protect* her from the apparent scheming? Blaz she could somewhat understand. He had been nothing but friendly to her since she first saw him. But Brannick?

After a not-so-gentle push, Elora moved herself away from the prince and his wolf. "I will play one song."

The wood felt smooth and enchanting under her touch. The rich brown didn't seem to match any of the tree trunks she'd seen in Bitter Thorn. Pulling the harp's pillar down to her shoulder, she reached for the strings. "Usually one plays sitting on a stool or chair, but I can play like this for a short time."

Plucking the strings felt more like tapping the stem of a flower. They bent to her instruction and let out glorious sounds. She chose a mournful song to play. Lyren always seemed to hum those songs the most. But maybe her own heart had chosen something mournful too.

Her parents were gone. With a wedding in the future, her childhood was almost gone too. The sad notes echoed through the hall, sending grief and pain along with them. Her pulse slowed to match the melody, making the song feel like a part of her.

Truthfully, she had always liked playing the harp. But she liked torturing her mother during lessons a little more. Her mother was always getting after her to sit straight and be polite and curtsy low. Harp lessons were the only time Elora had more control than her mother. And of course, she wasted it by picking fights and complaining loudly.

But now her mother was gone forever. She could never get through a lesson without fighting. She could never even apologize. Just like the harp and her book of drawings, those chances had burned up in the fire.

The ending notes of the song hung low and tight in the air. They brought the same hardness through her that existed when she first saw her burning cottage. When she first saw the charred bodies of her parents.

They were gone forever.

And not even Faerie could bring them back.

No one noticed when she caught a tear as she set the harp back upright. The fae surrounding her seemed unable to move. Their faces were blank. They looked like they wanted more, but they didn't know how to reach it.

"I can see why you tried to hide her talent, Prince Brannick." Lyren's voice came out in a whisper. In the silent room, it pierced through the air like a shout. "You will have to protect her well, or another fae might try to steal her away."

The prince stared at Elora, seeming to ignore every voice and body in the room. His eyes shimmered like always, but his gaze had never felt so intense.

A gentle nudge came at the back of her knee. Blaz used his snout to urge her forward, toward the prince.

She complied without a fight. Brannick was probably eager to train with her once again. Though her chest pounded with the pain of her past, it only made her more ready to wield a sword.

When she reached the prince, he gestured and guided her out of the room.

Just before they left, Quintus whispered into the thick silence. "I have never heard such a beautiful song."

CHAPTER 20

The prince didn't speak to Elora as they traveled through the halls. It was a stark contrast to how he had gazed at her in the entrance hall. Now, he wore a stoic mask that didn't hint at cracking.

When they reached the armory, he pulled the vine to open the stone door without acknowledging her presence. Inside the octagonal room, the wolf tilted his head to the side while his ears twitched.

Brannick gazed at her again with that same strange intensity that twisted her chest in knots. He rubbed a hand over his wolf's neck as his eyes narrowed. "You actually *do* know how to play the harp?"

It felt good to be the one smirking. "You thought I was lying?"

He shrugged. "Lying is a uniquely mortal trait."

Her eyes narrowed. "Wait, so did Lyren and Quintus not believe I could play the harp either? Is that why they were acting so strange?"

The slightest flex went through the prince's jaw before he answered. "They suspect you are here in Bitter Thorn for another reason. But now that they have heard your music, they will be less suspicious." He eyed her more closely than ever. "I still do not understand. You are a master of swords. How do you also know how to play the harp?"

She wanted to roll her eyes but managed to suppress it. "I'm cultured."

Blaz tilted his wolf head at the exact same moment Brannick did. They wore the same half-open mouth paired with scrunched up eyes. They looked supremely confused, as only a Bitter Thorn prince and his wolf could.

A sigh escaped her lips. "My father taught me sword fighting. My mother taught me to play the harp." She shook her head as an even more important thought took over. "Wait, a *uniquely* mortal trait? You mean fae can't lie?"

He waved the question off before his face grew serious again. "Lyren is right. Faerie will be more dangerous for you now that others know you have skill. Some fae collect skilled mortals and treat them…"

Blaz tensed, showing a bit of his teeth as he glared across the room at nothing in particular. The action almost stole her attention completely, but an even smaller action managed to catch her eye. Brannick's fingers twitched at his side, almost as if he wanted to curl his fist but controlled the impulse.

Her eyes went from Blaz then to Brannick and back again. Their emotions and reactions were always so in sync. Did they share a connection? Or perhaps Blaz had just been around the prince so long that they thought the same things about people.

After clearing his throat, the prince gestured toward the back wall that hid the stone compartment with her sword. A hand wave from the prince opened the compartment. He allowed her to retrieve her sword and then pulled out a second sword hidden inside. "Does this one meet your standards?"

For a moment, Faerie stopped existing. She closed her eyes as she balanced the sword and ran a finger over the blunt side of the blade. With no sight, she could almost pretend she stood in her father's forge testing one of his recently made weapons. The hilt, the pommel, the cross-guard. Every part of the sword was just as important as the last.

With a thrust, she sliced the sword through the empty air. Every muscle in her body was attuned to its movement to check its quality.

"It's good." She pushed it into his hands, ready to pull her own sword from its sheath. It had been too long since she'd held it.

But the prince was staring at her again. His gaze felt even more captivating than ever. When he had stared before, she had been entranced by him, but now? He seemed to be mesmerized by the sight of *her*.

"What?" All the staring made her stomach writhe.

His eyes narrowed as he took a step closer. "You express so much emotion in your features."

Her stomach did a flop. Maybe him staring wasn't the worst thing that could happen.

With a grimace, he jerked his gaze away. "It is disgusting."

She rolled her eyes back hard. *There* was the prince she knew too well. "Show me your stance. Now that you have an acceptable sword, we can begin."

Blaz settled down next to a stone wall that held spears. He watched them intently as they fought, as if danger might leap out at any moment.

The prince did better than she expected. Much better. After the second perfectly timed parry, she let out a grunt that made him chuckle. After a few more moves, his improvement sent a flurry of heat through her limbs.

It probably wasn't becoming for a master to be impatient over her student's rapid growth, but she didn't care. "Do you have faster reflexes than me?"

"Yes."

The answer came so swiftly, she almost missed his next strike.

He let out a chuckle and glanced toward his wolf, as if seeking approval. "My eyesight is also better. My hearing is better. I'm stronger, my taste is more sensitive." He sliced his sword through the air with perfect form. "I truly do not understand how mortals survive with such inferior bodies."

His sword fighting form was perfect, but so was his ability to get under her skin. *Inferior?* She let out another grunt. Brannick was so arrogant. Which meant he probably *didn't* want to know that she was being extremely easy on him. It wouldn't take much effort on her part to overpower and harm him. But that probably wasn't the best way to teach sword fighting.

As she threw another strike his way, it reminded her of a much more important conversation they should have been having. Asking while the prince was distracted might be more effective too. "Have you determined the exact words for your vow yet? The one that you will give to the high king?"

The thinnest shimmer of sweat glistened across his brow. "We are getting close. Lyren sees more loopholes and intricacies than I do. It helps, but it is taking more effort than I anticipated."

Hopefully the prince didn't see her grin as she blocked a blow. "Can I help?"

His hands immediately lowered while his eyes narrowed. During his moment of hesitation, she jabbed the sword toward his gut. Against her father, she would have moved much faster, but the prince was still a clumsy beginner. Even if he was a fast-learning one.

The slow speed gave him time to block and improve his stance. He still managed to raise one eyebrow at her as he moved. "You scream at me in front of my trusted council one day and another day you offer to help?"

She let out a huff before spinning into an attack stance. "And you only seek to understand me when it benefits you?"

"Yes." His sword shook as he nearly lost his grip on it. "I see no shame in that. I must take care of myself. And you hate me, so I do not understand why you would help me."

Raising a hand, she indicated that they should rest. He hardly seemed winded, but Brannick nodded eagerly. Her sword sang as she dropped it into her sheath. "I'm sure if you thought about it really hard, you could think of a reason I want to help."

He stared back at her without moving. Rolling her eyes, she decided to interact with the only creature in the room that she actually liked. Blaz bounded toward her once he realized her intention. He licked her fingers and nuzzled his nose into her leg.

A grunt sounded at the back of Brannick's throat. His eyebrows pinched together as he folded his arms over his chest. "We hate her. What are you doing?" he asked the wolf.

Blaz paid him no mind, which sent a giggle to Elora's lips. A crease appeared between the prince's eyebrows. "Do you feel sorry for me?" He spat the words out while glaring at her.

She laughed and rubbed a hand through the softest fur she had ever felt. "No."

One eyebrow raised on Brannick's forehead. "You want to help Blaz?"

She gave the wolf one last rub before returning back to her position in front of the prince. "You are impossible."

He shifted his feet, still wearing a glare that looked capable of wilting flowers. "Our bargain only requires that you teach me sword fighting."

She slapped a palm against her forehead. "And the sooner you win the testing, the sooner I can go home to my sisters." As an afterthought, she added, "And so I can marry my betrothed."

His gaze did not shift away from her for several moments. The crease between his eyebrows had vanished, but his eyebrows were still pushed down. Finally, he glanced at Blaz, who had settled back onto the stone floor. The wolf almost seemed to give a nod in the prince's direction.

Throwing his arms into the air, Brannick let out a huff. "Oh, why not? We have determined that the high king's statue will contain a magical essence that spontaneously grows roses all around it. The statue itself, of course, will be of the high king."

When she raised her sword, he mirrored the movement. Their practice continued again. "Why roses?"

Brannick moved into a perfect stance before swinging the first blow. "High King Romany is from the Court of Noble Rose. He has been the only ruler from his court, even when it was known as Rarerose."

The blades clashed as she sent slow strikes at the prince. "The court used to have a different name? Why?"

Once again, the fighting seemed to lower the mask of stoicism the prince often wore. "Before this court became known as Bitter Thorn, it was known only as the High Court. At that time, Romany's court was called Rarerose. When Bitter Thorn was cursed, Rarerose became the new high court and was renamed Noble Rose."

"*Noble* Rose and *Bitter* Thorn?"

A twitch went through the prince's nose as he glanced away. "Yes, the names were chosen to mock my court. To highlight its disgrace."

The sharp reflexes and swift movements he had at the beginning of their training had dwindled. Apparently, even a fae prince could get tired. "Is that when you became prince? When Bitter Thorn was cursed?"

He pierced her with a hard stare, but his lips didn't move.

Sheathing her sword, she took a step forward. "Lyren said your mother created a portal between Faerie and the mortal realm. You said that portal brought unwanted emotions into Faerie. Did the other fae kill her for her mistake? What happened to her? Why are you in charge now?"

Each question seemed to hunch the prince's shoulders a little more. He took a step backward and glanced away. "She made a choice and suffered for it."

His defenses seemed more broken than ever. A decent person would have stepped away. Would have let him rest. But the red ribbon around Elora's ankle rubbed against her bare skin. She gripped her sword hilt and took another step forward. "How important are the exact words of the vow?"

"Very." He waved a hand to get her to step away, but she didn't. With a huff, he reached into a pocket of his shirt. At

174

least he hadn't removed it this time. He placed a small scrap of paper into her hand. "Here. This is what we have so far. We might change one or two words, but this is very close to what I will say to the high king."

Controlling her breath wasn't possible when her heart beat so wildly. She gripped the paper, trying to not give away too much with her expression. "Don't you need this?"

He continued to avoid her gaze. "I have it memorized." His eyes flicked over to hers for a brief moment before he shot them away again. "You must love your betrothed very much if you are so eager to return to him."

Just like that, her own defenses crumbled. The scrap of paper got tucked into a small pocket of her dress, but it didn't change how her heart twisted. Maybe being vulnerable would make him less suspicious. Or maybe she just had to get these words out because otherwise they might consume her from the inside out.

Slumping her shoulders, she said, "I don't even know him. He has a nice library, I guess. And he promised to let me practice my sword fighting after we get married." She shrugged, hoping the prince didn't see how her lower lip trembled. "But I've only met him once. And he's so old." She glanced toward him, allowing the tiniest smirk on her face. "Like you."

The reaction came even faster than she expected. Brannick's arms dropped to his sides like weights as he stepped forward. "I am *not* old."

She took a step closer to him. "You've been the prince of Bitter Thorn for a long time, haven't you?"

An exasperated burst fell out of his lips. "That is not..." He massaged his head with one hand. "In Faerie, age is measured by experience. You have experienced the loss of your parents. You are a master with the sword *and* with the harp. You even have wings. By fae standards, you are also old."

Looking him in the eye seemed suddenly impossible. Her eyes turned to the ground as she tucked a piece of hair behind her ear. Before completing the task, the prince grabbed her hand and pulled it up to his nose.

"Where did you get this scar?"

He rubbed a thumb over the lopsided scar on the fleshy part of her hand between the finger and thumb.

"Why?"

When she tried to pull away, he allowed it but only after he slid a finger over the scar once more.

"It looks like a troll bite."

She rolled her eyes at him as she hid her hand behind one leg. Why did it seem so warm now? "Have you had many trolls in the castle since my arrival?"

He raised an eyebrow. "Of course not. Trolls live in Fairfrost. They never travel outside its borders unless they are with the queen."

Though she had pulled her hand away, the prince still stood close. That intense gaze wouldn't shift off her. Except it wasn't the same as when they had begun training. A deeper respect seemed hidden under the layers of his arrogance.

The scrap of paper burned a hole in her pocket. With a swallow, she stepped away from him. "I don't remember where I got the scar, but I can assure you, it wasn't from a troll. It probably came from climbing a tree or something."

He nodded, but the way he looked at her sent a tingle all through her. Turning on her heel, she marched toward the exit. She couldn't let a look like that distract her now. The exact words to the vow were hers.

It was time to contact King Huron.

CHAPTER

21

E lora stood in the middle of her room, staring at the glowing lights that floated near the ceiling. The scrap of paper in her pocket contained the exact words she had promised to give King Huron. But now, she needed an offering for a sprite.

Her chest fell as she moved toward her large window. It seemed silly that she could have forgotten something so simple. The forest outside her window came to mind. Maybe she could peel a bit of moss off the rock she sat on when she first met Lyren. Hopefully that was personal enough to work as an offering for a sprite. Even with the scheming, Lyren was the closest thing to a friend Elora had in Faerie.

Thorns bit into her fingers when she grabbed the window ledge. She hissed at them, as if they could hear. Why did those things have to grow everywhere?

Using her boot, she snapped the vines of the briars until the thorns fell away. A fresh, green vine provided her something to hold as her feet stepped onto little ledges and spots jutting out from the black castle walls.

It didn't take long before she landed on the damp soil. Sucking in a long breath, she enjoyed the scent of leaves and dew and wildflowers. A clump of pink wildflowers reminded her of the frail sprite who had delivered her message to the Dustdune king. Her pink dress had sparkled against her glowing green skin and wings.

As Elora entered the forest, a part of her hoped that same sprite would be the one who sent her message again. Green lights lazily circled above her head. The sprites were everywhere in Faerie. Which probably meant her chances of seeing that sprite in the pink dress again were nearly impossible. But maybe that sprite had liked her too. She could have come back.

On her way to the moss-covered rock, Elora came near a tall tree with a thick, brown trunk. Familiarity struck through her at the sight of it. But it wasn't until Kaia's brown and green eyes blinked from inside the tree trunk that Elora remembered why.

The dryad stepped out of the tree wearing a gauzy white dress and several beaded necklaces. Her hair was parted down the middle and in two braids again. Except this time, the braids only went halfway down. It left plenty of glossy emerald hair to flutter in the breeze.

Her brown skin looked more like bark today. Variations of color stretched over it, but it still had the same smooth texture as skin. She smiled. "I was looking for you, my child. I was almost away from my tree for too long."

Without another word, the dryad disappeared back into the tree except for a few of her facial features. Her hair and dress couldn't be seen at all. Instead, it just looked like the tree trunk had eyes, nose, and a mouth.

"Why were you looking for me?" It probably wouldn't be polite to mention how disconcerting it was to be talking to a tree.

"Prince Brannick told me you played the harp in front of a large crowd today."

Elora bit her bottom lip and reached for her non-existent sword hilt. The dryad used her same gentle tone as always, but that hadn't stopped the words from sounding like an accusation. With her eyes on the ground, Elora nodded. "I did."

Even inside the tree, Kaia's eyebrows seemed to lower in a patronizing look. "The prince asked me to stay with you more often. You do not understand the danger you put yourself in by playing so well."

Reaching an arm across her stomach, Elora shrugged. "I didn't play *that* well. My sister, Grace, is much better than me, and she's only twelve."

"Hmm."

It wasn't even a proper response, but it still managed to pierce Elora with guilt. Maybe now was a good moment to change the subject. "Do you have any paper in the castle? Or parchment? And also drawing pencils or paints?"

Kaia sucked in a sharp breath. Though only a few of her features remained visible, it looked distinctly like she was about to faint. "Do not tell me you are a skilled painter as well."

"No." Elora nearly snorted on the word as it came out. "My skills are rudimentary at best. I just wanted to do a few basic drawings of the castle and clothes and a few other things."

She looked at the ground again, and her voice came out softer than before. "So I can remember Faerie after I go home."

A sparkle glittered in Kaia's brown and green eyes. "I can find you some paper and pencils."

As they continued to speak, Lyren wandered into the clearing carrying a painted clay pot filled with dark red beans. "They are seasoned perfectly," the fae said as she popped one into her mouth. "The brownies helped me make it. Such a delightful snack. We do not have such seasonings in Swiftsea."

Lyren held the pot out, allowing Elora to take a few. They did indeed taste delicious. She considered sneaking one into her pocket to use as an offering for a sprite, but she gobbled them up before she had the chance.

Both Kaia and Lyren snickered when they saw Elora's empty hands.

A wistful look passed over Lyren's face. She took the flower out from behind her ear only to stare at it with a sigh. "I do miss Swiftsea. The oceans and sands." She closed her eyes and breathed in deeply. "The salty air."

Giving a quick nod, Elora took a step back. This seemed as good a time as any for her to sneak away. She'd just have to find that rock and get a piece of moss from it.

Lyren slid a finger over the seashell necklace hanging from her neck. "I so miss my friend, Waverly. She is a mermaid and has the most spectacular blue and silver hair."

Just as Elora moved a step back, her foot went forward again. "There are *mermaids* in Faerie?"

The fae let out a titter in response. "Of course."

Part of Elora's mind was still on the scrap of paper in her pocket, but a much larger part of it couldn't release the wondrous idea of mermaids. Soon, she sat cross-legged on a clump of fresh moss while Lyren told tales of Swiftsea.

The dusky light of a Faerie night had filled the sky before Elora made it back to her room. She only barely remembered to gather a handful of yellow flowers as an offering for Fifer before she returned to her room.

When day dawned, the little brownie brought in her cleaned clothes. They looked richer than ever. The skirt was soft and slippery and gorgeous. The leather corset felt more flexible than ever, but somehow, stronger too. Elora spent the day searching for purple berries to bring to Fifer, as she had promised.

Another day was filled with doing drawings of everything around her. Lyren even helped. Her drawing skills were far greater than Elora's.

The dryad stayed with Elora almost constantly, only returning to her tree when Elora trained with the prince.

Suddenly, Elora sat on her bed at the end of another day.

And she had no idea how many of them had passed.

Why hadn't she been worried? How could she have forgotten so easily about her sisters and her marriage? Snatching the piece of moss from under her corset, she moved to the center of the room. It might have been evening, but she'd already wasted too much time enjoying Faerie.

It was time to send a message to King Huron.

CHAPTER 22

Heat flushed through Elora's cheeks as she raised her hand in the air.

For the first time since coming to Faerie, something held her back when it came to returning home. Of course the realm was cruel and devious with all sorts of rules that didn't make any sense. But it was magical too. Beautiful. Full of excitement that no tournament could boast.

She let out a sigh and clicked her tongue three times. At least now she would have something wonderful to remember for the rest of her life.

A glowing green light swirled down toward her hand. A pink sparkle of light moved along with it. When the sprite landed on her palm, Elora recognized the pink dress and velvety, grass-like hair at once.

"I remember you." Elora brought the sprite closer to her face. "I didn't think I'd see you again."

The sprite's red lips pursed, but not in a bad way. It was more like the sprite tried to hold back a smile.

Holding up the bit of moss, Elora said, "This moss comes from the spot where I met my first fae friend. Maybe you and I could be friends one day too."

The sprite's balance teetered once the moss was dropped into her hands. Her frail arms shook while examining the tuft.

"I wish you would tell me your name." Elora let out a sigh as the sprite continued to gaze at the spongy green moss.

With eyes flicking up, the sprite quickly glanced back at the moss again. She tucked it into her magical pocket, even though the tuft was at least five times the size of it. As she had done the first time, the sprite stood shoulder width apart and placed her hands on her hips.

Elora moved her palm close enough to her face that she had to be careful to not breathe too hard, or it might knock the little creature over. "No? You won't tell me your name?"

The velvety hair twists jiggled as the sprite shook her head.

Twisting her mouth to one side, Elora let out a short sigh. "All right then. I have a message for King Huron of the Dustdune Court. Tell him: I have the vow."

Before the sprite flew off, she pointed to her pocket and grinned. As her furry wings began flapping, she gave a distinct wink.

Delight coursed through Elora, which she had no ability to control. The sprite hadn't said a word, but she'd still communicated. In a way.

Leaning against the tree that stood in the middle of her room seemed like the only thing Elora could do. If she wasn't careful, she would grow far too attached to this magical realm.

It didn't take long for a door to appear. The orange, yellow, and copper lights that filled the swirling tunnel looked brighter than ever. Dry heat seemed to suck moisture from her skin as she stepped through the door.

Once again, large and colorful sand dunes greeted her on the other side. This was a new location yet again. A little pool of clear water sparkled in the dip of a sand dune. King Huron looked the same as always. His dark skin and mustache were beautiful against his yellow-orange silk tunic.

"What is the vow?"

Elora raised a single eyebrow at his eagerness. She folded her arms over her chest, ready to fight harder for her own desires than she had before. "Don't forget, I'm only helping you because I need to get back to the mortal realm. My sisters need me soon. It's urgent." She tried to puff out her chest like she had seen her father do when trying to exert dominance. "I need reassurance that helping you will get me home sooner." Especially since she had unintentionally let so much time pass.

A smile stretched across the king's face, but his eyes looked dead. "It seems you have learned to play your own game after all." He waved a hand through the air. "I will explain my plan to you, which will surely give all the reassurance you need. The testing is supposed to have three phases. The vow, the speech, and the tournament. Fae tradition dictates that each part will have long breaks between them."

"But." Her hands fell to her sides as her eyebrows pinched together. "I need to get home soon. I can't wait for long breaks between each phase."

King Huron nodded. "And I would like to win before the end of all three phases, trust me. But I have a plan. For my vow, I will promise High King Romany that my power is greater than half the Faerie realm. High King Romany may be

184

seduced by the thought of legacy, but nothing will appeal to him more than raw power. That is what made *him* High King."

Her head tilted to the side. "*He* took the title from Bitter Thorn? Did he curse the court also?"

The king's eyebrows rose into his silk crown. "You have learned some Faerie history, have you? Yes, High King Romany was part of a council that stripped High Queen Winola of her title and cursed her court. He became high king by demonstrating that he had the greatest amount of magical power of any high fae."

A skeptical thought twisted Elora's mouth to a knot. "And you now have more magical power than that?" It seemed unlikely, especially because Brannick's magic was supposedly renowned enough that he needed someone to teach him sword fighting instead. How could Huron be more powerful than that?

Rather than answer her question, he pulled something from his pocket. A golden shard sat on his palm. The shape of it looked like a piece of glass that had been cracked from a mirror. Its jagged edges looked sharp enough to slice through even strong materials like leather.

But the color was something else entirely. No, color couldn't even describe the sight she beheld. It did look gold. But it simultaneously looked glittery, shimmery, and even glowy. It gave off an energy that crackled through the air.

"Have you seen one of these before?" The king's voice sounded far away compared to the captivating shard.

Her hair brushed against her cheek as she shook her head side to side. But even that seemed far away.

He closed his hand over the gold object and tucked it into his pocket again. "It is called a balance shard. Two types exist.

The gold shards can turn fae into mortals. The pink shards can turn mortals into fae."

Elora sucked in a breath when she realized she was still staring at the king's pocket. Her eyes flicked to his. "How does that help us?"

King Huron stood a little taller before he spoke again. He didn't even try to hide the devious nature of his grin. "When a fae turns into a mortal, their magic is absorbed by the fae who offered the shard."

It took a few breaths to gather her thoughts. She ran a thumb across the tips of her fingers as she spoke again. "So, you plan to turn a few powerful fae into mortals? And then you'll have their magic?"

A wicked chuckle left his mouth. "Well, a little more than a few."

The energy in the air changed again. Even in the warm Dustdune air, a chill ran through her. "What does that mean?"

He let out another chuckle as he adjusted the ends of his sleeves. "My plan will not harm any fae in Bitter Thorn, if that is what worries you. The protections around its border are too strong for my shards to get through."

Her head nodded, seemingly of its own accord. She was oddly comforted by that knowledge, but it didn't calm her racing heart.

The king gave a sweeping gesture over the sand dunes around them. "The fae within my own court will obviously be safe as well. So will the fae from Fairfrost."

"Why Fairfrost?"

A twitch went through one of his eyebrows when she asked.

But the memory of her first meeting with him answered her own question. "It's because the queen of Fairfrost is working with you, right?"

His eyes narrowed to slits. "Why do you say that?"

Tension twisted through her as she tried to gulp. "You sent her that message when you showed me how to use the sprites."

After a short sigh, calm settled over King Huron. "I had forgotten about that." He pinched the bridge of his nose. "Anyway, only the courts of Mistmount, Noble Rose, and Swiftsea will be affected."

Her chest tightened all at once, which sent her heart down to her stomach. Pain lined her throat when she tried to swallow. Hearing the name of Lyren's court only exacerbated the symptoms. Elora tried to swallow again. "Does it hurt? The shards?"

When the king looked at her, he didn't seem upset by the question. Rather, he seemed intrigued by it. "You are sympathetic to fae now?"

She shrugged. It was harder than she expected to make it seem casual. "Maybe."

His eyebrows lowered as he leaned forward. "Once I enact my plan, even High King Romany himself will be affected. No other fae will be able to fight against my raw power. I will be undisputed as high king."

Her heart refused to beat as another chill slithered up her spine. So much power in one fae couldn't possibly be a good thing.

With a patronizing tilt of the head, King Huron gave her a pointed look. "And *then* I will help you return to the mortal realm."

One foot stumbled as she took a step back. "Why do you need the words to Brannick's vow then?"

187

He glanced up with a mild expression. "I need Prince Brannick's vow because I must find a way to exploit it. I need to make High King Romany believe the Bitter Thorn vow is unworthy of the high king's greatness. Knowing the words ahead of time will make it easier to do that."

She gulped before taking another step back. "I don't know if it's going to help you that much. It seems like you have things figured out."

The muscles in his forehead twitched. "I need to make Prince Brannick's vow look bad so the high king will be convinced to allow me to do a presentation." He shook his head which shook the feather on his crown. "We have a bargain. You *must* share the words of the vow."

Just like that, her feet froze. The sand beneath her feet seemed to crawl up the soles of her boots, trapping her in place. How had she forgotten yet another Faerie rule so easily?

A bargain was impossible to break.

The king responded with a subtle smile. "As long as you tell me the vow, I will do everything in my power to get Brannick out of the testing. Then, you can go home."

Home.

Hearing the word was bittersweet. Thoughts of her starving, vulnerable sisters brought her hand straight to the scrap of paper that contained the vow. But thoughts of her marriage and the boring life she'd have to live made her fingers falter. What harm would these shards really cause? Would it hurt Lyren to be turned mortal? Would it hurt her mermaid friend?

It didn't matter. The truth hit Elora harder than a pommel to the chest. She had already made the bargain. All she could do was fulfill her part.

The scrap of paper felt prickly between her fingers. She pushed it into the king's hand, angry that he took so long to read it.

When he opened a door at her side, she bounded through it faster than she ever had before. After running into her room, she threw herself onto the bed and curled into a ball.

What had she done?

The drumming in her heart did not bode well.

CHAPTER 23

Elora spent the night running a thumb over the silk ribbon around her ankle.

Memories fought for her attention throughout the night. Chloe dancing through their cottage, reciting poems as she went. Grace closing her eyes while her fingers plucked the harp strings in sweeping melodies.

They needed her.

But every day in Faerie made it more difficult to determine how long she'd been there. The events of each day muddled in her mind. It all felt like one day and every day and not any day at all.

Rubbing a finger over the red ribbon helped. It grounded her and reminded her of the mortal realm where time wasn't so difficult to decipher. It had been at least two weeks. Maybe more.

But had it been longer than three weeks? Had she missed her wedding? Even if she hadn't, what if Dietrich arrived early to retrieve her, and she wasn't there? What would happen to her sisters then?

Kaia had come into the room. She used her motherly voice and pulled the soft green blanket off Elora.

When the dryad pushed a flat piece of fried bread into Elora's hands, it didn't seem real. She couldn't feel it. The emerald-haired fae begged her to take a few bites, which she did. But it tasted like sand in her mouth.

Using one hand, Kaia led Elora out into the hall. Prince Brannick was waiting for her in the armory. The walk passed by in a flash as she tried to count the days again.

How close was the wedding? If Huron's plan worked, she might barely get home in time.

The prince was talking to her now. His mouth moved. Blaz stood at his side with an intense expression. But it took so much effort to nod in the appropriate places that Elora couldn't possibly process the words too.

All at once, a sword dropped into her hands. Her sword. She rubbed a finger over the raised shield symbol her father had marked the pommel with. Her sisters needed her. Nothing else mattered.

Even when she started training, her mind had wandered far away. She worked through the moves using muscle memory alone. She hardly even noticed if the prince was following along.

A swipe. A jab. Shield. Block.

But then the prince's sword cut through her defenses and nearly pierced her leather corset.

She gave a sharp gasp and stepped back.

In a single moment, the world came rushing back at her, splashing against her like a sea of freezing water.

Sliding a hand through his long hair, Brannick grinned. "Am I getting better than you already?"

"Have you heard of a balance shard?" The question came out with no conscious decision on her part. Apparently, spending the whole morning trying to convince herself that Huron's plan didn't matter had only convinced her it did.

Metal clattered to the stone floor as Brannick's arms fell at his side. His mouth hung slightly open while his ever-changing eyes turned decidedly hollow. "Who told you about that?"

Her breath shuddered as she tried to suck it in. Even holding tight to her sword hilt couldn't stop her fingers from shaking. "Can you please just answer my question?"

The prince's sword remained at his feet. The rest of his body had gone impossibly still. In the corner of the room, Blaz's ears perked up. Tense muscles ruffled his black fur.

Brannick's eyes narrowed. "Was it Lyren? I thought I could trust her, but she has taken a greater interest in you than I expected. You need to watch out for her. Many fae *do* keep mortals as pets."

"It wasn't Lyren." Terror skittered across Elora's nerves. "Do you think her intentions are insincere?"

A new look crossed the prince's face. Now he seemed to be the teacher instead of her. "Lyren's intentions are selfish, just like every fae's intentions. But maybe she still likes you. Fae *are* capable of friendships." His eye twitched as he leaned forward. "We are not as evil as you seem to believe."

It was easy to brush off the accusation. He was clearly trying to distract her, which wouldn't work. "So, you *have* heard of balance shards?"

From the corner of her eye, she noticed Blaz tense again at the mention of the shards.

On the other hand, Brannick let out an annoyed sigh. "I assume someone is tempting you with the promise of becoming fae, correct?"

After a bombardment of thoughts, it seemed best to avoid answering his question directly. Instead, she asked, "Does it really work?"

His demeaner relaxed again. After plucking his sword from the ground, he gripped the hilt and spun it in circles. "Technically, the balance shards do have the power to turn a mortal into a fae. But it never works. You would die a slow and painful death if you tried."

The breath went out of her then. Even the blood seemed to stop coursing through her limbs. When she spoke, the words felt sticky inside her mouth. "But then why are they rumored to have that power?"

Brannick stopped spinning the sword. He rested the tip of the blade on the stone floor and then rested his elbow on top of the pommel. "They *do* have that power. The process is what kills. The shards meld with your heart. They make you experience every negative feeling you have ever had, but at an unbearably high level. If you have ever been sad over something small, like losing a button, it would feel five times more painful than seeing your parents' dead bodies. The grief kills more completely than a spear or sword."

At some point, her heart had started beating again. Now it hammered in her chest as a sheen of sweat popped out over every surface of her body. If it got any colder, she'd start shivering. "Is it the same for fae? You don't feel emotions like mortals, right? I know the shards can turn fae into mortals. Is that process less painful?"

A laugh parted the prince's lips, but it didn't hide how his shoulders hunched. "That is even worse. The shards cause fae to experience the feelings they would have felt in their lifetimes if they had been mortal. And again, the pain is greater. No one can survive the process."

"No one?" A squeak pinched through her words as her voice broke.

His eyes turned down to his sword. "There are tales of survivors, but they are few and far between. I doubt their accuracy anyway."

Her head dropped into her hands as she tried to grapple with this knowledge. In a whisper, she repeated his previous words. "No one can survive."

She couldn't tell how long she'd been standing there, or how many movements happened around her. In her head, she could see Lyren writhing in a corner somewhere, screaming for an end to the pain. Pain that Elora had let happen.

"Shall we continue?" Brannick held his sword out, but his face seemed more passive than usual.

She buried her face in her hands again, shutting out the room along with him. "I need to think." Her fingers curled against her face, ending in fists that she pressed into her closed eyes. "What happens to the magic of the fae?"

Peeking above her fists, she saw Brannick glance at his wolf, both looking even more confused than ever. "If a mortal survives the shard, Faerie itself will provide magic to turn the person fae."

Ice lined her throat when she spoke again. "And if a fae turns mortal?"

"Their magic is absorbed by the fae who offered the shard. You may realize, the shards only work if a fae offers one to you."

The screaming fae in her mind wasn't limited to Lyren now. Elora imaged a sea full of mermaids, a sandy beach covered in fae, all writhing and screaming.

Dying.

She took a deep breath, which Brannick seemed to think meant she was ready to fight again. As he raised his sword, she dropped words from her mouth as heavy as iron. "King Huron of Dustdune knows your vow."

His grip faltered, nearly dropping the sword in his hand. "What are you talking about?"

Her shoulders rolled back, but it didn't help. "You know that paper you gave me with the words of the vow on it?" A hard gulp bulged through her throat. "I gave it to King Huron."

For a moment, he stood there without moving. Little by little, the anger slowly seeped in. First, he gripped his sword hilt tighter. His knees vibrated as his leg muscles tensed. Red heat flushed his cheeks. He clenched his jaw so tight a vein in his neck popped out. She could *feel* his shout even before it left his mouth.

"You lying…" His nostrils flared. "Deceitful." He raised the sword into the air. "*Mortal.*" His blade swung toward her with more venom than he'd ever shown before. "How could you?"

She dodged the blow easily, but it made talking more difficult. "I have to take care of my sisters. Huron promised to help me get home sooner if I gave him the vow."

A low growl sounded at the back of Brannick's throat as he swung his weapon again.

When she blocked his strike, she used a little more velocity than necessary. "My sisters will *die* without me. I just wanted to go home."

The prince responded with a hard slash in her direction.

It only took a few light steps to get away. "I know his plan. Just calm down, and I'll tell it to you."

Brannick swung at her again, but he seemed to realize his skill was no match for her own. "Why would I believe anything you tell me?"

"Because I knew you might kill me when you found out about my deception, and I still told you anyway."

Without any force behind it, the prince pointed the tip of his sword toward her. "That makes you stupid, not trustworthy."

"No, it makes me compassionate." She dropped her sword into its sheath and glared at the prince. "I'm guessing that's a uniquely mortal trait too."

His sword clattered to the ground as his mouth pinched in a knot. "You think betraying me and conspiring with my enemy is compassionate?"

He could pretend to be belligerent all he wanted, but at least he'd dropped his sword. Now she could tell him everything. "King Huron is planning to give golden shards to every fae in the Mistmount, Noble Rose, and Swiftsea Courts. He is going to use the power he absorbs to take control of Faerie."

The prince's nose wrinkled at her words. "Even if he gives shards to all those fae, he cannot force them to pierce their own hearts. No fae would be foolish enough to do such a thing."

She stepped forward, moving as close to him as she dared. "I don't know how he plans to do it, but I know he's confident it will work. He's going to use the words of your vow to convince High King Romany that your vow is secretly harmful to Faerie. He hopes that Romany will then allow Huron to perform an unplanned presentation. *That's* when he plans to release the shards."

The prince's nose continued to wrinkle as he used one finger to push her back. "How did you even meet King Huron?"

Her feet stumbled. "Oh. I forgot about that." Reaching for a lock of hair, she looked at the ground. "Your friend, Vesper, is also betraying you. He opened a door to Dustdune, and I followed him through without his knowledge. King Huron called Vesper his *favorite spy.*"

Brannick spat out a laugh.

"You believe Vesper was working for Huron?" He didn't say another word as he yanked her sword out of its sheath. After plucking his own sword from the ground, he hid them in the stone compartment. Her sheath went in next.

Blaz bounded to the prince's side as he hid the compartment with magic. While marching toward the exit, Brannick spoke in an authoritative voice. "Training is over. I need to meet with my council."

CHAPTER

24

A cool breeze blew through the council room, making it colder than Elora remembered.

Leaves rustled in the trees growing alongside the council table. Brannick insisted she sit in the chair nearest to him, though nothing about it seemed kind or protective. He sneered at her as he snapped away the briars growing on the arms of his throne.

Even Blaz eyed her with a hint of suspicion. When she reached out to him, he flashed his sharp teeth and sat closer to the prince.

The others gathered, each wearing varying expressions of confusion and fear. Lyren sat on Elora's side and Kaia sat across from her. They didn't smile or preen over her, but they didn't seem to hate her either.

That wouldn't last.

Soren came to the table grumbling about a splintered spear. Vesper and Quintus entered together. Their laughs filled the room until they caught sight of the prince's face. Silence fell as everyone settled into their chairs.

Brannick shot another glare at Elora before speaking across the table. "I have solved your mystery, Vesper. I found out who followed you into Dustdune."

The curly-headed fae blinked before his gazed shifted to the prince's side. "The mortal?"

So, they were back to calling her *mortal*. Her hands twisted in her lap as she looked down at them. This time, she probably deserved it.

With eyes shimmering, the prince spoke through his teeth. "Tell her what you have been doing with King Huron."

Vesper glanced at the prince once more before he began speaking. "I have planted false information, tried to discover his plans."

Brannick sneered, turning slowly to face her. "And what have *you* been doing with King Huron?"

Fire burned in her throat as she tried to swallow. The words boiled in her mouth, but she couldn't get them to come out.

The prince cocked up an eyebrow. "You will not tell them? No matter, I will." His eyebrows twitched as he turned to face the others. "The mortal gave King Huron the exact words to my vow."

A tiny gasp escaped Lyren's mouth and she clapped a hand to it. Her eyebrows pinched together. She flashed her teeth at Elora.

The scrutiny only served to harden the guilt in Elora's heart. Slapping her palms on the table, she leaned toward the prince. "I also found out King Huron's plan, which is more than the rest of you were able to do."

Spears seemed to shoot out of Brannick's eyes as he rounded on her. "I should imprison you for the rest of your life for what you have done."

Her heart beat so fast, she had to put a hand to her chest. Still, her stomach dropped. "You can't do that. You promised to take me—"

Tightness filled her throat, choking her as soon as she got too close to mentioning her bargain. It took several hacking coughs before she could breathe again.

While she tried to clear her throat, the prince sat back in his stone-carved throne. He stared down his nose to look across the table. "Soren, get this mortal out of my sight. I will retrieve her when she is needed again."

The fight went out of her when Blaz gave a low growl in her direction. Every eye in the room narrowed as she got to her feet. Their features hardened with her every step. The thumps in her chest pounded hard enough to cause pain.

Through the halls of the castle, Soren led her in silence. His white beard sat stiff beneath his chin, as if his steps couldn't affect it. The fae's all-black eyes glared ahead, never once glancing her way or acknowledging her presence at all.

No grumbling passed through his lips. Thick silence hung between them, only their footsteps breaking through it.

An angry Soren would have been better. Even a livid one. But this complete, glaring silence made her insides writhe.

It came as a surprise when he delivered her to her room. Despite the bargain, she had been expecting a dungeon. She didn't fight when he gestured inside the room. The moment she passed through the threshold, the fae's short, pointed hat shook as he released a shimmery, golden light. The gold traveled through her room until it lined the walls. It gave one last glow, sealing the exits before it vanished from view.

Her stomach continued to sink as she ran a hand through her hair. How had she gotten into such a huge mess? How had she gotten Faerie into such a huge mess?

Collapsing onto the floor, she reached for the red ribbon from Chloe. It was still tied as tight as ever around her ankle. What would happen to her sisters now? Would they die of starvation? Would they live on the streets?

An ache strained in her heart as she curled into a ball on the stone floor. Even the patches of moss felt colder than usual. It had been right to tell Brannick about the Dustdune king's plan. Or had it? Were half the fae in Faerie worth more than two mortals?

Trembles passed through her arms. But those *mortals* were her sisters. How could she jeopardize her return to them?

As they always did, the glowing lights floated above her. A pink sparkle moved along with one of the green lights. Whether it was the same sprite she had met before or not didn't matter. Elora desperately needed someone to talk to and that silly sprite was the closest thing she had to a friend now.

She pulled herself to a sitting position with her back against the large tree. Hugging her knees to her chest, she watched the pink sparkle as it moved across the room. "King Huron of Dustdune is going to kill half the fae in Faerie. He's going to absorb their power."

With a sniff, she dropped her chin to her chest. "Three whole courts." Her arms gripped tighter around her knees. "I know it's not completely my fault, but I did help him." She touched a hand to her forehead. "It doesn't even matter if I'm at fault or not; I still want to stop him." Tears welled in her eyes as she sniffed again. "But now I'm stuck in my room. Useless."

The sprite with the pink dress flew down close enough for Elora to recognize her, but she kept her distance.

Elora's lip trembled when she spoke again. "I'm scared for you. For all fae. The king will have so much power afterward. There's no telling what he'll do with it."

After each word, the sprite flew a little closer. By the time she finished, the sprite hovered a hand's length away from Elora's nose.

Her fuzzy wings buzzed so fast, they blurred in a bright green glow. Her face looked conflicted. She held her hands behind her pink dress.

Gazing at the sprite, Elora rubbed a wrist across her nose. "I don't know what to do."

At that, the sprite glanced up at the green lights above her. In response, the lights twinkled with a brighter glow. A soft sparkly sound erupted above them.

Elora pulled her knees closer to her chest again. "I bet you're sick of me asking, but what's your name?"

"Tansy." Her voice came out high but not shrill. Instead, it sounded silvery and clear.

It took three heartbeats before Elora recovered. Her jaw had dropped at the sound of it. "What?"

The sprite hovered in gentle drifts as she stared back. "King Huron is going to use sprites to deliver the shards."

Putting a hand over her heart, Elora checked that she was still breathing. Her voice came out in a whisper. "I thought you couldn't talk."

Soft, green eyebrows lowered over the sprite's eyes. She slammed fists onto her frail hips with a deeper glare. "Of course we can talk. How else could we deliver messages?" With a flippant head toss, she looked to the side. "We simply choose to not speak to other fae except when delivering messages. It is against our code."

This probably wasn't a good time to point out that the sprite was now breaking that code. Or maybe mortals didn't count. But at least she had a name to pair with the pink-dressed sprite. Tansy.

Moving her legs into a crisscross position, Elora gestured to urge more conversation. "You said King Huron is going to use sprites to offer the shards?"

Tansy's eyes darkened as she gave a hurried nod. "On his signal, we will travel to the three courts of Mistmount, Noble Rose, and Swiftsea. We will approach fae and say, 'I have something for you from King Huron of Dustdune. Do you accept?' Thinking it is only a message, the fae will agree. Then, we will pierce their hearts with the shards, and they will die."

Once all the words were out, the sprite stared at the ground with a look that made her eyes droop. She even lowered in the air as she hovered.

Elora bit her lip. "Can't you just... not do it?"

The sprite responded with a deeper frown.

While closing her eyes for an extra moment, Elora let out a sigh. "You have a bargain, don't you?"

Tansy responded with a nod. "King Huron's greatest magic is with bargains. He can make any bargain tip in his favor. You are lucky to have that ward around your ankle, or your bargain with King Huron would have turned out much worse."

A bit of hair twisted around one of Elora's fingers as she tried to think. "What *can* we do? How can we stop him?"

The green lights glowed all around her now. A faint breeze from the sprites' wings kissed her skin. The other sprites didn't look her way or acknowledge her presence, but their flying indicated they did indeed know she was there.

With her pink dress sparkling, Tansy's face shifted to one of hardened steel. "We do not believe King Huron has collected the shards yet. If High King Romany begins the first phase of testing before day dawns, it will prevent King Huron from collecting the shards."

Something passed through Elora that almost felt like victory. "Convince the high king to begin the testing?" She got to her feet and ran a hand over the tree trunk, as if it might give her courage. "I might be able to do that."

CHAPTER 25

Elora twisted her hands together as she looked up into the leaves of her bedroom tree.

Shifting from one foot to the other, several questions passed through her mind. How could she convince the high king of Faerie to begin the testing right away?

The pink of Tansy's dress sparkled as she hovered and weaved around Elora's head.

A wave of homesickness hit Elora all at once. "I wish my sister, Chloe, was here. She would know exactly what to say to the high king. She's so much better with words than I am."

Tansy responded with an exaggerated eye roll. "Maybe it would be best to consult with a master of words for such a task."

While sucking in a breath, Elora's arms dropped to her sides. "I forgot about Brannick. He doesn't even have a vow anymore." She glanced at the door of the room and narrowed her eyes. "You know how Soren put that enchantment on the room that locks me in?"

The sprite's velvety hair bounced as she nodded.

One of Elora's eyebrows quirked up in response. "Can you get through it, or are you stuck in here with me?"

The scoff that left the sprite's lips sounded just as proud as it did offended. "Of course I can get through it.

A smile stretched over Elora's mouth. Even without seeing it, she knew it probably looked devious. Faerie had officially gotten to her. And she didn't mind in the least. "Can you send a message to Prince Brannick for me? Tell him we can probably stop King Huron if we convince the high king to begin the testing before day dawns."

The furry green wings of the sprite flapped before Elora waved the sprite down again. "And tell him I already have a message to convince the high king. I just want his blessing to send it."

While the sprite zoomed out the open window, Elora pressed her forehead against the tree trunk. Now she just had to think of the perfect words.

Her chest tightened. She scowled at it in response. It had no business making things more difficult for her in a time like this. As a last-ditch effort, she reached for the low branches of the tree and hoisted herself onto them.

Once settled onto a wide branch, she glanced over the room. It looked different from high up. The patches of moss growing over the stone floor and walls looked smaller, yet brighter too. Briars twisted around the window ledge and along the door frame. The wall of vines that hid her bath from view fluttered gently in a light breeze.

With a deep breath, Elora lifted her palm into the air and clicked her tongue three times. A little sprite zoomed down to her palm before she could take a breath. This one wore a teal vest and bright green pants. He had a little beard and dark brown skin.

After peeling away a piece of bark from the tree she had come to love, she turned to the sprite. She offered a smile along with the bark, which the creature seemed to like. "I know what I want to say to High King Romany. Can I say it now but have you wait to deliver the message until after I know that Brannick approves?"

The sprite gave a hurried nod and tucked the bark into his pocket.

"Good." Elora settled deeper against the tree, trying to breathe in its barky scent before she continued. "Here is my message to High King Romany of the Court of Noble Rose." She cleared her throat. "There is a plot to take away your life even faster than the poison will. Begin the first phase of testing before day dawns if you want to survive until the end of the testing."

The sprite stood so still, he seemed to be made of stone.

Her lips fell into a frown at the sight of it. "Is it good enough, do you think?"

Perking up, the sprite nodded again.

While he did, another glowing green light came darting toward her. Soon, Tansy's wings beat wildly as she hovered close to Elora's face.

"This is Prince Brannick's message. 'You may do whatever you wish, mortal. It will not make a difference.'" Tansy had the decency to look down as she said the words.

A lurch went through Elora's gut. Her jaw clenched as the statement settled into her. *Mortal.* And that wasn't even the most offensive thing about the prince's message.

Her jaw clenched again, tight enough that her teeth almost cracked. She gave a pointed look at the bearded sprite on her hand. "Send the message."

The sprite's eyes widened before he vanished through the open window.

Maybe Brannick wouldn't have much time to prepare a new vow, but at least this plan would prevent King Huron from killing half the fae in Faerie.

If it worked.

Her stomach dropped again, but she just reached for a tree branch and swung herself down to a lower one. In her mind, she ran through a list.

High King Romany just had to begin the testing before day dawned.

King Huron wouldn't have time to collect the balance shards.

Brannick might not do so well in the first phase of the testing.

Her teeth bit down on her bottom lip so hard it almost drew blood.

But at least half of Faerie wouldn't be dead.

When her boots landed on the stone floor, the red ribbon shifted on her ankle. All at once, the tightening of her chest and the dropping of her stomach were nothing to how her heart ached.

"Tansy." Elora glanced toward the sprite, hoping the creature couldn't see tears welling in her eyes. She swallowed. "When all the sprites bargained with King Huron to deliver the shards, what did he offer you in return?"

The sprite's pink and green eyes flicked upward at the lights floating around them. A silvery sound went through the air. At the sound of it, Tansy winced. "I should not say."

That seemed to be the end of it until Tansy hovered closer. Her frail arms gripped Elora's ear, which felt very much like a bug landing on it. The sprite whispered, "He promised to free our brothers and sisters. Queen Alessandra of Fairfrost does not allow sprites to fly freely in her court like we do in all the other courts. She keeps us caged in a dark room in her palace. When fae of her court want to deliver a message, they have to go through the queen and then she delivers the message. All sprites that enter her lands are forced by magic to travel to her first. After that, they are trapped in her cage."

Elora shook her head. "But King Huron and Queen Alessandra are allies. Why would she help him if he planned to free her sprites?"

A shudder shook through the sprite before she answered. "Queen Alessandra does not know his plan."

Cold slithered up Elora's spine. After a tight swallow, she asked, "Do you know any sprites who are imprisoned there?"

With wings fluttering against Elora's cheek the sprite landed on her shoulder. "I was trapped in Fairfrost for so long, I lost most of my essence."

Though high-pitched and silvery, the words felt like a knife to the heart. Was that why the sprite looked so frail?

"And if High King Romany starts the testing, it might prevent King Huron from using the shards…" Elora glanced over at the sprite on her shoulder. "But your brothers and sisters will still be stuck in Fairfrost."

The little sprite flapped her wings enough to send a flap of wind through the air. "We do not want to kill half the fae in

Faerie either. What concerns us more is that the bargain will still be in place even if the testing begins this evening."

Elora blinked for an extra-long moment, afraid of the answer to the question she had to ask. "Is there any way to break a bargain?"

Tansy shrugged. "It depends on the bargain. Usually, the one who proposed the bargain can revoke it. Or if one party dies, the bargain usually ends. But it all depends on the exact language used."

The wheels in Elora's head turned so fast, it made her stomach churn. Idea after idea hit her like the blast of hot air from a flame. She jerked her head toward the sprite. "What if we're wrong? What if King Huron collected the shards already?"

The sprite responded with a confident shake of the head, which quickly turned into a fearful look.

"Do you know where the shards are? Can you make sure they haven't been collected yet?"

With a single bounce of the head, Tansy floated toward the window.

Elora's heart lurched in her chest as she leapt for the door. She only had one chance to test her theory. Her hand wrapped around the leather door strap, watching the window carefully. Just as the sprite exited the room, Elora yanked on the strap.

To her pure delight, the door swung open. It had been a wild guess to assume the sprite had a way of breaking the enchantment inside the room. The sprite's magic could have just as easily passed through the enchantment instead of breaking it. But fate must have been on Elora's side today.

She crept into the deserted hallway outside her door. A true idea hadn't formed in her mind yet. In fact, she probably wouldn't know what she was going to do until she actually did it. But one thing she did know.

She needed her sword.

Whatever adventures or mysteries were ahead, she would need that sword at her side to get through them. Maybe she didn't need a tournament to sword fight after all.

At the end of her wing, the bustling voices of the other fae in the castle filled the hallways and rooms. But Brannick and his council were certainly still in that room meeting with each other.

Holding her head high, Elora traipsed past the nearest group of fae. A pair of high fae were examining a few gauzy tablecloths. They had seen her before. Most of the fae ignored her anyway, probably because she was mortal. So why should now be any different?

Her breath caught in her throat the whole way to the armory. But no one stopped her.

She entered the octagonal room and went straight for the stone compartment holding her sword. Standing in front of it, she quickly realized only magic could open it. Even wedging a spear from the wall into the edge did nothing to help.

That only seemed to give her more determination. She *wasn't* a piece in someone else's game. Her eyes flicked up to the glowing lights above her. "Can any of you open this?"

The lights twinkled at the sound of her words, but they continued floating around. She shook her head. Asking wouldn't work, she had to think like a fae. Fae were selfish.

"I can give you something in return. If you open the compartment, you can have my boots."

The boots had been hers for almost a year, which definitely made them personal. But they weren't exactly important to her either. The sprites seemed to agree. They twittered around in the air, still floating away from her.

It had to be something important. Something emotional but not something she needed. Sucking in a breath, her head shot up.

"What about my belt with the sheath? It would take several of you to carry it, but you can have it."

In a flash, they zoomed toward the compartment, opening it in no time. She pulled her sword free and offered them the sheath.

They swarmed around it, each grabbing a different part of the leather belt. For some reason, they refused to touch the sheath. With so much going on, she didn't really care why.

Now her eyes went to the door of the armory. Getting there hadn't been much trouble— but returning? The other fae were sure to notice if she carried a sword through the hallways.

Biting her lip, she tucked the sword into the folds of her skirt. Once it was covered, she held the hilt with one hand but carefully positioned it, so it looked like she was simply lifting her skirt to walk.

She held her breath almost the whole way back to her room, only allowing herself a few careful breaths. When she reached her door, she opened it with no trouble, but she couldn't step into the room. The enchantment still blocked her, apparently even when she was trying to get back in.

After slowly releasing the folds in her skirt, she poked her sword through the doorway. It passed through without issue. Just as she discovered that, footsteps sounded from nearby.

Before she could even take a breath, Brannick appeared around the corner. His black hair swept in thick strands behind his shoulders.

Without thinking, she tossed the sword into her room to the side. She hoped it would land hidden somewhere behind the hanging wall of vines.

The prince narrowed his eyes as he moved closer. "How did you get out of your room?"

Perhaps an attempt at humor might soften the situation. "I learned to do magic while you were gone."

His eye roll managed to tilt even his head.

She stood up straighter. "Is there a reason you're here? Did you decide to bring me home early?"

After a wave of his hand, the golden shimmer around the edge of her room glowed before it disappeared. He gestured inside. "There is news."

CHAPTER

26

Once Elora stepped into her room, Brannick barreled in after her. He slammed the door shut behind him and narrowed his eyes at every visible surface and crevice.

Soft fur tickled her fingers. She started when Blaz's body appeared at her side. "Where did you come from?" she asked as she rubbed behind his ears.

The prince continued to examine her walls, this time touching them with varied amounts of pressure. "Blaz can put on a glamour that keeps eyes from looking at him. It is how he hid from you in the mortal realm."

It felt nice to have the wolf giving her attention again. She hadn't realized how much it hurt to have him growl at her until he nuzzled up to her leg. She gave him an extra rub in return. Perhaps the prince and his council had decided the knowledge she shared was valuable after all. Why else would the wolf be kind to her again? "What's a glamour?" she asked.

"It is how fae disguise themselves." His voice sounded faraway as he ran a hand over the stone wall next to the door. "I used a glamour in the mortal realm as well. It made me appear mortal, but glamours are versatile. They can do many things."

His eyes shifted upward at the glowing lights above. The sprites flew more freely after her conversation with Tansy. Silvery whispers danced between them now. Their lights seemed to glow brighter too.

The prince folded his arms over his chest. "Did one of these sprites help you escape your room?"

"No." It wasn't *technically* a lie since Tansy hadn't returned from checking on the shards. She was the one who had aided in the escape.

Brannick raised a skeptical eyebrow in response.

What good was avoiding lies if Brannick didn't believe her anyway?

She took a step forward. Maybe that would distract him from figuring out how she escaped. "What is the news?"

Blaz padded across the floor toward his master before the prince answered. "High King Romany has requested our presence for the first phase of testing. We are to arrive at nightfall."

A thrill went through her, and she clapped her hands together. "So, it worked?"

After screwing up his face, the prince shrugged. "The high king requested we meet at the Dustdune Castle instead of his own. So, King Huron has the high king's ear. At least in some regard."

Her stomach sank at the thought. Still, as long as he hadn't collected the shards, it probably didn't matter where the first phase of testing took place.

Brannick continued to look around her room but with a different sort of expression. Before, he had been searching for an explanation for her escape. Now, he simply seemed interested in what the room held. It seemed strangely intimate to have his eyes wander over the window she had snuck out of so many times. When he glanced over her bed, it brought a jolt to her stomach.

A tingle spread through her skin as he continued to stare. When he turned toward the wall of vines and the wardrobe, the sensation felt more like needles.

What if he found her sword?

With a hard swallow, she slowly stepped in front of him.

He gazed so intently at her wardrobe, he didn't even seem to notice the movement. But a moment later, he looked at her. More accurately, he looked at her clothes. His eyes pulsed with impossible colors, drawing her attention as they always did. Then he glanced back at the wardrobe again.

A frown tugged his lips down. "You do not behave the way I expected you to."

Droplets of sweat broke out on the back of her neck, proving how completely his eyes could mesmerize her. Trying to gain some control back over herself, she too glanced at the wardrobe. "Because I don't wear the clothes you gave me?"

"Why do you not?" Once again, his piercing, shimmering gaze brought shivers through her. He gestured toward the wardrobe. "There are many styles of clothing inside, including styles popular in the mortal realm. They are much finer than the clothes you wear. Your wardrobe even has jewelry with gems and gold and every sort of luxury. We do not care for such jewelry in my court, but they are easy enough to conjure. I thought you would be delighted."

For a moment, she forgot to be mesmerized as her eyes opened wide. "You can conjure gems and gold?"

That same wicked smile that had entranced her from the beginning spread across his lips. "Not all fae can, but for me it is easy."

His shoulders looked broader than ever when he carried himself with such pride. The black hair fell to his shoulders in straight, glossy strands. His light brown skin perfectly complemented the chiseled features in his face.

She glanced away with a silent huff. It was such a cruel trick of Faerie that he should be so handsome.

"I wear these clothes because they are from my mother."

The prince raised an eyebrow.

Her hand slid over the folds of her skirt. "They help me remember her."

His eyebrow only raised higher. He stepped toward the tree growing in the center of her room and placed his palm against the trunk. "Your memory is not enough?"

She let out a sigh, resigned to the fact that no fae would ever understand.

But the prince no longer seemed interested in a response. He closed his eyes and took a deep breath, as if smelling the tree. His palm pressed against its trunk. "Have you climbed this tree?" he asked with his eyes still closed.

She reached one arm across her stomach and held tight to her opposite elbow. "Yes." And then she gulped. "Is that bad?"

Brannick opened his eyes and gave a quick shrug. "No. Kaia said you liked climbing trees. She chose this room for you."

Elora blinked in response, but the prince wasn't looking.

How did the dryad know about her love of tree climbing? Elora had never done it when they were together.

She didn't have much time to contemplate the question because Brannick leaned one shoulder against the tree and pinned her with another mesmerizing stare. "We chose another vow for me to give to High King Romany."

Flutters bounded all through her stomach, which she tried desperately to ignore. "Oh?" Did the prince hear the higher pitch in her tone? Maybe a quick swallow would help. "Do you think it will be enough to stop King Huron from doing a presentation for the high king?"

Brannick shrugged. "Against a fae who magicks in bargains, one can rarely win the fight."

Her head jerked toward him. "A fae who magicks in bargains?" The words felt familiar on her tongue, but she couldn't remember why.

The prince didn't seem to notice her reaction. He leaned into the tree, not quite looking at her as he spoke. "Instead of a statue, we will give the high king something else to honor his life." From his magical pocket, the prince pulled out a glass orb slightly bigger than his palm. Though the glass seemed to be transparent, Elora couldn't see anything in or through it.

"This orb can record a memory." When he looked at the glass, a slight grimace passed over his features. "They are extremely rare. I paid dearly to obtain this one, which I planned to use for another memory." He let out a sigh that pierced her with guilt. "But with little time to prepare, it is all we could think of to entice the high king."

The longer she stared at the orb, the more it sizzled with energy. "How does it work?"

"A request lined with magic will make it record the memory of choice. Once recorded, the memory will last forever.

Afterward, a fae need only touch the orb to be transported to the moment the memory was made. Anyone can experience the memory as if there when it first happened. High King Romany will adore the idea of a moment from his life being recorded in such a way. Then, he will never be forgotten."

Remembering how her sword still sat somewhere on the ground behind the wall of vines, she moved herself more directly in front of the prince. "Will you just give it to him then? You'll let him decide which moment to record?"

Brannick's eyes had been gazing at the orb, but he slipped it into his pocket. "No, I have already chosen what will be recorded. The moment will be part of my vow." He stretched his arms out, which reminded her how strong he was. "A song will be played in the high king's honor. The song will forever be associated with his life... and death."

The prince shared a look with his wolf before he glanced at her again. His gaze seemed more pointed than before. "It will be a mournful, beautiful song, sure to make all fae listen in awe."

It took another pointed stare before she finally caught on. "You mean the song I played on the harp? You want me to play it for him?"

A shiver went through Blaz, ruffling his black fur.

The prince's eyes shimmered in response, somehow looking more frightening than ever. "Yes," he replied in an even tone.

The word melted into her. Even swallowing did nothing to dispel the writhing strands of fear that wrapped through her limbs. "But didn't you say it was dangerous for me to play in front of other fae?"

He let out a chuckle which felt more like a punch to the gut. "It will be very dangerous for you." And then came that devious smirk he loved to wear. "But that is not my problem."

With a sweeping turn, the prince marched out of the room. After passing through her doorway, he snapped his fingers and a shimmer went through the room, glowing when it reached the edges. It looked just the same as the other enchantments that had locked her in the room, but this time it was silver.

Her stomach sank. Something told her *this* enchantment would be impossible for her to sneak through.

The sinking only deepened when she considered the new vow. She gripped her skirt with two tight fists and forced herself to take even breaths.

How bad could it be? She only had to play the harp.

The beating of her heart increased despite her attempts at calming breaths.

She'd just play a mournful song that had already entranced a roomful of fae. A gulp did nothing to assuage her fear. And this time she'd play in front of an even larger roomful of fae. Ones even more selfish and devious than ever.

Okay, it was probably pretty bad.

But the thought of such danger only struck her with an intoxicating thrill. Only one thing could distract her now.

Snatching a piece of parchment from the pile near her bed, she began making a list of everything she had done since being in Faerie. Though fear still gripped her like a knife to the neck, she managed to smile at all the whimsical things.

Make friends with a sprite.

Climb a tree inside her room.

Climb a much larger tree in a Faerie forest.

Gather offerings for a friendly brownie named Fifer.

The list grew, which made her heart flutter in a wholly different way. Faerie certainly had downsides, but the adventurous side of her could find nothing but perfection in all its delights.

Now came the terrifying part of making this list.

She grouped the items together into days. No matter how she tried, she had never been able to keep track of the days she had spent in Faerie. Keeping track of the events was much easier. Now she just had to remember which events had happened together.

It didn't take long to organize everything into days, but the result sent her heart into a tangled mess.

The prospect of playing the harp was nothing now. Air stilled around her.

Three weeks.

She had spent three weeks in Faerie. Her heart stopped as she stared at the deceitful list.

Her wedding was tomorrow.

CHAPTER

27

The paper felt like crusty earth in Elora's hands. Her eyes scanned the handwritten events over and over again, trying to discover a flaw in her accounting.

In Faerie, the days truly bled into each other. They all seemed to be happening at once. As Brannick had often said, time didn't seem to exist in Faerie.

But it still existed in the mortal realm. Maybe everything was happening at once in Faerie, but her sisters still had to live day after day without her.

Elora had been in Faerie for three weeks. Her sisters had been alone for too long. They had bread, but the Bakers only promised to help until Elora's wedding.

Which was supposed to take place tomorrow.

The truth of it choked in her throat, leaving a hardness that couldn't be swallowed away.

Being in a magical world had helped her forget her troubles. Her responsibilities. But that didn't mean they had disappeared.

As she had always known it would, her wedding had come to haunt her.

She focused so much on the paper, it took a moment to realize a glowing green light had appeared outside her window.

The light flew forward, but when it reached the open window, it bounced backward. The silver enchantment around her room gave a shimmer at the same time. The sprite's light flickered for a moment.

A shiver seemed to pass through the sprite just before the green light glowed bright. With another zoom toward the window, the light continued to grow outward. This time, it passed through the silver enchantment with no trouble.

By the time the sprite flew close enough to recognize, Tansy's eyebrows were already knit together. Her expression only darkened the closer she got to Elora.

Her furry, green wings flapped as she flew, but quivers seemed to shake them much more than usual.

The sprite landed on Elora's shoulder. Rather than stand upright as she had always done, Tansy collapsed into a sitting position as she let out a heavy sigh. "The shards are gone."

If Elora had had any energy left inside her, she probably would have gasped. "King Huron has them?"

Even turning awkwardly to look at her shoulder, Tansy's body visibly hunched over. "Yes." Her voice no longer sounded silvery. It was high-pitched and croaking instead. "I don't know how. He never could have collected the shards that quickly on his own. Even with their strength and speed, fae cannot get to the balance cliffs easily. Wings are the best way to travel there, but the dragons will not go near them. Unless he got help from the trolls, I do not see any way he could have done it so quickly."

The words triggered a conversation she and Brannick had during one of their training sessions. Elora looked to the side. "I thought all trolls live in Fairfrost."

Tansy's fuzzy green wings hung limp as she pulled her tiny knees up to her chest. "They do. But they have an alliance with Queen Alessandra, and this plan will make her lose the control she has over her sprites. I do not understand why she would help King Huron. We thought she did not know about his plan."

Elora narrowed her eyes at the sprite. "The balance cliffs are in Fairfrost? I thought you said sprites couldn't enter Fairfrost without being sent to the queen."

A tiny sob escaped the sprite before she buried her face in her knees. When she spoke, her high voice came out muffled. "The balance cliffs are on the border of Dustdune and Fairfrost. I stayed on the Dustdune side but could still see where thousands of golden shards were broken off the cliffs."

It didn't help that all the questions had a logical answer. That only meant this problem was getting worse. After urging the sprite to move into her palm, Elora set the sprite down. Next, she curled into a ball at the base of her tree.

Being in nature, especially around trees, had always brought her comfort. Brannick would probably say it was their essence. Maybe he was right. Elora tucked her chin to her chest and crumpled the paper with events into one fist. With her other hand, she hooked a thumb over the silk ribbon around her ankle.

Those reminders of her life in the mortal realm did nothing to hide Faerie. Tansy still sat in front of her, her tiny body and wings shivering in fear. The magical enchantment still trapped

Elora inside her room. King Huron still had the shards and the sprites would still be forced to deliver them.

Her heart throbbed in pain. She held tighter onto the ribbon and crumpled the paper even more. The tears she'd been holding back flowed down her cheeks. Every part of her trembled as pain sank into her skin. Her limbs. Her heart.

The two fists she held were the only things keeping her grounded during her anguish. Every sniff and sob sent a hard shudder through her body.

It wasn't fair for the prince to hate her. She had sacrificed her deal with King Huron to tell Brannick the truth. If she hadn't told the prince about the shards, she could have returned to the mortal realm that evening. Right when her sisters needed her.

Instead, she chose to protect Faerie and tell Brannick about the plan. And he had repaid her by making a plan that would put her life in danger. Playing the harp might not get her killed, but it certainly wouldn't make her life in Faerie any easier.

Her fingernails dug into her palm as she gripped the ribbon tighter.

And yet.

She gulped.

And yet, that wasn't even the thing that hurt the most.

A pain had burrowed into her chest many weeks ago, and that pain only pulsed in agony now.

Even if they found a way to stop King Huron, even if she got home to her sisters in time, even if everything worked out the way she dreamed, she still wouldn't be happy. Because one truth inside her heart refused to settle.

Her parents were gone now. As much as their deaths pained her and left her heart hollow, it also left her with a responsibility that was almost too much to bear. Elora *wanted* to save her sisters. She wanted to protect them and help them. But...

She *didn't* want to get married.

It didn't matter how nice Dietrich Mercer's library was. It didn't matter how much money he had or how quiet he promised to be about her sword fighting. She didn't *want* to settle for a life she had no part in choosing.

Her body rocked in jerky motion as tears continued to fall. Her parents had fallen in love with each other, hadn't they? Why couldn't she fall in love and make some stupid decision for love like they had?

On that point, why couldn't she just stay in Faerie? All her life she had dreamed of a place with adventure and intrigue and a chance to use her sword. Now she had finally found one, and she was supposed to give it all away?

Why couldn't she stay and help the sprites get out of their bargain? Why couldn't she enjoy the magical world without the threat of returning to a life she didn't want?

Just like a needle piercing her heart, words came back to her that had hurt her so much when she heard them the first time.

You will always be a piece in someone else's game, but you will never play your own.

Her gut rocked as she clenched both of her fists tighter. Her fingernails dug deeper into her palms, nearly drawing blood. It only fed fuel to her fire.

How had King Huron been so right about her? How had she given up so much of her life just because someone else told her she had to?

Her chest swelled as she jumped to her feet. She threw the paper onto the stone floor and crushed it under her boot. With the backs of her hands, she wiped away the trail of tears that slid down her cheeks.

Touching the tree, she sucked in the deepest breath of her life. Her chest had never expanded so much. And air had never tasted so sweet.

I am not a piece in someone else's game. She repeated the words in her mind until her arms shook at her sides. Until the mantra thrummed through her with more energy than sword fighting. More than her wings. It buzzed through with more force than the responsibility she felt to her dead father.

Breaking through the shields she didn't know she had put up, clarity hit her like it never had before.

Just because she loved her father didn't mean she had to do what he wanted.

Just because she had to take care of her sisters didn't mean she had to get married.

Now, when she admitted to herself that she didn't want to get married, it came with an even brighter realization.

I don't have to get married. I won't.

The air around her sizzled. Her wings broke out of her back, flapping and sparkling like they never had. When she moved away from the tree, her feet didn't brush over the stone floor. Instead, her wings kept her floating just above the ground. The motions were still jerky, but her sudden realization seemed to improve her flying skill the tiniest bit.

Ideas came to her the moment her feet lifted off the ground. How strange that it only took a decision to find a way out of her prison.

Elora stood in front of the wardrobe, putting her wings away. The simple wood had been carved with triangles and diamonds, similar to those on the green wool blanket on her bed. For so long, she had refused to look inside the wardrobe. Now, it would provide her salvation.

The doors thrust open easily. Sparkling, shimmering fabrics spilled over her arms. Velvet, lace, brocade, organza. Some of the fabrics she had only heard of but never seen. Their threads shone brilliantly; their drape fell with perfection she had never dreamed of in mortal clothes. Each piece of fabric had the thickness of a sturdy corset but the softness and lightness of a feather.

And the colors! She had never ogled over clothing the way some others did, but even she couldn't deny how rich and exquisite these dresses were. Such finery was fit for royalty. Not just mortal royalty but fae royalty too.

Even more importantly, they were fine enough to fetch a high price in a market.

All at once, the dresses transformed in her mind into little piles of gold. After examining them, she knelt and retrieved the wooden box at the bottom of her wardrobe.

An involuntary gasp escaped her when she lifted the lid. Gems twinkled back at her. Necklaces, bracelets, and earrings in every possible design. Strands of pearls, diamonds, and sapphires sat in the box as unassuming as flowers in the forest. And there was *so* much gold. Strand after strand, pendant after pendant.

Even the king in the mortal realm couldn't boast such wealth.

She lifted a simple necklace with emeralds and black pearls. That alone could buy an entire cottage for her sisters. Food would never be a problem for them again.

The grin on her face grew tighter with each moment. She snatched the wool blanket from her bed and spread it out flat on the floor. It took some time to gather all the dresses and jewelry into a neat pile on the blanket. When she finished, she tied the four corners of the blanket together until it sat neatly in a bundle.

It might be heavy to carry, but maybe her wings could help if she needed. Staring at it, her heart soared again.

No matter what happened, the marriage with Dietrich was off.

Saying it in her head brought joy like she had never known.

It wasn't until that moment that she noticed Tansy buzzing around her head, probably trying to get her attention. Elora gave a pointed glance in the sprite's direction. "I'm going to help you."

The muscles in the sprite's shoulders seemed to relax, but she didn't say a word.

Elora sucked in a breath. "Brannick needs me to play the harp for High King Romany." Her hands curled into fists as she felt freedom in making her own decision. "I'm going to do it because I don't want half the fae in Faerie to die."

Rather than respond, Tansy cocked up one eyebrow and glanced at the blanket stuffed full of dresses and jewelry.

Stepping toward it, Elora tried lifting the homemade bag off the floor. It was heavy but not too difficult to manage. "I will help you, but there is something I have to do first."

Her energy must have charged the air itself because Tansy's wings perked up. "What are you going to do?"

It felt oh so glorious to be the one to don a devious smirk. Elora tilted her head toward the open window. "You can get out of this room even with the new enchantment, right?"

Tansy gave a hurried nod.

The smirk on Elora's face only grew. "Good. Tell Prince Brannick I need to speak with him immediately."

When the sprite began flying toward the window, Elora lifted one hand with a jerk. Her lips pursed as she thought for a moment. "If he says *no*, tell him I refuse to play the harp unless he comes immediately."

CHAPTER

28

A twist went through Elora's gut when Brannick appeared in her doorway.

Instead of using the subtle hand wave he usually used, he punched through the silver enchantment that trapped her inside the room. He didn't wince, but a grimace grew the longer he stared at her.

At least he hadn't seemed to notice how she hid her hand behind her back. Sweat made her sword hilt slippery, but she had learned to hold it tight despite sweat long ago.

While the prince was busy glaring at her, the makeshift bag full of dresses and jewelry caught his attention. For the briefest moment, his piercing eyes softened. "What is that?"

Her grip on her sword hilt tightened at the exact moment she gulped. "It's all the dresses and jewelry from my wardrobe."

His eyes moved slowly back to hers, the confusion clearly growing. "But why is it gathered up like that?"

She rolled her shoulders back. "I'm stealing it."

It only lasted for a second, but his mouth tipped up in smile. He quickly smothered it with another glare. "One does not usually inform the person she is stealing from."

"It won't disappear in the mortal realm or anything, will it?" It seemed best to ignore his statement. The muscles in her fingers were beginning to twitch with how hard she gripped them. "The clothes and jewels will be the same there as they are here?"

No matter how he tried to glare, he couldn't hide the pique of interest that tilted his eyebrows. "Of course they will be the same in the mortal realm. My magic is not some parlor trick." He raised one eyebrow higher. "But you are not going to the mortal realm until after the testing."

She stood higher, which didn't make much of a difference since he was so much taller than her. But it wouldn't stop her from trying. "That brings me to my next point."

With a sharp twist of her arm, she swung her blade until its tip pressed lightly against the prince's chin. "You are going to take me to the mortal realm right now."

After lifting his jaw, his entire body slouched. He seemed to be lounging on a sofa, not standing in a closed off room with a sword at his chin. With a sigh, he even managed to examine the cuticles on one of his hands.

Unfortunately for him, their sword training had taught her exactly how he hid his fear. And how it actually came out. Despite his great show, one eyebrow twitched above his darkening eyes.

He glanced to his side where Blaz usually stood, and the twitch pulsed harder.

Was Blaz not there?

Maybe the wolf was using his glamour to hide himself, but if that was the case, Brannick probably wouldn't have been more frightened after failing to see the wolf.

After clearing his throat, the prince's fear only became more tangible. He donned a patronizing smile. "Do you really believe your sword skill is strong enough to defeat my magic?"

She shrugged. "Obviously I do, or we wouldn't be here, would we?"

His eyes narrowed. When he took a step to the side to get away from her blade, she moved it in perfect time to keep it in place. The fear around him didn't grow. Now anger took hold. "You would condemn Faerie, with no regard for the fae King Huron plans to kill? Where is your compassion now?"

Her feet mirrored his as he tried to step away. With every movement, she kept the tip of her sword just under his jaw. "I *am* going to help you. I will play the harp. I will continue to teach you sword fighting."

He gave a pointed glance at her sword before locking eyes with her.

She lifted her chin. "But I have some requests first."

Now he rolled his eyes, as if that could change how *he* was the one whose life was in danger. "You are a mortal. You are in no position to negotiate."

It only took a gentle nudge with her sword to shut him up. "I wasn't finished yet." She clenched her jaw. "I am going to help you, but I'm only going to do it because I want to. Not because I'm forced to."

He tried to glare but a twist of confusion passed through his eyes.

After easing the pressure on his jaw slightly, she said, "I want you to revoke our bargain."

A puffy chuckle escaped his mouth. "And all this time, I thought you were intelligent. It seems you are truly a fool, after all."

Her natural instinct was to push her sword forward again, maybe just enough to draw a droplet of blood. Instead, she held her hand steady, letting her words pierce him like the sword never could. "You are going to revoke our bargain. And then you will open a door to the mortal realm." She gestured toward the blanket holding the contents of her wardrobe. "Once there, I just have to deliver these things to my sisters and inform my betrothed that we are no longer getting married."

At the mention of her betrothed, a whole new kind of look passed over the prince's features. He raised an eyebrow, pairing it with the subtlest of smirks. And of course, a thousand butterflies filled her stomach at the sight of it.

Only glancing away from him could clear her head again. She pointed her nose toward the ceiling. "When I am finished with those things, I will come back with you to Faerie. I will help you, but it will be by choice, not by bargain.

He tapped his chin once and pressed his eyebrows together the way he always did when he was thinking. She realized a moment too late that the expression only served as a distraction. With his other hand, he waved and caused a root from her tree to twist around her ankle.

Her body came crashing down toward the mossy stone floor. Only years of training allowed her to keep a firm grip on her hilt. Brannick reached for the sword, thinking she had lost hold of it. She swiped the blade at his legs in response.

With impossible speed, he jumped away from her strike.

Though she feared he would use the tree roots against her again, she decided to catch him off guard by running toward her tree. His head tilted, and he froze for the briefest moment to watch what she did.

Clutching the low branches, Elora hoisted herself up only to fling herself on top of the prince's back. They crashed to the floor, but he threw her off him a moment later.

When he flicked his hand upward to perform more magic, she thrust the pommel of her sword against his wrist with as much force as she could manage.

He let out a hiss as he cradled the wrist with his other hand. "I knew you would be more trouble than you were worth."

It only took a few breaths before he whipped his hand upward again.

Tree branches sliced through the air, snapping against her back and arms. Her loose hair tangled across her face from the force of a lashing branch.

A quick swing of her sword cut the branches away and freed her from their attacks. Both she and the prince panted when they glared back at each other. Apparently, they had *both* been holding back during their training.

They circled each other then, feet mirroring each other and both glaring as they waited for the other person to make the next move. Her years of training taught her well how to defend herself against a sword.

But now she used a sword against magic. Magic she didn't fully understand.

The next few strikes happened so fast Elora only registered them after they happened. Brannick used the roots to trip her again and then sent his fists toward her. Two parries and a quick jab with her sword obliterated the threats.

Twisting her sword toward the prince, errant thoughts filled her head. Maybe Brannick wouldn't take her home. What would happen to her sisters then? Would Chloe be forced to marry Dietrich? Would her sisters assume Elora had just abandoned them? Would they be sent to the streets?

Energy sizzled around Elora and the prince as the fight took on a new edge. She swung her sword, very nearly piercing the prince's gut. When he waved a hand, it wasn't the tree that moved.

Instead, she felt a jolt inside herself. Not from her muscles or bones. Rather, her soul itself seemed to crack and fracture. Her essence?

The grip on her sword tightened hard as she sucked in a breath. Maybe the prince could use her essence to make wings or trick her into a bargain, but she would *not* allow him to attack her resolve. The next strikes with her sword came with a fury she had never known before. She wasn't truly trying to kill the prince. Yet, he had done something to her insides that made her far less hesitant of the idea.

His magical defenses were no longer enough to keep her back.

Soon, he stood pressed up against a wall with her sword across his throat. Her elbow dug into the stone next to his chest, her knee pressed into his leg. After a fruitless attempt to get away, he gulped.

Though fear pulsed in his eyes, a deep level of awe definitely sparked inside them too.

She leaned in close. "Revoke our bargain and open a door to the mortal realm. Now."

He gave short nod, but it didn't hide the devious smirk twitching beneath his lips.

Her eyes narrowed as she leaned closer. "Open a door to the *right place* in the mortal realm."

"And if I refuse?"

She glanced at the blade kissing his throat. "You aren't the only one who can open a door to the mortal realm. If I kill you, I'm pretty sure our bargain will be revoked, which means I can go home whenever I want."

A soft chuckle from his lips brought heat into her face.

"Am I wrong?" she asked, careful to not let her stance waver.

No answer came in return. He simply lifted one hand, and a swirling tunnel appeared at their sides. The smudges of green, brown, and black looked clearer and brighter than she remembered. A cool breeze seemed to blow through the door with the sound of fluttering leaves moving with it. Even the forest outside her window didn't have the perfect scent of crisp rain and wet bark like his door had. A whiff of wild berries trailed through it, silently declaring this door the most magical one a fae could create.

When he spoke again, the whispered words tickled the hairs across her forehead. "I revoke our bargain."

His eyes captivated her for a whole breath before she forced herself away. Why was it suddenly so difficult to breathe?

"I have another proposal for you."

She whipped around to face him, already rolling her eyes. "I will not enter another—"

"It is not a bargain." His gaze came steady, sending a jolt through her stomach. "Just an idea. Whatever you do, it is your choice."

Skepticism crept through every corner of her body, ready to reject anything that came from his mouth.

"What if I let you stay in Faerie?" He leaned toward her. "Forever."

The breath was completely stolen from her chest. Her heart pattered as she stared into his impossible eyes. How did he know? Had it been that moment when he touched her essence? Despite her insistence to be sent home, somehow, he knew the true desire of her heart.

Her fingers curled around the tied ends of the blanket holding the dresses and jewelry. The possibility of never-ending adventure filled her mind.

The smile curling the prince's lips indicated he knew exactly what he offered. "You have proven yourself useful. You found out King Huron's plan. Even more impressive, you resisted me when I tried to attack your essence. There are not many fae who could do that. If you choose to stay, you will have a position at the castle and the protection of my court."

"Can my sisters come too?"

Even before the words left her lips, she knew the answer that would come.

Brannick's smile turned wicked. "No. If you go through that door and return to the mortal realm, the offer is gone."

She let out a huff. "But what about the testing? What about—"

He raised a single finger, silencing her without a word. "If you return to the mortal realm, I will still require your assistance for the testing. You still must play the harp for High King Romany. You still must train me in sword fighting for the final phase of testing." He gave a nonchalant shrug. "But after the testing, I will take you back to the mortal realm. Faerie will be nothing to you but a distant memory."

It became clear then what he was really asking. Would she play by his rules or her own? Would she abandon her sisters and do the prince's bidding just for the chance at having grand adventures?

The hairs on her neck bristled at the thought of such a life. It was better than anything she had ever dreamed of. Faerie was more magical, more magnificent, more exciting than any life she could have in the mortal realm.

But.

Of course there had to be a *but.*

As a mortal, she would always be lesser in a court full of fae. Things would never truly be equal between them, which meant she would always be playing by *their* rules.

One final truth dawned clearer than any sunrise or any cut of diamond.

Adventure was not the same as freedom.

Though she craved the excitement of Faerie, it could never give her what she truly wanted. It didn't matter how much adventure Brannick could offer, all she really wanted was to make her own rules.

A glow of warmth burst inside her chest. With eyes locked onto the prince's, she snatched the makeshift bag off the ground and marched into the swirling tunnel. Walking through the tunnel sealed her fate. Now the prince would return her to the mortal realm once the testing ended, whether she liked it or not.

Though she would soon return, her heart still said farewell to Faerie forever.

CHAPTER

29

After Elora stepped through the door, her feet landed on a familiar road. She stood in the middle of the dusty street that led into her village. The Bakers' morning bread filled the air with yeasty goodness. Whiffs of brittle leaves and sticky tree sap floated along next. It smelled so much like home she could barely stand it.

Brannick stepped to her side, silently eyeing the buildings that lined the street.

Dry, cracked dirt sat beneath her boots as she stomped forward. Everything looked exactly the way it had the morning she had left. The familiarity brought peace to the homesickness inside her. But then a twinge of regret beat in her heart.

She had forgotten how boring the mortal realm could be.

The sky was a dusky charcoal with the sun just barely peeking over the horizon. Glancing above, a red hue brightened the still-visible moon. A slant went through her gut. "There's a blood moon."

Keeping up with her strides, the prince managed to throw her a sidelong glance. "You said it is not usually like that."

"It's not." Her heart pattered as they continued down the street. What were the odds of having two blood moons only three weeks apart? They were supposed to be rare. A lump formed in her throat when she tried to swallow.

If a blood moon was an omen for change, what did it mean for the upcoming testing in Faerie?

As they passed the Baker's open door, Brannick gestured inside. "See? I delivered the barrel of apples as I promised."

The barrel sat just inside the door. But the apples must have been gone by now. She had gathered them weeks ago.

When they reached the Rolfes' home, Brannick turned up his nose and gave a grimace. Still, he followed her inside without a word. Mrs. Rolfe and her son were nowhere in sight. They must have been in their bookstore already.

The pattering in Elora's heart only grew as she got closer to the room where she and her sisters had been staying. What would they say to her?

Swallowing became impossible when the door to the room came into sight. "Stay here," she told Brannick before bursting inside.

Grace's auburn hair bounced when she let out a gasp. But then a wide grin appeared on her face. "Elora. You're here."

"I'm sorry for leaving." The words came out tight when she tried to push them past the lump in her throat.

At least Grace's expression looked more pleased than angry. Elora turned slowly, fearful of the emotion on her other sister's face.

Chloe brushed her blonde tresses up into a loose bun. She barely spared a glance in her older sister's direction. "I thought you were going to gather apples for the Bakers."

"I…" The rest of the words caught in Elora's throat. She shook her head. "What?"

After brushing the wrinkles from her skirt, Grace lowered herself onto the bed. "You told us before we went to sleep last night that you had to gather apples for the Bakers in the morning."

Elora's eyes narrowed. "I did. I…" Her head jiggled as she tried to find sense in this conversation. "What day is it?"

Chloe tied a green ribbon into her hair as she let out a chuckle. "It's three weeks before your wedding, silly. Don't you remember moaning about it yesterday?"

It took several moments before Elora could move again. Her body seemed frozen as realization washed over her. With her jaw flexing, she stepped into the hallway. The prince leaned casually against the wall, picking at his nails.

Even though she whispered, she still shot accusation into her tone. "Today is the day I left the mortal realm? It's the same day here?"

"Yes." He sent a shrug along with his answer.

Tilting her head toward him, she clenched her teeth. "And you didn't think to tell me that?"

He raised an eyebrow, looking almost affronted. "I promised I would return you to the same place. How did you think we would return?"

Before she could grunt at him, Chloe's footsteps moved toward the hallway. "Who's out there?"

"Nobody." Elora's reply came swiftly but not before her sister got one foot in the hallway.

Her eyebrows flew up toward her blonde hair at the sight of Brannick. "Hello." Now a grin was forming.

Elora shoved her sister back into the room. "Go get me some paper. I need to write to Dietrich Mercer and tell him our wedding is off."

This time, both Chloe's and Grace's heads popped out from around the doorframe.

Chloe gave a long glance at Brannick. "Well, that makes sense. *He* looks like a much better husband than Mr. Mercer."

Heat burned into Elora's cheeks as she forcefully pushed her sisters back into the room. Grace giggled in response.

When Brannick snickered, the heat in Elora's cheeks burned even hotter. Now *he* peeked around the doorframe and into the room.

Placing a hand to his chest, he said, "I would make a *much* better husband. Mr. Mercer is so *old*, is he not?"

"Exactly." Chloe gave a bouncing nod as she retrieved a sheet of parchment from the desk.

Elora flicked Brannick's shoulder. "Stop talking."

Her reaction amused him enough to bring another snicker to his lips.

She let out a groan and looked back into the room. "Chloe, get me that paper." Now she lifted the makeshift bag and threw it into the room. "Grace, I need you to take this bag and put it on the bed."

Grace wrapped her arms around the bag and tottered as she carried it across the room.

When Chloe handed Elora the parchment, she took it immediately and began crafting a letter for Mr. Mercer. Brannick edged into the room while she worked.

Even with her head down, Elora could tell her sisters were ogling the prince again.

Of course, Chloe was the first to pipe up. "If you're going to marry my sister, I think we should at least know your name."

He sucked in a breath Elora knew well. She glanced over her shoulder at him, and sure enough, he had just puffed out his chest. That ridiculous regal voice was about to come out of his mouth.

"I am Pr—"

"Brannick," she finished. The prince glared at her interruption. Elora only sat taller in her chair. "Don't look at me like that. You aren't a prince here, so Brannick is the only name that matters."

Chloe's eyes went as wide as plates. "A *prince?*"

Elora turned her gaze toward her sister. "And he is *not* going to marry me, so hush."

With the bag now on the bed, Grace poked at it with one finger. "What's in here?"

Elora let out a sigh as she went back to her letter. After a few furiously written lines, she asked, "Chloe, where is that poem you read to us a few weeks ago?" Her head tilted to the side. But if it was still the same day in the mortal realm as when she left... Elora shook her head. "I mean a few days ago. Yesterday?"

A frustrated grunt left her mouth. She glared at Brannick like it was all his fault. "How do you keep track of this?"

He let out a chuckle. "We don't."

With another grunt, she went back to her letter. It was almost finished now.

"Keep track of what?" Grace's bright voice flitted across the room.

Rather than attempt to answer, Elora waved a hand toward Chloe. "You know the one. It's that poem with the strange line about bargains."

244

The blonde bun bounced along with Chloe's nod. "I know the one."

While Elora finished off the letter, Chloe dug through a drawer in the desk. She set the poem onto the desk a moment later.

Elora scanned it quickly until she reached the line she'd been so eager to find. Reading out loud, she said, "Against a fae who magicks in bargains, one can rarely win the fight."

Brannick jerked his head toward her.

She continued to read. "Only the truest weapon against him can win, and that is always the weapon of sin."

He snatched the poem from her hands. "Let me see that." His eyes scanned the paper quickly before he glanced toward her. "You knew this was here? This was why you were so eager to return?"

"Not the only reason," she said, gesturing toward her sisters.

But Brannick was already looking at the poem again.

Elora turned her attention away from him. "What does it mean, Chloe? What is the weapon of sin?"

Chloe shrugged flippantly. "The rest of the poem explains it. You have to use the fae's own weapon against him. Whatever he uses to try to kill you, that is what you have to use to kill him."

In an instant, Elora and Brannick locked eyes. Her next words came out in a rush. "We have to get him to use a shard against one of us."

Brannick responded with a frown. "Not one of us, against *me*. A golden shard would be useless against you. And we might not have to do it. If we can find where he has the shards hidden before he delivers them, we can destroy them. It would be much safer that way."

245

Biting her bottom lip, Elora glanced at her sisters. Then she turned back to the prince. "Can you do it again? Can you return me to this same day?"

"Of course."

Chloe wrapped her arms over her stomach as she eyed them both. "What's going on? It's just a poem." She gulped. "Isn't it?"

Grace was poking the bag again.

Elora shot her youngest sister a pointed stare. "Stop touching that. Chloe, I need you to deliver that letter to Mr. Mercer for me."

She reached under her corset for the pouch of coins from her father. But she didn't have it anymore. It still sat under her pillow in Bitter Thorn.

Brannick watched her hands before looking into her eyes. "How much?"

Elora was already trying to remember the pieces of jewelry inside the bag. But all of them were worth far more than a simple letter delivery. When the prince repeated his question, Elora barely managed an answer. "A few gold coins. It depends on the messenger, but it's usually less than five gold coins."

He reached into a pocket of his soft leather coat. Though she had seen that pocket do magical things on several occasions, now it simply looked like a pocket. She glanced over his features and realized those looked less striking than usual too.

She realized all at once that the prince was wearing a glamour to make himself look mortal. By the time the realization hit her, he dropped something into her palm.

A warm tingle spread through her arm as he pulled his hand away. Five gold coins sat in her hand. When she looked into his eyes, not even the glamour could keep her from staring too hard. She almost thanked him before remembering the rules of Faerie.

He must have seen the question in her eyes. Closing her hand over the coins, he said, "For your help with the testing."

Nodding was the only response she could manage. Even then, it took a few swallows before she could speak again. Her voice croaked when she tried. "Chloe, deliver that letter first thing this morning." She swallowed again. "If I'm not back by tonight, you can open that bag. But I'll be back."

Her attention turned back to Brannick. "Right?"

He moved toward the hallway. "We should go."

The words sent a twist deep in her chest. Elora couldn't even bear to look at her sisters before following the prince into the hallway. She had promised to help, and she intended to keep that promise.

But now the truth braided through her insides in an unpleasant knot. They were about to face a fae who planned to kill half the inhabitants of faerie.

Anything could happen.

CHAPTER 30

Walking through Faerie doors had become so commonplace, Elora barely even felt a thrill as she walked through this one. Although, maybe impending doom had something to do with that.

She *didn't* expect to be transported to Prince Brannick's own bedroom. Four thin trees stood at each corner of his bed, creating a leafy canopy over the green and brown patterned blanket. Feathers hung from leather strings tied at random spots over the trees' branches and trunks.

The bed was large enough to befit a prince. Heavy velvet pillows lined one end. One of them had a strange indent that looked suspiciously like Blaz's wolf head. Two large windows sat on either side of the bed, open with mossy trees standing outside them.

At the end of the bed sat a dark wooden trunk with black, leather straps. A desk carved from smooth stone stood against the opposite wall. Moss grew up the sides of the desk and vines twisted around the legs of the chair. On the other side of the room, several wooden chairs had been gathered together, probably for the prince's private meetings.

A wall of vines intermingled with a line of trees, which blocked one corner of the room from sight. Even without taking a deep breath, the smells hit her strong enough to bring a smile to her lips. Wet bark, crisp rain. It smelled breezy and cool with a barely-there scent of wild berries.

It was rugged with a hint of tenderness. It smelled like Brannick.

"Has Blaz returned?"

She sucked in a breath at the prince's voice. Before she could ask why he expected *her* to know such a thing, another voice filled the air.

"No, my prince. I believe he is still in Dustdune."

Elora recognized the brownie's voice at once. It took a few steps to peek around the trees growing at the base of Brannick's bed. Was he now working for the prince as he had dreamed?

Fifer wore leather gloves as he snapped black briars and thorns away from the trees and stuffed them into a suede bag. Considering how near the brim the thorns came, the brownie had probably been working for some time.

Brannick nodded before sitting on the wooden trunk to remove his shoes. "You have done well, Fifer. You need not continue with the thorns. I will be in Dustdune all evening."

The brownie gave a deep bow, which jiggled his bulbous chin. Before leaving, he snapped away one more briar that had just spontaneously grown around the leg of one chair.

When the door shut behind him, Elora turned back to the prince. "Do you have to remove thorns from your room every night?"

He winced before tugging off his second boot. "Yes. They follow me wherever I go in Bitter Thorn. It is part of the curse on my court."

His boots landed on the ground before he moved toward a large wardrobe that was halfway hidden behind the hanging wall of vines. But her attention was stolen by the bearskin rug covering part of his stone floor.

The rich brown fur seemed nice enough, but it didn't seem *too* remarkable. Still, her stomach jolted at the sight of it. All at once it seemed familiar and... She knelt down and touched one of the paws. Enchanting.

"Where did you get this rug?"

The prince's voice came from behind the wall of vines. "It is a trophy."

Her eyebrow cocked up. When he reappeared from behind the vines, he wore a dark green coat with a short fringe around every edge. The front pieces wrapped closed with a brown woven belt holding them in place. Part of his chest was exposed at the top of the coat, showcasing the four-layered necklace around his throat.

His long, black hair was parted down the middle and landed just past his shoulders. Though the clothes were simple, he still looked grander and more regal than any royalty she could imagine. His eyes shimmered with a thousand colors when he glanced at the bearskin rug.

"I stole that rug when I escaped from Queen Alessandra's court."

She had seen her share of arrogance from the prince, but the pride in his eyes now seemed more invigorating than cocky.

Touching the paw made Elora's stomach flip in an all new way. For no reason at all, she touched a finger to the lopsided scar on her hand. The one Brannick had said looked like a troll bite.

With a gulp, she jerked her hand away and got to her feet. "You had to *escape* Queen Alessandra's court? Tucking her hand behind her back, she tried desperately to wipe away the feeling in her gut. "Tansy escaped it too. She said being there nearly drained her essence."

Brannick shoved his hands through his hair, which somehow made it look glossier. "Who is Tansy?"

"A sprite." Elora dropped herself onto the trunk at the end of Brannick's bed, as if that could settle her beating heart. "Did it drain your essence to be in Fairfrost too?"

His fingers froze halfway through his hair, and a shiver shook his body. The mention of Fairfrost seemed to have caused it. "Sprites only speak to other sprites, except when they are delivering messages."

She gave him a pointed stare. "Or when a king is planning to use them to deliver shards to every fae in three courts." Her arms folded over her chest. "And you didn't answer my question about Fairfrost."

A twitch went through his jaw when he flexed it. Then came another shiver. Apparently, Fairfrost was a sensitive subject. "King Huron is going to use sprites to deliver the shards?" He shook his head. "But he has to be the one to offer the shard, or else he will not absorb the dying fae's power."

Looking at the mossy desk seemed to be the only safe place in the room. The prince's stupid eyes kept mesmerizing her, and the bearskin rug made her feel oddly adventurous. "The sprites will say, 'I have something for you from King Huron. Do you accept?'"

Brannick let out a groan as he massaged his temples. "That is annoyingly brilliant. Then everyone will accept because they will think it is only a message."

Before Elora could respond, the prince turned on her with his eyes narrowing. "Why would the sprites agree to help like that? They usually only speak to other sprites."

"They have a bargain with King Huron."

The prince let out a scoff. "But what could King Huron offer them? Why would..." His nose wrinkled as he trailed off. A darkening gloom passed through the prince's eyes. "He promised to free the sprites trapped in Fairfrost, did he not?"

One side of her face scrunched up. "You know about them?"

He gave no answer as he stared off at the rest of the room.

Elora continued. "Tansy made it sound like fae from other courts don't know about the sprites in Fairfrost."

The hair on Brannick's head whipped as he turned away. His voice came out darker than she had ever heard. "I only know because I spent far too long in Fairfrost myself."

Her feet seemed to move of their own accord as she stood and stepped toward him. "And you nearly lost your essence there? Does that happen to everyone who enters Fairfrost?"

He clicked his tongue before casting her with a short glare. "It is not the land itself that did it. The circumstances..." His veins pulsed as he tightened the belt around his waist. "What Queen Alessandra did..." His shoulders hunched forward as the lines in his face drew tighter.

All at once, he let out a sigh and his muscles relaxed. "Ah, Blaz. What did you learn?"

When she turned around, the black wolf entered through an opening cut from the stone wall near the door. How had the prince known he was there?

The wolf padded across the stone floor, giving a soft nudge to both her leg and Brannick's before stopping in front of the large wardrobe. After some obviously practiced nudges from the wolf, the door to the wardrobe flew open. A moment later, he used his teeth to pull out a dark green dress.

Brannick's face fell at the sight of it. "Ansel is in Dustdune?"

The wolf gave a short nod.

Elora fought the urge to grab the prince's arm after hearing how his voice wavered. Luckily, she still had her sword to grip. "What does that mean?"

After a nose wrinkle, Brannick said, "Ansel has more mortal pets than any other fae. He is always looking to add more to his collection. Even worse, his best musician recently died."

She took a step back as nausea rocked her gut. "Please don't tell me what I think you're about to tell me."

Brannick offered a knowing look in response. "Ansel will only leave you alone if a more powerful fae has already claimed you." He gave a short, mocking bow. "A prince, for example."

A gag yanked in her throat. She could barely even move when the prince tucked the green dress into her hands.

He raised both eyebrows. "It is for your protection. And it is only for show. Because of my vow, I cannot call you my pet. So, I need you to say it if anyone asks."

The dress might have felt soft and luxurious between her fingers, but it hadn't stopped her from noticing how it matched the prince's coat.

When Brannick swallowed, his neck bulged against the beaded necklace around his throat. "If necessary, you should imply a…" He swallowed again, as if the words couldn't find a way out.

"Don't say it," she said through clenched teeth.

"Physical relationship." A twinge of pink went through his cheeks before he could turn around.

Her own cheeks burned as her stomach flipped.

"I do not keep pets myself." Brannick flicked his hands away from his body, as if washing himself of such things. "I find it unsettling. But I need you to play the harp, and this is the best way to protect you. If we did not have to leave immediately, I might have found a better way." He gave her a pointed stare. "But *you* seemed to think it was necessary to begin the testing right away."

She huffed at him before stomping off behind the wall of vines with the green dress in her hands. "You're going to find me a sheath then. And you're going to use that glamour trick, or whatever it's called, to hide my sword, so I can keep it with me."

Just by the sound of his voice, the prince seemed to be lounging on something with no hint of care. "If I hide the sword with a glamour, it will not make it go away. It will still be at your side. Others could bump into it if you are not careful."

"Then I'll be careful," she hissed back as she slipped the dress over her head. The soft green fabric felt like a combination of leather and suede. And yet, it had a softer drape and lighter touch than chiffon. Embroidered vines trailed just above the fringed hem. A full skirt lay neatly on top of her purple skirt.

The fitted bodice looked a bit lumpy over her leather corset, but hopefully the other fae would just assume she had a strange mortal shape to her. No matter who would be in Dustdune, she wasn't about to remove her corset and leave it in Brannick's room.

While she changed, a knock sounded at the prince's door. When it opened, familiar voices filled the room.

"I made a few final tweaks to your vow. Here it is." Lyren's voice sounded tight. "Did she agree to help? The vow is worthless if she will not play the harp and then King Huron will kill all the fae in my court."

"She will help."

Lyren let out a sigh of relief in response to Brannick's words.

Vesper spoke next. "I just returned from speaking with King Huron. I told him you are excited about your vow. He still believes you will present a statue of High King Romany."

In the moment of silence that followed, Elora could imagine all the heads turning to the last face in the room. As she expected, Quintus's voice filled the void. "I added carvings to the harp I crafted. I mostly added roses to represent Noble Rose. High King Romany will surely be pleased when he sees it. It has already been delivered to Dustdune Castle as you requested."

Something tapped against stone, probably a shoe. "Where *is* Elora?"

Lyren had asked. It felt better than Elora expected to hear her name from the fae's lips. A part of her expected them to continue calling her mortal forever more.

"I'm here," Elora called out from behind the wall of vines. When she bent to grab her sword from the ground, her body froze. "I, uh. I just need…" She blinked twice as she stared at the sword. "Prince Brannick, I'm not sure which color belt I should wear."

In truth, the woven brown belt that matched Brannick's was already tied around her waist. Luckily, he didn't question her explanation.

A moment later, he appeared next to her behind the wall of vines. He retrieved a brown leather belt from the wardrobe. It didn't have a sheath, but it would bear the weight of her sword better than the woven belt could. After putting it around her waist, she tucked the sword inside with the hilt poking out.

He gave it a long glance before waving a hand at it. In a flash, the belt and sword disappeared from view. Standing next to her on the same side as the sword, he lowered his voice to a whisper. "I need you to stay near me to keep the glamour in place."

"Fine." Her jaw flexed before they both emerged from the wall of vines.

Lyren let out a gasp as she brought shimmery blue fingernails to her mouth. Her flowery dress glimmered between blue and teal every time the light caught it. Her black curls looked tighter and shinier than ever. "Beautiful," she said with a smile. "But your hair could use some braids."

She traipsed across the floor. With lightning-quick fingers, she made a thin braid on either side of Elora's head to frame the face.

While she worked, Brannick turned to Vesper and Quintus. His tone seemed darker than ever. "When we get to Dustdune, I will offer my vow as planned. The harp playing should be good enough that King Huron will have nothing to say about it. After the vows of the other courts are offered, the revel will begin. I will spend that time looking for the shards. Quintus, you need to stay near High King Romany and answer any questions he asks about the harp. Give *long* answers. Vesper, you try to distract King Huron, so he cannot speak to the high king and convince him to allow a presentation. Lyren."

The dark-skinned fae nodded just as she finished braiding Elora's hair. "I will keep Queen Alessandra busy and attempt to learn the nature of her alliance with King Huron." Lyren retrieved a white flower from her pocket and tucked it behind one of Elora's ears. Smiling, she touched the flower with one finger. "For Swiftsea." She gave a short nod. "For saving my court."

Elora made a fist at her side since she couldn't grip her sword hilt without making it obvious that she was wearing a glamour. With a heavy gulp, she returned Lyren's smile.

Now Lyren slid a finger over the dark silver chain of her seashell necklace. Her eyes seemed alight with excitement. Nudging Elora in the shoulder, Lyren spoke again. "Maybe tonight I will finally earn my necklace for bravery."

Vesper opened a door in front of them. It looked as misty as Elora remembered. No clear shapes formed inside the tunnel, except a rose every now and then. Rather, it seemed to take on a different look every time she blinked. The overall color changed from red to gray to green to blue with hints of orange and white at less frequent intervals.

The others stepped through the door, but Brannick held Elora back. With the back of his hand, he moved her hair away from her neck. "Good. You still have the feather from Soren."

Blaz gave a stoic look as the prince pulled a white feather from his coat. Brannick put it in her hands while fiddling with a piece of black string. "This feather will enhance any skills you have."

"Like my harp playing?"

He nodded as he took the feather from her and tied it to the hair behind her neck. "It will also enhance your other skills." He gave a pointed glance toward her sword, even though it was invisible. "Should you need them."

With those final words, they stepped through Vesper's door and entered Dustdune Castle.

CHAPTER 31

Sandstone walls towered high above Elora's head. Every corner, edge, and ridge in the walls was gilded in gold. Gilded swirls and patterns stretched over the sandstone. The dusty air had an underlying herbal scent. Thick, orange and gold rugs with intricate patterns lined the hallway.

Glowing green sprites floated above, giving off light as usual. The gold in the walls and the rugs shimmered whenever they caught the light.

As they walked down the halls, Brannick stayed close enough that his shoulder brushed against hers after every step. He never reacted when her sword bumped against his leg, but based on how close he stayed, he clearly didn't want any other fae bumping into it.

Blaz walked on the other side of the prince. His nose and ears perked with every step, as if eager to take in the smells and sounds. When they walked through a gilded doorway, everything ahead hit Elora like a torrential rainfall.

Fae of every size and shape flitted around an enormous ballroom. Some wore straight, colorful dresses with large prints, similar to the ones Lyren always wore. A handful of fae wore heavy brocade dresses with dense beading around the collars and all the way down the front of the dresses. A few other styles were present in fewer numbers.

Most of the fae wore rich silks like King Huron always wore. Though skin of every color filled the ballroom, the ones wearing the rich silk clothes mostly had brown skin, also similar to King Huron. The fae men wore long sleeved tunics in shimmery silks, often with a metallic sash draped across their chests. The fae women wore long sleeved tops, often in plain colors. Those were paired with sweeping full skirts in rich silk or brocade. Metallic threads created intricate patterns through the shiny skirts. Scarves ranging from sheer to opaque complemented the dresses. Each fae wore her scarf differently, many wrapped it around the neck, some around their arms and some over the shoulders.

Platters filled with rice and meat dishes were passed around. Those carrying the dishes wore plainer, cotton clothes in cream or tan. Brownies mostly held the platters, but there were some high fae as well, and even a few mortals. Some dishes boasted dates and mangoes while others had lentils and peas. The scent of heavy spices like cinnamon and cumin filled the air. Subtle notes of coconut drifted through it. One particularly delicious-looking dish held rice with small chunks of meat, all covered in a bright yellow sauce.

At the head of the room, an opulent golden throne commanded attention from atop its wide gold platform. King Huron stood next to it in a spectacular golden tunic with a brilliant orange sash wrapped diagonally across his chest and then around his waist. A smile lingered underneath his mustache, but it failed to light his eyes. Probably because someone else was sitting on his throne.

A young man with blue eyes and light brown hair lounged on the golden throne. He must have been High King Romany because he wore a red velvet and gold crown trimmed with white fur. He wore a purple velvet cape and even held a scepter with a large ruby on top.

Only the high king could get away with blatantly using King Huron's throne right in front of him. But the high king looked younger than Elora had expected from a fae who had always been king over his court. Then again, all the high fae were the same. They had impossibly stunning features with young and healthy bodies. Yet, their eyes always seemed to have seen too much.

Looking at the throne, Elora didn't notice anyone coming toward her until the woman had already bumped into her side.

The woman wore a long white dress with opalescent threads that gave off a rainbow of color when they caught the light. Thick beading decorated her collar and down the front of her brocade dress. Each bead had the same opalescent quality as the threads in her dress. A heavy white crown adorned her head. Several strands of white beads hung down from the crown and over her forehead. She looked even younger than the high king.

At Elora's side, Brannick tensed hard enough to bounce their shoulders together. His breathing had stopped completely.

Brown curls tumbled halfway down the woman's back. Her fair skin contrasted with her flushed pink cheeks. When Elora's elbow met the woman's, the contact released an icy chill into the air.

This woman was, without a doubt, Queen Alessandra of Fairfrost.

"When will that Bitter Thorn prince get here?" the queen muttered under her breath. She didn't even seem aware that she had run into Elora.

Even through her dress, Elora could feel the muscles in Brannick's arm and shoulder tense even harder. He didn't move, but his eyes began glancing at the exit like it could save his life. The hair on one side of his head fell over one of his eyes. It didn't look like an accident. Was he trying to avoid the queen's gaze?

As if on cue, Queen Alessandra whipped her head toward Brannick. Her eyes locked onto his, despite his apparent eagerness to get away. Seeing him sent a scrunch through her face. Her eyes narrowed at him, but she didn't seem to find anything recognizable in his features.

After a glance that grew more puzzled by the moment, the queen turned to scan the rest of the ballroom, as if still searching for the prince of Bitter Thorn.

When she stepped away from them, Brannick let out a breath of relief that he probably wished had been less audible. Blaz's ears were still perked up, but even he looked considerably more relaxed.

The prince ruffled the fur over the wolf's neck. "Go on, Blaz. Use your glamour."

Without another word, the wolf disappeared into the crowd. For some reason, Elora sucked in a breath at the sight.

Brannick raised an eyebrow that tilted up just as much as the corner of his lips. "Are you worried for him? His glamour will make sure no eyes look at him unless they know exactly where to look."

Why did the prince have to stand so close? It was beginning to make her palms sweaty. In an effort to gain back some control in the conversation, she raised one eyebrow of her own. "Didn't you live in Queen Alessandra's court? Why doesn't she recognize you?"

With shoulders hunching forward, his features went rigid. He leaned in close enough to whisper, but that didn't stop his words from feeling like daggers. "Hush, mortal." He shook out his shoulders before running a hand through his black hair. "High King Romany is waiting for us. Remember to stay close to me so I can keep the glamour hiding your sword."

Neither one spoke again as they moved across the ballroom floor. Using tentative movements, they stepped up the gold platform that held the throne. When Queen Alessandra came to the platform as well, Brannick moved himself behind Elora to stay just out of the queen's eyesight.

The other king on the platform wore a gray coat that paired well with his navy pants. A braided gold and silver crown sat on his blonde hair. He must have been the king of Mistmount.

She noticed then that only royalty stood on the golden platform, except for her. She turned to the prince and whispered. "Won't everyone wonder why I am up here?"

Brannick kept his eyes forward, his lips barely moving when he answered. "They will assume you have something to do with my vow, which you do."

When all the leaders had been accounted, High King Romany rose from the golden throne and lifted his ruby scepter into the air. Every voice and noise in the ballroom cut off in an instant.

Elora shifted on her feet as she glanced past the platform. In the crowd, Lyren's bright blue dress made her stand out. She stood among other dark-skinned fae who had gathered near the platform.

A tall woman with a blue-green dress stood next to Lyren. The woman's black hair had been shaved close to her scalp. Silver metal encrusted with sapphires twisted around her head to form a dazzling crown. Twisted white and shimmery seashells acted as tines amongst the silver and sapphires. A single silver chain with a blue pendant fell from the crown to the middle of the woman's forehead.

Queen Noelani of Swiftsea.

It occurred to Elora that Brannick was the only leader *not* wearing a crown. Was that by choice… or part of his curse?

The queen of Swiftsea gave a pointed glance at the sea flower in Elora's ear before she nodded.

Elora barely had time to nod in return before High King Romany's regal voice filled the room.

"Welcome, fae, to the first phase of testing." His voice came out tight and burdened. Upon hearing it, Elora gave a closer look to the high king. Red rimmed his eyelids and stretched over the whites of his eyes. Twitches spontaneously moved through various part of his body as he stood.

It seemed strange to see a fae of any kind visibly displaying weakness. Then again, the high king *had* been poisoned and by his own son no less. Seeing him lounge on the golden throne, she had almost forgotten High King Romany was dying.

After clearing his throat, he continued. "Each vow will be offered in the order of my choosing. When all have been offered, the revel will begin. We will dance and feast while I contemplate the vows. The revel will end when I am ready to declare a winner."

A few murmurs went through the crowd, but most fae seemed ready to begin.

High King Romany stumbled back to the throne. Once seated, he gestured toward the king wearing the gray coat and braided crown. "King Jackory of Mistmount, you may proceed with your vow."

King Jackory moved to the front of the platform. Murmurs danced around at the sight of him. Elora heard enough to know the fae were predicting what vow they were about to hear.

Without any ceremony, King Jackory said, "I vow to make my court of Mistmount the new High Court should I become High King."

A wrinkle appeared across High King Romany's forehead while his lips pursed.

In the lowest whisper she could manage, Elora spoke to Brannick. "That didn't seem like much of a vow."

Heat seeped through her dress when Brannick placed a hand on the small of her back. His whisper tickled in her ear. "It is a political move. King Jackory and High King Romany have always been allies. Everyone knows High King Romany wants his ally to win the crown. But King Jackory does not want it. He only participated in the testing because the high king asked him to. His vow is making it clear that someone else should win."

With a growing frown, the high king asked the stunning Queen Alessandra to go next.

Brannick whispered again. "The order indicates who High King Romany believes should win. He chose Queen Alessandra next because he believes her to be more powerful than King Huron or myself."

After a sweeping hand motion toward the many fae in the room, Queen Alessandra stood tall. "I vow that after your unfortunate demise, all fae in your great court of Noble Rose will feel loved by me."

High King Romany touched his mouth as he gave a short nod toward the queen. He said nothing, but he did seem pleased with the vow. At least more than he was with King Jackory's.

King Huron was called upon next. He offered a charming smile before straightening his back. "I vow that your son's despicable act of poisoning you will always be remembered."

As he spoke, a fae in a simple cotton tunic and pants climbed up the platform. He carried a sandstone sculpture that depicted an evil-looking fae dropping the contents of a vial into a fancy goblet. High King Romany's eyebrows rose high as he examined the sculpture before him. A wicked smile covered his face as he touched one finger to the sandstone vial.

Elora's face scrunched up at the sight. She nudged closer to the prince and kept her voice low. "A sculpture to commemorate something from the high king's life? He basically stole your idea."

Brannick cocked up an eyebrow, failing to hide the amusement that flitted through his eyes. "Did you expect anything different? I am sure he planned to accuse me of stealing *his* idea. He knew High King Romany would make me go last."

She didn't have time to mention how lucky it was that they had come up with a new plan because now it was Prince Brannick's turn to present his vow.

His chin tilted upward as he moved to the front of the platform. He eyed the crowd then turned to the high king. He held himself with such regal arrogance, it could only be labeled as elegant. His lips parted, as if ready to speak, but then he merely continued to stare.

By the time he finally did use his voice, every fae in the room seemed to be holding their breaths. "I vow…" The prince gave another sweeping look over the room. Scores of heads leaned forward at the sight. Now he glanced toward the high king and gave a devious smirk. "To preserve your memory."

The words caused a collective head tilt throughout the crowd, as if every fae was trying to work out the meaning of Prince Brannick's words. When he pulled the glass orb from his pocket, the head tilts turned into a collective gasp.

High King Romany's jaw had dropped.

Glints appeared in several eyes. Hushed whispers of delight accompanied them. Everyone looked astonished and pleased at the sight of the orb.

Everyone except King Huron.

His face flushed with red under his silk crown. He threw a glare toward Elora.

She did her best to ignore him and turned to Brannick instead.

The prince wore an even more arrogant smile as he lifted the orb high into the air. With a twist of his wrist, the orb gave off a soft red glow. He lowered the glass and looked toward the high king. "Do you have anything you would like to say, High King Romany?"

The High King's face lit up at the prospect. He sat taller in the golden throne and puffed out his chest. Holding his scepter high, he said, "While I was high king, peace reigned in Faerie." His head tilted to the side while he smirked. "Well, mostly." He let out a chuckle. "That is as good as any fae can claim."

At those words, a chorus of chuckles rippled through the room.

Still holding the orb toward the high king, Brannick gestured toward Elora. "As part of this memory, I present a song to be played in your honor, High King. Throughout Faerie, this song will forevermore be known as High King Romany's last ballad."

While he spoke, Quintus and Lyren carried the harp Quintus had crafted to the platform. Vesper followed behind them, setting a red velvet topped wooden stool behind the harp. The sweat in Elora's palms turned cold as she sat down to play. With a heart racing so wildly, breathing was a chore.

Those harp lessons with her mother had taught her more about pushing her mother's buttons than about performing. Still, the lessons had inexplicably taught her to play as well. Now she could only hope it would be enough to please the high king.

CHAPTER
32

The first pluck of a harp string sent a resounding note through the crowded ballroom. Fae and creatures alike paused and turned toward the sound. Elora leaned into the harp's pillar to pluck the next strings.

All around her, bodies froze, and jaws dropped. The mournful notes of the melody sent a gentle sway through many creatures all around. Her heart tightened with every pluck. Remembering her mother sent a wave of emotion through her fingers and into the music.

Behind her neck, the feather from Brannick seemed to tingle with energy. Upon noticing it, her fingers danced over the strings in a complicated run without a single pause or hesitation. With each slow note, emotion from deep inside her pulsed into the dry air.

At the end, a long breath went through the crowd, as if they were holding onto that last bit of feeling. High King Romany touched a knuckle to the corner of his eye, though it seemed only to be for show. No tears filled his eyes.

As moved as the audience acted, none of them seemed to be touched quite the same as Elora. Their faces were so still. Like they could sense the emotion was just... *right. There.* But they couldn't quite grasp it.

After a deep breath, Elora stood from the stool with a tiny curtsy. Her sword knocked around her knee with the movement. Just when she worried the sound of it might alert another fae, Prince Brannick appeared at her side.

The fabric of his dark green coat brushed against her arm. His leg was close enough to bump the sword. He held the glass orb out to the high king. With a twist of his palm, the glowing red dimmed until it vanished completely. But now the orb looked different.

Before, Elora had not been able to see through the glass. Now, a figure in a green dress sitting behind a harp was distinct.

High King Romany's eyes were full of awe as he took the orb from Brannick. Already, things in the room began moving again. Servers wandered through the crowds, holding their platters high. Someone blew into a little flute while many of the fae started tapping their toes and heads to the sound. Murmurs and whispers grew into rolling conversations.

With eyes still glimmering, the high king tucked the orb into a hidden pocket inside his shirt. King Huron in his rich silk tunic leapt to the high king's side. He gave a heated glance toward Elora before donning an exaggerated smile for the high king.

In a loud but tight voice, High King Romany addressed the crowd again. "The vows have been given, and now I need time to contemplate them."

Smiles twitched on every face in the room. They leaned forward, eyes wide with delight.

Even the high king's face held a hint of enchantment. He raised both hands high with a flourish. "Let the revel begin."

A cheer broke through the vast ballroom, one part thrilling, the other part wild. Music from several instruments bounced around the sandstone walls. Many fae jumped and twirled to the sounds in peculiar dances. King Huron swooped even closer to the high king with his mouth already parted.

Before he could utter a single syllable, the high king waved him off. "Go enjoy the revel, King Huron." The high king's eyes narrowed with a gleefully devious smirk. "I must speak with this mortal."

The smile that filled Brannick's face could only be described as dashing. But along with it, he pushed himself even closer to Elora's side.

Luckily, High King Romany didn't seem to notice or care. He steepled his fingers under his chin with a grin as wide as someone who had just discovered cake. "Where did you learn how to do that *thing?*"

It took far too much effort to hold back the confused squeak at the back of her throat. Elora managed to disguise it as a cough before attempting to answer. "You mean play the harp? My mother taught me how to play."

The high king let out a short chuckle before waving his hand through the air. "No, silly. We have masters of the harp in Faerie. I mean, where did you learn to put that…" His eyes narrowed and he held two fingers close together in front of his face. "That *thing* into your music? It was almost tangible. It was that quality that made it…" He held a hand over his heart. His eyes wandered over the crowd, as if searching for the indescribable quality.

Shrugging probably wouldn't be the most polite response, but she couldn't very well explain *the thing* when she had no idea what he was talking about. In desperation, she turned to the prince at her side.

"Emotion." Brannick spoke without contemplation.

At the sound of his word, the high king's eyes lit up again. "Yes, emotion. That was it." He took in a deep breath followed by a long sigh. "We do not have much of that in Faerie." Now he gave a slanted grin in the prince's direction. "And for good reason—right, Prince Brannick? A taste of it is all we need."

He dropped back into the golden throne with his chest already heaving from standing up too long. With a snap of his fingers, a fae in a tan linen dress and scarf brought him a platter of food. King Huron hovered at the bottom of the platform, clearly ready to speak to the high king as soon as he was free.

Giving a carefree head tilt, Brannick took a step toward the throne. "High King Romany, would you like to speak to the master craftsman who created this harp?"

At the sound of those words, Elora whirled around and began pulling the harp closer to the throne. "He carved roses onto it just for you."

The high king stayed sitting back with his chest heaving. Still, he gave a delighted nod. His eyes lit up when he traced a finger over one of the wooden roses.

Quintus appeared from nowhere and ran a hand over the pillar of the harp. "I retrieved this wood from the Noble Rose countryside itself. Nothing was better suited for such an instrument."

High King Romany sat a little taller in the throne while Quintus explained more about the construction of the harp. Elora and Brannick moved away slowly, ready to jump in if their plan didn't work.

Fortunately, the high king seemed immensely eager to discuss the harp, and Quintus gave *long* explanations as he promised.

King Huron huffed at the bottom of the platform. He seemed ready to climb it again to reach the high king, but Vesper managed to pull him to a corner to talk instead.

Brannick held out a hand to help Elora off the platform. It probably looked sweet, but he was mostly likely only concerned with making sure no other fae came anywhere near the unsheathed sword at her side. Regardless, her hand still shivered at his touch.

When they were both at the bottom, he spun her straight into his arms, right in time with the music. She resisted as he danced into the crowd. Her heart leapt as he leaned close enough to whisper in her ear.

"Everyone dances at a revel. We need to fit in, so no one notices when you and I sneak out to find the shards."

The last bit of her resistance dropped away when his breath hit her cheek. Her feet moved in time with the music, but it couldn't distract her from the prince's impossibly strong arms moving her with ease. An all new pattering jumbled her chest, but it had nothing to do with the testing.

Perhaps looking around would give her something else to focus on. Goblets were being passed around now. Each was filled with a thick, orange liquid that smelled sugary and tropical.

Following her eyes, Brannick's shoulder tensed beneath her hand. "Do not drink any of that."

She raised an eyebrow, ignoring how perfectly the prince could twirl her without any effort at all. "You should know by now, I like to make my own decisions."

His eyes tilted upward as he let out a scoff. "Fine, drink it then. But do not complain to me when mortal food tastes like dust to you until the end of your days."

Instinctively, she moved closer to him. "Is that really what it does?"

"Yes." He fell silent then, staring intently at a corner of the room. A patch of black fur seemed to materialize in that corner before it would disappear again a moment later.

Blaz was probably hiding over there, but she decided to keep looking through the ballroom. She and Brannick were supposed to get out as fast as they could so they could look for the balance shards King Huron had collected.

Though they seemed to just be dancing, Brannick had skillfully moved them closer to the doors with each step.

"Lyren is speaking to Queen Alessandra. Do you think she'll learn anything about her alliance with King Huron?" Elora asked.

A shudder went through the prince at the sound of the queen's name. His graceful steps turned stilted as he pulled her toward the gilded doors leading to the hall. They were very nearly there now. "I do not know." He leaned away from the ballroom as he spoke, as if that could move him farther away from the queen.

Elora moved with him, but that didn't stop her from giving him a pointed stare. "Why doesn't she—"

The prince pressed a finger to her lips and moved in close enough that she could feel the heat from his forehead. Every muscle in his face was tight. "Not here."

She could barely even swallow with him so close. When he dropped his finger from her lips, it left a lingering tingle that refused to be settled.

Her stomach seemed to think that was the perfect moment to perform a series of acrobatic jolts inside her gut.

"Prince Brannick."

Elora nearly jumped out of her boots at the sound of the unfamiliar voice.

A jovial-looking fae stood right between them and the exit. The fae's ears pointed higher than others. His sharp chin tilted up as he glanced at the pair of them. The look in his eyes was greedy enough to twist terror through Elora's chest.

"Ansel." Brannick wore an even face as he nodded at the fae.

The name brought another twist that sent Elora's heart scampering. When the prince put his hand on the small of her back and tugged her close, she responded by leaning even closer into his chest. The prince *did* say she should imply a physical relationship.

It didn't stop Ansel from roving his greedy eyes up and down her body. "Where did you find this magnificent mortal? Is she...?" He gestured between them.

Attempting to don a carefree smile, Elora gave the answer she knew she must. "I am the prince's." Even under such circumstances, she couldn't bring herself to use the word *pet*.

A crease formed between Ansel's eyebrows as his lips fell into a frown. The expression lasted only a moment before the frown was replaced with a teasing pout. He looked at the prince when he spoke again. "But you never take pets. Everyone knows this."

Her shoulders tensed. Or maybe Brannick's did. They were so close, she couldn't tell. Had they moved closer together too?

With an impressively carefree eyebrow raise, the prince asked, "Did you hear her play? I think that answers your question."

But Ansel didn't look convinced. "Mortals can lie and fae cannot. Why is she the one who said she is yours? How am I supposed to believe it?"

The greed in his eyes grew with every word he uttered. Even with Brannick at her side, terror sliced through every defense she had. Something told her now was the time to act. If she didn't convince this fae that she had been claimed, he might never stop hunting her.

She moved without thinking. Desperation fueled her actions as she wrapped her arms around Brannick's neck. Pulling him close, she moved up to her toes. It barely even registered when their lips met. She could only hope that something so dramatic would convince the greedy fae.

But then it hit her all at once. The prince's lips were too perfect. How could she ever breathe again knowing she'd never experience another moment as blissful as this? Without really meaning to, she moved closer. Leaned deeper. Gave more of herself to the kiss.

And nothing had ever felt so perfect.

Brannick reacted. She could feel him tense and then relax. For a moment, they were two separate beings merely touching. But then the hand on her back moved lower. He pulled her closer, kissed harder. Then they were one.

Everything changed again. A flutter moved between them. Or maybe a flicker. The prince's entire being seemed to flash or vanish or *something*.

When he pushed her away, it almost felt like a shove. A smile had been painted onto his lips as he carefully moved every part of his body until he no longer touched hers. Despite his strange reaction, he gave a convincingly hungry look toward her before turning to Ansel. "See? You may *not* have her."

Though the fae nodded and stomped off toward the crowd, he didn't seem happy about the outcome.

Brannick gestured her out the ballroom doors, which they both exited without a word. After walking over the orange and gold rugs of a few hallways, they finally found an empty one. The prince immediately rounded on her, forcing her to back into a sandstone wall.

His nose twitched as he leaned close enough to leave his breath on her face. He spoke through clenched teeth. "*Never* do that again."

She let out a scoff as she pushed him away and continued down the hallway. "Why would I ever *want* to do that again?"

Tension rocked between them like it never had before as they resumed their stomping down the hallway. They had to find those shards. But could they do it without speaking? Without feeling?

CHAPTER 33

Elora walked on one side the hallway, doing her best to ignore Brannick walking on the other side. They stepped in silence. Both refused to make eye contact.

Blaz had appeared. He moved from Elora to Brannick, nudging his nose against their legs. Was he trying to get them to speak to each other?

It angered her how much that stupid kiss had gotten under her skin. How much she couldn't forget it. After a few turns through the hallways, she wondered if the prince even knew where they were going.

As always, she had just been following along. She huffed to herself at the thought. Brannick certainly *acted* like he knew where he was going, but maybe it was his way of pretending that kiss had never happened.

Without warning, he stopped in his tracks. His eyelids closed, and he took in a long, deep breath. He stayed still for so long, she was tempted to flick him in the arm.

Instead, she opted not to touch him. "What are you doing?"

The sound of her voice made him start. He peeked through one eyelid wearing a scrunched-up mouth. "I am trying to find the shards."

She folded her arms over her chest. "By breathing?"

He let out a scoff before closing his eye again. Another deep breath moved through him. When he spoke again, it was in a lower, softer tone. "Can you not feel them?"

With a scoff, she turned and rubbed a thumbnail over the sandstone wall of the castle. Grains of warm sand drifted to the rug beneath her feet. "What are you talking about?"

The prince marched forward, his black hair whipping behind him. "I will never understand how mortals survive with such inferior bodies."

It didn't do any good to roll her eyes at Brannick's back, but she did it anyway.

He glanced over his shoulder wearing a stupid smirk. "I suppose you do *not* survive with them."

Since Blaz happened to be walking next to her at that moment, she rubbed a hand through the fur on his neck. It seemed like a nice moment to remind the arrogant prince how his ever-loyal wolf seemed to like her almost as much as him. "Excuse me?" she asked, raising one eyebrow.

As she hoped, a twinge went through Brannick's forehead when he saw how his wolf nuzzled against her. He responded by whipping his head forward, refusing eye contact yet again. "That is the difference between mortals and fae. Your bodies age and die. Ours can live forever unless we are killed." He looked back with another smirk. "But it takes a lot more to kill a fae than it does to kill a human."

Twisting her mouth up, she glared at the walls they passed. "You seem so confident despite the fact that your high king couldn't even identify emotion as the thing that made my harp playing so striking. No wonder you fae are all trying to curse and kill each other. You don't even know common decency."

On his side of the hallway, Brannick stopped in place. Waving a hand, a delicate bunch of purple wildflowers grew straight out of the sandstone wall. A sweet, floral smell drifted to her nose. Glitter seemed to burst from the petals as the prince plucked them from the wall.

With an amused chuckle, he pushed the flowers into her hand. "Do you still think being mortal is so great?"

Though she took the flowers with one hand, she shoved Brannick into the wall with the other. Holding her head high, she marched ahead of him without looking back. After a few stomps, the wildflowers vanished in a burst of purple light. When they reached the end of the hallway, she chose which direction to go next.

The prince immediately insisted they go the other way. He probably just did it to prove his *superiority*.

But then he raised a hand and took in another deep breath. "We are getting close."

Their argument seemed to disappear completely from his mind as he brought a hand to the sandstone wall at his side. He stepped forward with measured steps. Walking carefully, he touched the wall like it could tell the future.

It probably wasn't a good time to interrupt, but at this point, she didn't care. "If we *do* find the shards, what do we do then?"

His eyes narrowed as he glanced down the hallway. "Destroy them."

She trailed behind him at an angle, still afraid to walk directly at his side. "I know, but what about the testing? Can we tell the high king about the shards so King Huron will no longer be eligible to win the throne?"

A snort erupted from Brannick's lips. "High King Romany would never listen to such accusations. He only believes what he discovers himself. That is why he executed his son for poisoning him despite the fact that Queen Alessandra organized the whole thing. She will still be eligible for the throne after this, and she would be much worse than King Huron. Anyway, we still have two phases to beat them."

Somewhere along his explanation, Elora's feet had rooted to the ground. With a tiny shake of the head, she jogged to catch up with him. "Queen Alessandra poisoned the high king? How do you even know that?"

He didn't answer. He had the decency to narrow his eyes a bit more, as if looking harder for the shards.

At least Blaz was walking next to her again. She patted his head as she looked at the prince. "So, *why* doesn't Queen Alessandra remember you?"

"Memory elixir." Brannick placed his palm against a wooden door with intricate gilded designs. He closed his eyes and took in a deep breath. "I believe this is it." He gestured up at a little window that decorated the top of the door. "Can you fly up there and check inside the room? You should be able to see the shards if they are inside."

She blinked at him twice. "Right. Wings." Shaking her head, she popped them out of her back. "I can fly because I have wings."

The prince rubbed his temples. "If you were staying in Faerie, I might suggest you find a sprite or a pixie to teach you to use them better. Alas, you clearly decided you would return to the mortal realm after the testing."

Now she blinked back at him for a whole new reason. After he read Chloe's poem, Elora had been hoping he might change his mind about forcing her to return home after the testing. Unfortunately, that didn't seem to be the case.

He raised his eyebrows and gestured up toward the window again. "Go on."

Yes, he was probably just trying to distract her from asking more questions about Queen Alessandra. But for some reason, she didn't care. Any excuse to move farther away from him seemed like a good thing to do.

Her glittery wings let out a tinkling sound as she fluttered off the ground. It didn't take long to reach the window. She glanced into the room, which was mostly empty. A wooden trunk sat on the sandstone floor. Gold rivets wrapped around the edges of the trunk. The lid was open.

Her heart stammered as she tried to catch her breath. Piles of golden shards shimmered inside the open trunk.

When her feet hit the rug below, she put away her wings and reached straight for the golden doorknob. "This is it."

The door wouldn't open on her first try. After a quick hand wave from Brannick, it swung inward. He leapt to the trunk's side. Pride at finding the shards was quickly overcast with a shudder as he drew nearer to the metallic shards.

"How do we destroy them?" Elora asked. She reached for the hilt of her sword. "Should I—"

"No." Brannick turned his hand in a swirl, muttering under his breath and taking deep breaths every few moments.

Blaz moved to the wall and sat on his haunches. He eyed the room with suspicion while the prince worked.

Brannick's face scrunched up. His hand formed a fist. With a punch to the air, he let out a grunt.

But when he finished, nothing happened.

She glanced at the shards, then tentatively glanced at the prince.

He grimaced toward the trunk, eyeing the shards like they were planning his murder. In a flash, the gold vanished and the shards turned to orange sandstone. He glanced toward his wolf, but they both stared at each other with equally confused expressions. Narrowing his eyes, the prince's voice lowered. "That should have worked."

A familiar chuckle sounded from behind them.

Suddenly, King Huron stood in the doorway holding a golden key. "It would have worked if those were the real shards. Sadly for you, they are not. And doubly sad, High King Romany has agreed to allow me to give an unscheduled presentation."

Twists and knots and hammers slammed through Elora's chest. She reached for her sword, but King Huron's gold tunic caught the light as he turned his back on them.

"You two are not invited." With that, that Dustdune king slammed the door shut. A loud click sounded through the air a moment later.

They were locked inside.

CHAPTER 34

Letting out a loud grunt, Elora glared at the prince. "I thought you said you could feel the shards."

His shoulders tensed at the exact moment that a grimace twisted his features. "King Huron tricked me. He imbued that sandstone with a fake essence so potent that I could not sense the real shards." Snarling, he glared at the ground. "I can feel the real ones now. Sprites are carrying them all over Faerie, but none of the sprites in this room have shards."

Her muscles strained when she drew her sword. Since she had been separated from the weapon for so long, using it to relieve her anger felt even better than usual.

She screamed and swung the sword at the silk curtains hanging over a window. The blade left a nice deep slice in the sturdy fabric. It took another grunt to rip the sword back and whip it across another portion of the curtain.

In the corner of the room, Blaz sat on his haunches. He lowered his head at the sight of her, almost as if he was embarrassed by her actions.

That only sent her sword flying faster. Her blade cut and sliced the silk, leaving deep gashes and slices. Each one brought another grunt from her lips.

Unlike his wolf, Brannick seemed highly amused. He leaned against a sandstone wall with one shoulder. "This reminds me of when we first met."

When her sword hit a corner of the window, it rebounded backward, nearly making her lose her balance. She sent him a huff. "Too bad I can't use wings to magically solve all my problems now."

Her arms dropped to her sides as soon as the words left her lips. "The door has a window at the top. What if I fly up there and break it? I can get us out of here."

The prince did little to suppress his chuckle. He gave a pointed glance toward his wolf. Blaz returned it with an amused smile that looked far too expressive for a wolf. Brannick threw his head back to move the hair out of his face before he turned back to her. "That would not work. The lock King Huron used put an enchantment on the entire room." He gave a casual shrug, but it didn't hide the twinge of frustration in his eyes. "Besides, even without the enchantment, Faerie glass is not easy to break."

They could make fun of her all they wanted, but this seemed like yet another perfect moment to swing her sword. At least it gave her something to focus on.

Though he leaned against a wall wearing a decidedly disinterested face, Brannick still watched her every move. His eyes followed not just her sword but also her arms, her feet.

Her face. The hairs on the back of her neck prickled, feeling his every stare.

After a few moments, he cleared his throat. She stuffed her sword back into the leather belt around her waist. It didn't help that the prince's eyes looked wilder and more enchanting than ever. They pulsed in every hue with ripples of shimmering black. He tipped up one eyebrow, clearly unable to hide his excitement. "Maybe I could destroy the shards from here."

With a deadpan, she folded her arms over her chest. "Are you serious?"

"What?" He gave a casual shrug, but something about his expression seemed very much like he enjoyed her agitation.

She let out a scoff and drew her sword again. This conversation would only be bearable if she could hack through a piece of silk while they were at it. Rolling her eyes, she asked, "Why did we even go looking for the shards then? Why didn't we stay in the ballroom? We could have avoided Ansel."

A twitch went through the prince's nose for the briefest moment. "It may be unsuccessful. I locate the shards by feeling for their essence. Since I made a mistake with these fake ones," he gestured toward the trunk, "I *could* make a mistake again. But I am fairly certain that destroying the shards will not harm the sprites carrying them."

Her eyes couldn't roll back far enough in her head. "Do it then. Destroy them. I'm just going to keep cutting into this curtain because I haven't gotten to use my sword enough today."

He didn't respond. He didn't even move.

The stillness in the room was enough to make her lower the sword. She glanced over at Brannick, who now wore a face which didn't look sure at all.

285

Since they were looking at each other, she glanced at Blaz next. The wolf had lowered his head, staring at the prince with piercing eyes. Was he *talking* to the prince? Maybe the prince's essence magic allowed that sort of thing.

The silence lingered until she could take it no more. "What is it?"

Brannick turned away only to glare at the ground. "Destroying the shards in this way will drain energy from me. Blaz worries that trying to destroy so many shards at once will diminish my essence completely."

Even with the prince turned away, she could still see how his shoulders slumped. "I think Blaz might be right."

Pain danced in his eyes when he glanced back at her. He seemed to recognize the danger in destroying the shards, yet he clearly still considered the plan anyway. No matter how standoffish and cruel he acted, this moment proved he wasn't nearly as selfish as he wanted her to believe.

The silence continued. Dread filled too much of her heart to allow her to lift the sword again. It weighed heavy in her fingers as they tried to keep a firm grip.

They couldn't get out of the room, and Brannick couldn't destroy the shards.

But that didn't mean it was over. It couldn't be.

Elora hadn't used her sword against the prince only to lose her freedom now. She jammed the sword back into her belt and tapped her toe on the richly designed rug beneath her feet. With a smile, she whipped her head around. "What about the poem?"

Brannick narrowed his eyes but didn't utter a response.

Stepping toward him, she raised her eyebrows. "My sister's poem said we can defeat King Huron with the weapon he uses against us."

Brannick shook his head. "King Huron does not carry any weapons with him. He only uses magic or bargains."

"What about a shard?"

A scoff erupted from the prince's mouth. "And where are we supposed to get a shard?"

The question felt like a pommel to the gut. After a long huff, he turned away from her and sat cross-legged in a corner of the room. Blaz padded over to sit next to him. When the prince spoke again, he used a faraway voice, as if he could barely bring himself to speak to her at all.

"I will attempt to locate the shards. The real shards. I may not be able to destroy all of them, but hopefully I can destroy some of them."

Again, not nearly as selfish as he claimed.

When she opened her mouth, his hand shot into the air above him. "Do not interrupt me. You must be as quiet as possible."

A few choice words tickled the back of her lips, but she managed to keep them inside. Moving to the opposite side of the room, she glanced around again for a way out.

When her eyes wandered upward, a thrill shot through her. Glowing green lights floated near the ceiling. Even that set her mind spiraling with all sorts of ideas. But then one glow stood out for the pink sparkle inside it.

Elora held out her hand, knowing the smile on her face probably looked comically large by now. But she didn't care. When the tiny body of her sprite friend landed on her palm, she whispered a quick hello.

Tansy's body looked a little taller today. Her limbs looked stronger too. It no longer seemed like the sparkly pink dress would force the sprite over if a wind caught it wrong. The sprite's fuzzy wings flapped as she flew next to Elora's ear.

"I know where you can get a shard."

With eyes wide, Elora opened her mouth to ask more. But the sight of Brannick's tensed body turned toward the corner silenced her again.

The sprite must have been watching them because she seemed to understand. Tansy swooped down. With two hands, she grabbed Elora's pointer finger and tugged it upward.

Elora lifted her hand at the sprite's insistence, but it didn't seem very helpful. When her hand was high above her head, the sprite pointed to her wings.

Was blinking a good enough response?

Tansy pointed to her wings again and then flew behind Elora only to touch her back with a featherlight touch. The sprite flew in front of her again and pointed to her own wings a second time.

It dawned on Elora then. Taking in a quick breath, she released her wings until they flapped hard.

With a smile, Tansy started tugging Elora's finger again.

Fear wriggled through Elora as her feet lifted off the ground. It only multiplied as she moved closer to the ceiling. Going up a little higher, her heart started pattering with increased speed. This was officially the highest she had ever flown. The awkward movements proved she still had a lot to learn about flying, but the wings still carried her upward.

Before Elora could think about it too much, the sprite tugged her right into a glass window along the top edge of the room. Except they didn't run into it at all.

They went through it.

When the dry heat of Dustdune's air blew into Elora's face, she could do nothing but let out a delighted shriek. Her body flew lopsided with the help of her inexperienced wings. But still, she moved.

She flew.

Another shriek escaped her, this one filled with pure glee. The sprite looked over her shoulder with a finger to her tiny lips.

Elora tried to suppress her snicker by pressing a hand over her mouth. But how could she be quiet when she was flying? Actually *flying*.

Faerie looked so much bigger from up high. Dustdune's sandstone and golden castle rose above a swirling sand dune landscape. Scores of round white houses with thatched roofs surrounded it. There had to be at least five times as many houses there as there were in her little village back home.

But as Tansy led her over the curving sand dunes and dry stretches of sand, Elora soon realized that village was only one of many. Trees with thick trunks and even thicker branches dotted the landscape. Stiff, needle-like leaves stuck out in a tuft at the end of each branch. Scrub bushes and thin streams broke up the sandy, orange landscape.

Despite the dry heat, everything seemed magical.

At one point, they flew right past a bird with bright red feathers and a golden beak. It seemed like a pretty enough creature, but when Elora realized the bird was almost as big as a horse, she couldn't help but gasp.

Tansy gripped tighter and looked over her shoulder. The wind carried her voice back, but it sounded so small this high in the air. "Firebirds will leave you alone as long as you leave them alone. Just don't go looking for their nests."

By the time they reached the balance cliffs, Elora was so full of thrill she could barely breathe. Two sets of cliffs stretched out in front of them, one gold and the other a shimmery pink.

Tansy stopped just short of the cliffs and pointed to a little ledge on the golden side. After so much flying, Elora's wings were better at bringing her to the ledge. Though, her feet still slipped when she tried to land. Grabbing onto a ridge helped slightly.

Pulling out her sword, Elora tried to chip away a golden shard. The material was more delicate than she realized. Her sword broke a perfect shard into her hand. But then a huge chunk started falling away from the cliffside.

The large piece fell heavy with a whoosh and only *just* missed hitting her wings. It took a moment of hovering before Elora could breathe again.

Tansy flew toward her with eyes wide. "How did you do that?"

The fear lining the sprite's voice melted into Elora. She loosened her grip on the shard in her hand. "I thought these shards couldn't hurt me because I'm mortal."

A loud snort erupted from Tansy. "The golden shards cannot begin a transformation inside you, but they can still fall on you and kill you. How did you move so quickly to avoid that chunk? You are not that good at flying."

With a gulp, Elora touched a hand to the feather behind her neck. Soren's feather was supposed to protect her from any accidental danger. She eyed the cliffs while a lump grew in her throat. Apparently, that was more useful than she thought.

The sprite urged her forward, and soon they were headed toward Dustdune Castle again.

With her wings flapping, Elora tucked her sword back into her leather belt. She tried to tuck the shard underneath her corset, but the dark green dress from Brannick stopped her. She glared at the soft fabric when she realized it had no pockets.

Her body continued to move in lopsided glides as she flew. "Hey Tansy, how do I get one of those magical pockets all you fae seem to have?"

A noise came from the sprite's mouth that sounded halfway between a snort and a chuckle. "You have to be fae to get one." She glanced back with a teasing look in her green and pink eyes. "I do not know how you mortals manage."

The words probably would have upset Elora if she weren't in the middle of *flying* over *Faerie*. As it was, it seemed like nothing could ever upset her again. Even the sight of Dustdune Castle couldn't sour her mood.

They had a shard now. That meant they could defeat King Huron.

As they neared the castle, a feeling deep inside Elora sent shivers through her. The hairs on her arms raised in an uncomfortable bristle. Even before the sprite brought her through the window, Elora knew something was wrong.

Her heart stopped once inside the room. The weight in her gut seemed to drop lower despite how her wings flapped. When her feet hit the ground, she put away her wings with a jolt. It didn't change how dread skittered across every bit of her skin.

In the corner of the room, Prince Brannick writhed and twisted with groans of pain. His veins pulsed, and he seemed completely unaware of his surroundings.

CHAPTER

35

Elora tripped over her feet as she stumbled across the floor. She was at the prince's side in a single heartbeat.

His eyes had rolled back in his head. He held both hands in tight fists. His back arched while his body tensed and twisted. When she said his name, he continued as if he had heard nothing.

"What's going on?" She tried to ignore how her lip trembled through the words.

In a graceful swoop, the sprite landed on her shoulder. Tansy took in a deep breath before she answered. "He is trying to destroy the shards."

A jerk shot through Brannick, nearly slamming his head into the castle wall.

The tremble in Elora's lip had spread out to her chin and jaw. "I thought you weren't going to do that." Her scolding had no effect on the writhing prince. Now her tone turned gentle. "What can I do?" She reached for Brannick's arm, his shoulder, anything.

But he continued to wince while pained moans escaped his lips.

Tansy's voice lowered to a whisper. "I do not know what to do."

Black fur nudged its way under Elora's palm. She looked toward Blaz, hoping he had an idea of some sort. The wolf gave her a pointed look before he nuzzled himself against the prince's side.

She bit her bottom lip, hoping she had interpreted the wolf's intention correctly. But maybe it didn't matter. Watching Brannick moan and jerk was too painful. In desperation, she reached for his hand.

It took some prying to get his fist open. When she did, she wrapped her hand around his and put her other hand around them too.

At first, nothing changed. His eyes stayed rolled back in his head as every muscle in his face twitched. She squeezed his hand harder, which only seemed to relax his muscles a fraction.

But it wasn't helping. Not enough at least, that much was clear.

Perhaps it was desperation or fear or something else entirely, but words came to her from deep within. They seemed vaguely familiar, though she was certain she had never heard them before. Even still, they seemed like just the words for an occasion like this.

Leaning close, she put as much emotion into her words as she possibly could. "Come on, Brannick. A prince never accepts defeat."

At those words, a very soft chuckle came from Brannick's mouth. His body went rigid, but then he took in a deep breath.

293

Tremors rocked through his body, each one slightly smaller than the last.

A hard shudder shook him. Afterward, his breathing evened to heavy pants. But even those seemed more controlled with each breath. His rolled back eyes wandered forward looking as bright and mesmerizing as ever. They didn't focus on anything in the room, but they didn't roll back again either.

After a tentative squeeze, Brannick's hand grew warmer in her grip. For the first time, he returned the squeeze. He took in a deep breath at the exact same moment, which seemed to give him strength.

When he closed his eyes and clenched his jaw, it didn't seem to be from pain. His concentration now seemed to be directed at some action Elora couldn't see. Probably something magical.

His breathing evened when he squeezed her hand again. But the action also caused his body to flicker. Or shimmer? Right before her eyes, Brannick vanished before reappearing less than a moment later.

With a hiss, he ripped his hand from her grip. He was on his feet faster than she could blink. Heavy pants huffed through his clenched teeth as he glared at her. "Do not touch me, mortal."

Heat seared through her face as she too got to her feet. Her lip trembled, attempting to match the anger in his voice. "Fine." She had to stop and brush a hand over her skirt because otherwise tears would have burst out. Only after looking away could she continue. "Next time you're screaming and writhing in pain, I'll just let you die."

He flashed his teeth at her before resting his hand against the wall. "I was not screaming." His lip curled. "And you will not be in Faerie long enough to experience another moment like this anyway."

The sprite flew up to the ceiling when Elora shoved both hands through her hair. She glared at the prince while a growl threatened to explode from her throat. She managed to keep it to a heavy puff through her nose instead. "You are insufferable."

Putting a hand to her forehead, she moved toward the door. Maybe speaking would be easier when she didn't have to look at him. "How do we get out of here?"

He was panting again, but she was determined not to look his way. When he spoke, his voice came out weaker than usual. Too bad for him. "The door is magically sealed. Only King Huron can open it."

She let out a scoff before turning her eyes to the ceiling. When she had located the glowing green light with a sparkle of pink, she asked, "Tansy, can you open it for us?"

The light swooped down until the sprite landed on Elora's shoulder.

Brannick raised an eyebrow before rolling his eyes. "That is just a sprite. What do you expect it to do?"

Both Tansy and Elora folded their arms at the same moment. With her jaw tight, Elora said, "In my experience, sprites have no trouble getting past any enchantments, including the ones you put on my room."

One of his eyebrows twitched. "That is impossible."

She raised an eyebrow. "Really? How do you think I got out of my room then? How do you think I got my sword back?"

He glanced at his wolf while the twitch in his eyebrow went faster. Blaz seemed to give him a shrug. The prince turned back to her looking even more sure of himself than before. "But they are just sprites."

Elora shook her head as she moved a hand to her hip. "And I'm just a mortal, yet I seem to be solving a lot of your problems lately. Including how to defeat King Huron."

She retrieved the golden shard from where she had dropped it on the ground.

Brannick's eyes widened enough to raise his eyebrows into his hair. "That…" He clapped a hand over his heart as he took a step back. "That is a real balance shard."

"I know." She turned and moved closer to the door. "Tansy and I just went and got it from the balance cliffs. If you hadn't been too busy trying to kill yourself, you probably would have noticed my absence."

He moved to her side but stayed more than an arm's length away.

After a quick glance at the sprite, Elora reached toward him. "Tansy can get us through, just hold my hand."

"No." He was staring at her hand wearing an expression that didn't make any sense at all.

After an exaggerated scoff, Elora reached out and touched Blaz's neck instead. "Fine, then she can take us through separately."

On the other side of the closed door, Elora had both hands on her hips and tapped her toe when Brannick finally stepped through. He glanced up and down the hallway with shoulders bunched, as if he couldn't believe it had actually worked.

She rolled her eyes at him before turning to the sprite on her shoulder. "You better go up to the ceiling with the other sprites so no one gets suspicious."

Tansy nodded with a sweet smile. The expression quickly turned sour as she glared at the prince. A moment later, she blended in perfectly with the other glowing green lights that floated above.

Examining the shard in her hand, Elora flicked her eyes toward the prince. "Do we even need this if all the other shards are destroyed?"

Brannick took in a breath before he answered. Considering how long he spent breathing out, it seemed likely he was taking his time just to annoy her. Or maybe he just didn't want to admit what he was about to say. Rubbing the back of his neck, he said, "I did not destroy all the shards. I could only locate a few of them. I *did*, hopefully, destroy the ones the sprites in the ballroom were carrying. The destruction of shards is explosive, so it should have caused a commotion."

"And that's a good thing?" She tilted an eyebrow up along with the question.

He responded by turning away from her and running a hand through Blaz's fur. "I do not believe it injured the sprites. But now the other fae know someone is trying to use the shards against them. They will not be happy."

Following him back down the halls seemed like the only thing she could do. And thinking out loud. She could do that all day. "If my sister's poem was right, you have to get King Huron to attempt to use a shard against you. Then you have to pierce *him* with it instead. That should defeat him, right?"

"Correct." Brannick held his hand out for the shard, which she gladly dropped into his hand. *Without* touching him.

With her eyes on the hallway ahead, a knot twisted through her chest. "How are we supposed to do it?"

He allowed their eyes to meet for only a moment before grinning. "I have no idea. We will have to figure it out as we go."

CHAPTER 36

Crashes and shouts from the ballroom filled the hallway where Elora and Brannick ran. Blaz had his fangs bared by the time they reached the chaos-filled room.

Weapons had been drawn, swinging through the air with rage and precision. All around the room, faces had transformed from stunning beauties to ones of cruelty and rage. Amid the madness, two fae used javelins to fight against a large creature in the middle of the room.

The creature had gray skin with orange undertones. It loomed at least a head taller than any other fae in the room. Its arms and legs looked thicker than tree trunks. Two fang-like teeth protruded out of its mouth from its lower jaw. A long tail with a tuft of orange fur poked out of the brown tunic covering it. The creature held a short, pointed dagger with a golden grip. The gold sat perpendicular to the blade with an H-shaped grip.

At her side, a low growl rolled in Blaz's throat. His furry black ears pointed upward while tension ruffled his fur.

After glancing at his wolf, Brannick shook his head at the large creature. "King Huron brought in an ogre." He pinched the bridge of his nose. "This will make things more difficult."

The ogre's arms hung down past its knees. When it jabbed its dagger at its attackers, the fae fighting it stepped backward at lightning speed.

But apparently, casualties had already fallen. At least one brownie and a simply-dressed mortal lay in blood-soaked clothes at the ogre's feet.

All around the ogre, fae fought against fae. They shouted, pointed fingers, swung weapons. Fear and anger laced the voices. Accusations could be heard rising above the roaring chaos. "*You* were going to use the shards." "I knew you had it out for me." "How dare you do such a thing?"

Every fae seemed quick to accuse, but the pandemonium brought them no closer to an answer.

From atop the platform at the other end the room, High King Romany sat in the throne with his hands gripping the arms so tight, it turned his knuckles white. His face was red from yelling. Queen Noelani of Swiftsea brandished a shimmery blue javelin, pointing it at King Huron. King Jackory of Mistmount was pointing at Queen Alessandra. She was yelling at all of them.

With a swift glance at Brannick, Elora and the prince pushed into the throng. When Blaz joined them, he didn't bother wearing a glamour of any kind. His snarling and teeth flashing were enough to frighten many fae away.

There didn't seem to be much of a plan except get to the platform and somehow get King Huron to use a shard against

Brannick. And survive. That was definitely an important part of the plan.

The moment they entered the crowd, King Huron whipped his head toward them from atop the platform. The feather in his crown rustled at the movement. A sneer crept onto his face as he locked eyes with Elora. In a louder voice than anyone, King Huron pointed toward the pair of them. "There he is. Prince Brannick is finally here, but only *after* those shards were discovered. Why would he appear now, only after the shards were discovered?"

All around them, faces turned in their direction. Weapons moved from other targets only to focus on the prince. When Elora reached for the hilt of her sword, she was more ready than ever to use it.

Brannick shot an arm in front of her, blocking the other fae from seeing how she gripped the hilt. His eyes stayed forward, but he whispered to her in a low voice. "If anyone sees you use that, they will guess my secret. I will lose the element of surprise in the third phase of testing. I ask that you do not use it."

Her teeth clenched together hard enough to bring a twinge to her jaw. "But everyone here wants to kill you."

The crowd was already closing in on them. Getting to the platform would be hard enough. But without her sword? It might be impossible.

After glancing at his wolf, the prince flashed her with a smirk. "I have more power than you know."

After slamming a fist into a fae who tried to tackle her, she raised an eyebrow at the prince. "Even after you destroyed all those shards?"

With a wave of his hand, the three fae charging him collapsed to the ground with simultaneous grunts. "I may be drained, but I am not dead yet. Just keep close to me so I can maintain the glamour on your sword."

He seemed overly confident for someone whose knees wobbled with every step. Despite his insistence, she could see how a tremble went through his hand every time he used his magic.

At least they still had Blaz. He sank his razor-sharp fangs into any fae who dared come near the prince. Blood dripped from the gashes he tore into arms and legs. Since he had always been so kind to her, Elora had almost forgotten he was a dangerous wolf and not just a kind creature. His ferocity could not be matched. But with each attack, the other fae only grew more determined. Soon, Brannick and Blaz both fought, but more fae charged them.

When a pair of fae bolted toward them from behind, she had to get creative if she wanted to avoid drawing her sword. Whirling around, she stood back to back with the prince. Maybe he didn't want her using her weapon at all, but she had already decided she was no player in someone else's game. She'd just have to be more discreet than she was used to.

Using her forearm, she pressed the pommel down so the blade went up. When the two fae tried to approach her, they were met with an invisible blade that slapped against their bellies.

Before they could look too hard for the weapon that hit them, Elora kicked them both to the ground. With her shoulder blade brushing against Brannick's back, she managed to keep pace with him as he headed for the platform.

Now a new group of fae rushed toward her. This time, she spun in a circle, making sure to slap her sword against their bodies. Two jabs to the gut were enough to drop the nearest fae to the ground. Her hand to hand combat clearly needed refining, but at least her muscles were toned enough to do a small amount of damage. It helped that none of her attackers could see her weapon.

"Get them!" King Huron's shriek was followed by the ogre lumbering over the ballroom floor toward them.

The creature pulled a weapon from its belt. At first it looked like a whip with several strands. Upon closer inspection, she realized the strands were actually thin, flexible blades. The ogre let out a growl from his fang-like teeth. The blades sliced through the air, cutting a gash into the arm of a nearby fae.

With a gulp, Elora glanced over her shoulder. Brannick panted. His eyes seemed more tired than ever. And they were still only halfway through the ballroom.

Her chest tightened when she tried to breathe. After turning back around, the fae had backed away to clear a space between her and the ogre. A lump formed in her throat. Swallowing did no good. Her fingers itched for the hilt of her sword.

At least she didn't have to worry about any other enemies to fight. Even Blaz's opponents stepped away. None of the fae seemed willing to be near the ogre while it wielded its strange weapon. Taking in a breath, she tried to convince herself that was a good thing.

Now she just had to fight off an ogre. And Blaz could help.

Her heart pounded as the creature slashed its whip at her.

With her forearm still on the pommel of her sword, she moved her body forward into a roll over the ballroom floor. During the movement, she arranged her sword just right so it slapped against the ogre's blades.

A clash sounded through the ballroom as her sword hit the thin blades away. While they flew high in the air, the wolf sunk his teeth into the ogre's leg. Once on her feet, Elora moved herself to stand back to back with the prince again. She jerked her head upward. The wolf immediately followed the command and raced to her side.

With spittle erupting from its mouth, the ogre raised the blade-whip again. "Your tricks will not last, mortal. I will grind you into dust and then eat every crumb."

Brannick pushed forward in the crowd just enough that she could jump backward to avoid the thin blades. The wolf moved along with her. But when the ogre raised the whip again, the extra space had vanished. He stepped closer. Pulsing shook her limbs. Would this be her doom?

In a clear voice, Brannick shouted above the crowd. "Do not fight *me*. King Huron is the guilty one."

This stayed the hands of a few fae. It seemed strange until Elora remembered fae could not lie. Was that simple statement all the proof they needed?

King Huron's voice filled the ballroom next. "If Prince Brannick is not guilty, then why did he leave the ballroom? Where was he when the shards were discovered?"

The fighting renewed with even greater vigor than before. The ogre had moved close enough now that avoiding his blade-whip would be impossible. In desperation, Elora reached for her sword, ready to finally use it.

From behind her, Brannick nudged against her shoulder and let out a grunt. Despite his frustration, her sword still seemed to be invisible. Though, if anyone watched her fight with it—even invisible—they could probably figure out what she was doing.

He could complain all he wanted, but they didn't have much of a choice at this point. At least the platform was a little closer than before. They just had to reach it.

The ogre raised his blade-whip, and she prepared to give herself away as a master swordsman. Just when she went to pull the sword from her belt, a shimmery blue javelin blocked the ogre's thin blades from reaching her.

Lyren spun her javelin in a circle, nearly making the ogre lose its grip on its weapon. With a sharp jab, she stabbed the ogre in one knee. It let out a yowl that shook the castle walls. Swinging the javelin again, Lyren blinked her dark eyelashes. "I tried to get here sooner, but this crowd is so wild."

Warmth spread through Elora's chest as she discreetly pulled her hand away from the invisible sword in her belt. Though all the fae she met claimed to be selfish, emotionless beings, they clearly had a small amount of honor. At least the fae Elora had met in Bitter Thorn did.

Nodding toward Lyren, Elora raised her fists ready to fight off any new enemy. Blaz bared his teeth with a ferocious growl.

It didn't take long to get to the platform after that. Other Swiftsea fae had joined the fight, clearly on Brannick's side. With every step, Elora's skill seemed greater than it should have been. When weapons whizzed past, just missing her, she knew the feathers in her hair were to thank.

Once they reached the platform, the prince turned toward Elora long enough to whisper in her ear.

"I have an idea. Draw your sword. I'll create a new glamour that hides the sword and makes it look like your hand is at your side."

CHAPTER

37

Sweat poured into the leather on Elora's sword hilt. Her heart hammered as she gripped, ready to enact the prince's plan.

Dark circles sat beneath Brannick's eyes. His knees trembled even when standing still, which was barely even noticeable because of how every muscle in his arms and shoulders twitched. The copper undertones in his light brown skin looked dull as he reached into his green coat.

Despite his disheveled appearance, he managed to command attention from the room. Brannick pulled a golden shard from his magical pocket. Gasps sounded throughout the room at the sight of it. Many fae seemed to believe the shard only proved the prince had indeed planned to destroy the fae.

He didn't even flinch at the whispers rolling through the room. He just held the shard out and gave a pointed stare toward the Dustdune king. "If you believe I am guilty, then hurt me the way I supposedly intended to hurt others."

With a great flourish, he placed the glimmering shard at King Huron's feet. Taking a few steps back, the prince made it clear that King Huron had all the power. That caused a wild grin to break onto the Dustdune king's face.

High King Romany rose from the throne, shaking his head with each step. "Put that disgusting thing away. I will not have my court leaders kill each other in the middle of a testing. Do I need to make it an official rule?"

But the Dustdune king couldn't tear his eyes away from the shard. His eyes kept flicking from it to Brannick. The wheels in his head seemed to be turning with every new breath.

Elora recalled King Huron's original plan. He wanted to use the shards to absorb power. With so much power, he could easily defeat High King Romany and become the next high king himself.

Similar thoughts seemed to be bouncing around in King Huron's mind now. After seeing how much magic Brannick was able to use, even after destroying those shards, maybe absorbing his magic would be enough to make King Huron the most powerful fae in Faerie all at once.

King Huron took in a breath. At that moment, everyone seemed to understand what he intended to do. The high king reached for him. On his other side, the Mistmount king reached for him.

Neither one caught him in time.

Gripping her sword tighter, Elora prepared for her part of the plan. Though her arm moved, the prince's glamour made it seem as though it remained hanging at her side.

King Huron snatched the shard off the ground. With lightning speed, he lunged forward and plunged the shard into Brannick's chest.

Or he tried to, anyway.

Elora's hand shook as she gripped her sword. She held the flat side of the blade directly against Brannick's chest. The shard slammed against it, rather than piercing the prince's heart like King Huron had intended. Still, the sword remained invisible.

King Huron's face twisted as he went to pull the shard back to try again. With a subtle move, the sharp edge of Elora's sword caught the delicate shard and held it in place.

While the Dustdune king tried to make sense of what was happening, Brannick plucked the shard from off Elora's sword. In a swift punch, he ran the shard into King Huron's chest.

A gasp went through the king. The shard let out an explosive crack that reverberated through the ballroom. Afterward, it burst into a cloud of golden glitter. While the gold pieces floated to the floor, King Huron gripped his chest. Soon, his hands moved up to his throat. He clawed at it, as if trying to pull away something that blocked his air.

Stutters erupted from his mouth as his knees fell onto the golden platform. A moment later, he collapsed into a convulsing mess. Stutters no longer left his mouth. Now, he simply coughed until no sound at all came out.

His body scrunched into ball only for his back to arch and his arms to flail out again. With one last moan, he went limp. The color drained from his face. A tiny light floated up from the king's chest. There it hovered with a pulsing orange glow.

High King Romany looked at the body like it was as pleasant as an ogre's spittle. His nose wrinkled as he lifted one foot and stepped away from the dead king. "That went faster than I expected. Most fae last until day dawns at least." After a quick head shake, he took another step away. The high king gestured toward the glowing orange light. "Prince Brannick, the magic of King Huron rightfully belongs to you."

Now it was Brannick who wrinkled his nose. "If I absorb his magic, I will also absorb his essence." A seemingly involuntary shudder passed through the prince's shoulders. "But his essence is filthy. I reject the magic and choose to return it to Faerie instead. May the land cleanse it before it is used again."

The high king replied with a quick nod before he started rubbing his forehead. "Did King Huron have any heirs? I am busy with a testing for my own throne. I would rather not have to organize one for *another* court."

A man from the crowd stepped forward wearing a tan linen tunic and pants. He might have been mortal, but a mop of thick, black hair covered his ears so it was hard to tell. "I believe he had a daughter who lives on the outskirts of Dustdune, though I do not know if she is still alive."

With a hurried nod, High King Romany waved the man away. "Very well. Find the heir and send her to me in Noble Rose. I will name her ruler if she truly possesses the same blood as King Huron. But she will not be eligible to win my throne. There is already enough going on with the rest of you."

He let out a sigh that seemed only related to King Huron's death. But considering that he then collapsed onto the golden throne with a heaving chest, it might have had more to do with his physical ailment than he wanted to let on. Rubbing his temples, he looked to the other rulers. "The rest of you, behave yourselves until the next phase of testing. I might send messengers to check on you if I need."

The high king gave a quick nod to a nearby fae with long golden hair. She quickly waved a hand which opened a door with red swirls and green vines. She and the high king stepped through it at once.

As soon as he left, Queen Alessandra glared at Brannick. She narrowed her eyes, examining his features carefully. The prince's shoulders hunched in response. He stepped behind Elora, once again using her as a shield to block himself from the Fairfrost Queen's sight. The queen huffed and disappeared through her own door.

King Jackory of Mistmount disappeared through his door a moment later. That brought a ripple of doors throughout the ballroom. Each door was unique. Fae of all shapes and sizes stepped through their doors, leaving the room even emptier than before. Several fae remained in the room, most of them wearing rich silks and brocades in a style similar to King Huron's.

Queen Noelani adjusted her seashell crown before pulling a long chain from a magical pocket inside her dress. Her whispers to Lyren were inaudible, but that didn't stop anyone from seeing how the queen draped the silver chain over Lyren's neck. Now a new seashell necklace hung clattering against the other. Glancing back at Elora, Lyren's eyes sparkled with silver bursts almost as big as her grin.

Despite their victory, Brannick stood in silence. Breathing. Hard. Even when Blaz nudged his leg, he didn't react.

Elora turned toward him, but he barely moved his eyes to look at her. She gestured out at the ballroom. Fragments of clay platters were scattered all over the sandstone floor. Goblets and bits of food were strewn every which way. Tables and chairs had legs broken off and lay at strange angles. That didn't even include the empty eyes of the Dustdune fae who now had no leader.

The ogre stood panting. Its grip on the blade-whip tightened as he glared at the prince. Perhaps he was even more eager than ever to finish Brannick off.

"What happens to them?" Elora asked under her breath.

The prince held his head high as he whirled around. "That is none of our concern." By the time he opened a door, Lyren, Vesper, and Quintus had come to his side.

They all walked through silently. After stepping through, they stood inside a hallway of Bitter Thorn Castle. Brannick gave a casual glance at Elora's waist. When he did, she looked for the same thing he did. Luckily, her sword was still invisible.

He had not taken them to the council room like she expected. Instead, the empty hallway before them led to her room. Kaia appeared from nowhere with a small clay pot that sat perfectly in the palm of her hand.

The dryad pulled a soft, brown rag from her magical pocket. Pouring the contents of the clay pot onto the rag, Kaia began dabbing the prince's forehead. She shook her head every time the rag touched his face. "You used too much of your magic."

Brannick gave a sideways glance at Elora before answering. "I had little choice."

Soren appeared from around a corner, his white beard jiggling with each step. He let out a breath of relief at the sight of the prince. Then he narrowed his eyes at Elora and seemed to see something no one else could. "I see my feather was useful."

She nodded in response, allowing a subtle smile onto her face.

"Where did you two go?" Lyren smoothed her blue dress as she looked from Elora to Brannick and back again.

With a wince, the prince moved away from the dryad's dabbing. "Trying to find and destroy the shards."

Both of Vesper's eyebrows rose. "Did it work?"

Kaia had stepped closer to the prince again, dabbing with even more vigor than before. After a small huff, he accepted her help. Whatever she was using, *did* seem to bring the copper undertones back into Brannick's skin. Frowning, the prince said, "I only destroyed some of the shards. I chose the ones in the ballroom, so it would alert the other fae that a sinister plot was in motion."

With one last dab, Kaia stepped away from the prince with narrowed eyes. "That is all I can do for now, but you will need more treatments."

Brannick nodded and waved everyone away. "Yes, fine. Later. Everyone go get some rest. We will have another meeting after day dawns to begin preparing for the next phase of testing."

After the others began walking away, the prince gave another short glance toward Elora's sword. It was still hidden, but he seemed intent on staying with her until they had reached her room.

It seemed like the perfect time to ask another question that plagued her. "What will happen to the other shards?"

One eyebrow ticked up Brannick's forehead. "I was hoping your friend might be able to answer that." He gestured toward her room, mostly at the ceiling.

With any luck, Tansy would be there waiting for them.

CHAPTER

38

Stepping into her room after everything sent a strange wriggling through Elora's stomach. She wasn't here because of some bargain anymore. She was here by choice. As thrilling as the adventure had been, freedom tasted much sweeter.

After a quick glance through the room, it seemed Tansy had not yet arrived. Brannick stood with a stiff back near the closed door. He clasped both hands behind his back looking more formal than she'd ever seen him. Blaz sat near, resting his head over his paws.

Reaching for the tree growing inside her room, Elora traced a finger over the striations on the bark. "How did King Huron know we were looking for the shards?"

Brannick shrugged, but the movement made him wince. In a flash, he went back to his formal posture. "Fae are selfish.

When he told you about his plan with the shards, he must have assumed the possibility that you would tell me about it. Clearly, he took precautions to be prepared if we went looking for the shards, which we did."

A smile broke onto her face as she rubbed a thumb over the rich bark of her tree. "He was definitely still surprised when you changed your vow though."

The prince's stiff posture vanished for a moment when he let out a chuckle. "Yes. I do not know if you realize how tricky that was of you. If you had given him my first vow with the intention of telling me his plan, the bargain would have alerted King Huron to your deception. But since you truly planned to betray me when you gave him the vow, the bargain allowed it. I am certain King Huron never expected you to change your mind like that."

She tried to smile, but it was difficult because she wasn't sure if she should be proud of herself or not. After all, she *had* intended to betray Brannick. That would have ended in disaster.

Luckily, a green glow with a faint pink sparkle floated into the room a moment later. Grinning, Elora held a palm toward the ceiling. "Tansy, we had a question for you."

The sprite came zooming down wearing the widest smile Elora had ever seen on her. She stood as tall as Elora's thumb now. Her limbs were stronger than ever. Even tiny, no amount of frailty seemed to remain in Tansy's form.

Gulping, Elora asked, "What will happen to the rest of the shards that weren't destroyed?"

The smile on Tansy's face only grew. When she spoke, her voice sounded as silvery and clear as ever. "Our bargain died with King Huron. The sprites are all bringing their shards to the balance cliffs to dispose of them."

Brannick let out a breath of relief.

Elora bit into her bottom lip as she turned back to the sprite. "But all those sprites are still trapped in Fairfrost, right?"

In an instant, the smile on Tansy's face fell. "Yes." Even the fuzzy wings on her back drooped with the word.

With every inch of her body, Elora wanted to help those sprites that were trapped. Maybe someday, she'd be able to.

The sprite fluttered upward and gave a quick nod toward the large window. "I must speak with more of my brothers and sisters. I am glad to see you safe."

Her green light glowed bright as the sprite flew out through the window.

Brannick must have thought that was a good moment to leave because he reached for the leather strap on the door.

"Wait."

Elora's voice stopped him from tugging the door open, but he kept his hand tight around the leather strap.

She pulled out her sword. Since it was still invisible, she swung it hard enough to make sure he could hear the wind whistle around it. "You can't take my sword again."

He gave a nod, as if he had been expecting this. "I will get you a new sheath, and I will put a glamour into it. The sheath will keep your sword hidden like it was this evening. I would have done it tonight, but I did not have enough energy to devote to it. Hide your sword until then, but I will get you the sheath as soon as I can."

That seemed reasonable enough, but it still didn't answer her biggest question of all. Sliding the sword back into her belt, she took another step toward the prince.

With a cringe, he dropped his hand away from the leather strap on the door. Was he expecting this next question too?

"I have no bargain with you now. I am only helping you because I choose to."

His jaw flexed before he responded. "Have you changed your mind?"

"No." She drew her eyebrows together. "But I need you to explain why you want the throne so much."

He casually leaned into the wall next to him, but it didn't hide the twinge that went through his nose. "It will take the curse off my court. Bitter Thorn will finally be the High Court again, as it should be."

The scoff that came from her mouth had exactly as much bite as she intended. "I know there's more to it than that. Why would you be better than Queen Alessandra?"

His shoulders shuddered as he moved closer to the wall. At his side, Blaz buried his head beneath his paws.

Elora stepped forward again. "Why doesn't the queen remember you? You lived in her court. And you're a prince. Shouldn't she know *of* you at least?"

Brannick touched a hand to his forehead as he let out another sigh. This time, he seemed to be resigned. The words came out even faster than she expected. "I was young when I first met Queen Alessandra. She told me that some people called her Less, so that is what I called her too. I did not know her true identity."

The hand against his forehead curled into a fist, which he pressed against his skin.

It almost hurt watching his reactions. So much pain seemed to guide his movements. Biting her bottom lip, Elora asked, "Were you two friends?"

The prince jerked his head toward the wall as he huffed. "We were worse than friends."

Her heart seemed to stop. Heavy silence stretched between them.

His shoulders hunched forward as he wrapped his arms over his stomach. With eyes firmly glaring at the stone floor, he finally spoke again. "I fell in love with her." Another shudder passed through his shoulders before he placed his forehead against the wall. "We decided to get married, but we chose to do a bargain first. Many fae do bargains before they get married—maybe all of us do."

Another silence went through the room. A prickling sensation had broken out underneath Elora's skin. Reaching one arm across her stomach, she grabbed her elbow. "What did you promise in the bargain?"

Brannick's whole body slumped at her question. His eyes, his lips, his arms. They all drooped in unison. Even his knees bent. With posture so precarious, a single touch could have dropped him to the ground.

Even his voice sounded weak when he answered. "Marriage bargains are unique. They are mostly one-sided to represent how love requires trust. Two bargains must be made. In each, one fae makes their promises and the other merely offers love in return."

After a long blink he continued. "My bargain came first. I promised to follow every order she ever gave me for the rest of my days." He shook his head, still glaring at the ground. "I thought the words sounded a bit strange, especially the following orders part, but I was in love."

Digging both hands into his hair, his voice broke. "Like a fool, I even added more to the bargain. She had recently discovered me with a woman fae and assumed the worst. Nothing happened between the other fae and me, but I wanted to prove I would always be faithful. I promised I would never

316

touch another creature—besides my Less—with romantic feelings in my heart."

The prince dragged both hands down his face, groaning through his words. "I thought it was so romantic."

For a strange moment, the urge to scold him overtook Elora. "And what did she promise you in return? Why would you do something so foolish?"

His throat bulged against the necklace at his throat as he pushed the side of his fist into the stone wall. "I was young and stupid. I thought love was always pure." His eyes fell to the ground again, not even able to look at his wolf. "I am sure many mortals have succumbed to their emotions in a similar way."

All at once, Elora's body froze. A chill swept through her at this first inkling into why Brannick detested emotions with such vigor.

He shot her a knowing glance before continuing again. "She was supposed to make a bargain too, immediately after mine. But as soon as she opened her mouth to begin, a group of trolls kidnapped my Less right before my eyes. With anger fueling me, it didn't take long to track the trolls down. But soon I learned the bargain, the love, everything, was all a trick. The fae I thought was helpless was actually the great and feared Queen Alessandra of Fairfrost. Even worse, she had scores of guards who had all fallen for her same tricks. They had made a marriage vow exactly as I had, only for her to get kidnapped before their eyes. Not only had she deceived me about her love to get me to do whatever she wanted, she had also done it many times before. All her guards are bound to her through bargains. They all must follow her every order without question."

At some point, Elora's hand had found her mouth. She pressed her fingers hard against her lips, searching desperately for something to say.

The prince let out a sad chuckle. He leaned against the stone wall and folded his arms over his chest. "As prince of Bitter Thorn, my magic made the bargain less powerful than it should have been, at least the part that had been her idea. The queen's orders only lasted until day dawned, but it didn't matter because she just gave me new orders every morning. My spirit broke immediately. I kept hoping that a small part of Queen Alessandra had truly fallen for me. It did not take long to learn the harsh truth. She only knows how to use love to her advantage. She does not know how to feel it."

"But how did you escape?" Elora pinched her chin now, dread rising inside her.

The prince let out a soft sigh. "Queen Alessandra was given a memory elixir that made her forget everything she ever knew about me. It fills in the gaps so she does not realize she has forgotten. She knows *of* me because I am Prince of Bitter Thorn, but she does not remember what I look like. She does not remember meeting me."

He shook his head. "I escaped at dawn one day when my magic released me from her orders." Touching a hand to his forehead, pain twisted the prince's features again. "If she ever remembers who I am, I will be forced to follow her orders again. Even now, she could give me an order, and I would have to follow it. Since she has no idea of our past, that is unlikely to happen." A wince scrunched up one of his eyes. "Though, since she is a queen, the memory elixir might not be as powerful as it should be. I will always be in danger while in her presence. Even tonight, snips of memories seemed to flash in her eyes when she saw me. She is probably in her palace right now, trying desperately to think of why my presence feels strange to her." He bit his lip, looking closer at the ground. "If I become High King, I should be powerful enough to break my bargain

318

with Queen Alessandra. I do want to remove the curse from my court like I said, but I want to be rid of *her* even more."

Breaths moved in and out of Elora's mouth while the words settled inside her. She stared until the prince finally looked her way. After a short gulp, she forced the words from her mouth. "You promised you would never touch another creature with romantic feelings in your heart."

His throat flexed as he glared back.

Violent flutters moved through her chest. She took another step toward him, firmly locking her eyes on his. "What happens if you do?"

He turned away, glancing at his wolf's black fur. "I disappear." He waved a hand. "I cease to exist."

She sucked in a breath before forcing words from her lips. "That's what happened when I kissed you."

His eyes shot toward her, but then he jerked his head away.

She stepped forward one last time, merely an arm's length away now. "And again when I held your hand. I saw your body flicker or something. You were beginning to disappear."

He flashed his teeth at her, slamming his palm against the wall. "It means nothing. Just because I have come to respect you—" The words seemed to stick in his throat, forcing him to cough. He looked away before he continued. "I may admire your courage and—" He let out a grunt and slammed his fist against the wall. "It means nothing. While in Fairfrost, I vowed I would never love again. After the testing is over, you will go back to the mortal realm, and everything will go back to normal."

Judging by how he gripped the leather strap on her door, he probably intended to storm out of the room. But before he could, a glowing green light landed on top of his hand.

The sprite who landed had a body so thin, he barely looked capable of standing on his own. He stood no taller than a thumbnail. In a wispy voice, he spoke to the prince. "I have a message for you from Queen Alessandra of Fairfrost."

Brannick gulped as he reached into his pocket. He pulled out a plump red berry, which the sprite accepted eagerly. The sprite took a large bite before stuffing the berry into his pocket. Red juice drizzled down his chin when he spoke again.

"Here are the words from Queen Alessandra. 'I can feel that I know you. Whatever you have done to my memory, I intend to reverse it. And soon. Your trick will not last.'"

With those ominous words, the tiny sprite flew out the window.

Elora's gut twisted in a knot as the prince glanced her way. She could do nothing. Say nothing.

As difficult as the first phase of testing had been, it seemed things were about to get much worse.

ACKNOWLEDGEMENTS

As always, I must begin by expressing my gratitude to you, the reader. This book was a year in the making. The research took me to all sorts of places I never expected. Even the plot had turns I didn't foresee. Thank you so much for joining me on the journey of this book! Readers like you make everything about writing worthwhile.

If you enjoyed the book, please consider leaving a review for it on goodreads or on the retailer where you bought it. Your review could help a fellow reader discover this story.

Another huge thanks goes to my book cover designer, Angel Leya. You were so awesome to create two completely different book covers for the same book. I love how unique the eBook and paperback covers are, and yet, they convey the perfect genre and feeling for the book inside.

Thank you also to my editor, Justin Greer. As always, your expertise made this book everything it needed to be. I appreciated all of your insight and your ability to see my vision. This book would not be the same without you.

Of course, I must acknowledge my dear author friends, Queens of the Quill. Your advice, encouragement, beta reading, etc. truly made this book a possibility. I must send an extra special thanks to my fae queens: Alison Ingleby, Clarissa Gosling, Hanna Sandvig, Joanna Reeder, Stacey Trombley, Tessonja Odette, and Valia Lind. You ladies rock!

Finally, I send the sincerest gratitude ever to my husband who has supported me more than I ever could have dreamed. Thank you so much for your love and your belief in me. I couldn't have written this book without you.

ABOUT THE AUTHOR

Kay L Moody is proud to be a young adult fantasy author. Her books feature exciting plots with a few magical elements. They have lots of adventure, compelling characters, and sweet romantic sub-plots. Most of her books have a dystopian flair. They include a variety of technology levels and lots of diversity.

Kay lives in the western United States with her husband and four sons. She enjoys summertime, learning new things, and doing her nails with fancy nail art.

MORE FROM KAY L MOODY

The competition could save her life... but only if she wins.

A divided empire. Manipulation of the elements. Torn between duty and freedom, Talise must learn that clinging to the past might destroy her future.

If you love royalty, romance, and intrigue, this addicting novella series is a must read.

THE ELEMENTS OF KAMDARIA

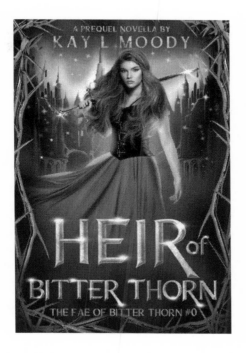

Visit kaylmoody.com/bitter for the complete prequel

Heir of Bitter Thorn is a prequel to The Fae of Bitter Thorn. Discover how Elora got the mysterious scar on her hand, how Prince Brannick escaped Fairfrost, and why the two of them don't remember their first meeting.

ELORA NEVER felt more alive than when a sword swung toward her body.

This one aimed for her heart, but she parried the blow. As always, her sword acted as a shield as much as a weapon. The two blades clashed midair. It took her a moment to regain a ready stance.

In the precious second she lost, her opponent managed to sneak in another strike. The lethal point of his sword kissed her bare arm on its way to her heart. It was too bad for him that she knew the move well.

Her steady footing gave just the right angle to slide her blade against his until the tops of their hilts clanged. With a great shove, she pushed the sword away from herself.

Her opponent stumbled backward for three steps and then landed on the dry, cracked dirt of the clearing where they fought. Faced with his defeat, Elora's father let out a chuckle as he smoothed wispy brown strands back over his balding spots. His silver eyes shined as he reached for the leather-wrapped hilt of his sword.

"I don't know how much more I can teach you, Elora." Hearing his gentle voice always jarred a bit with the ferocity of his sword fighting. He let out another soft chuckle and shielded his eyes from the sun, looking toward his forge.

The little clearing in the woods had always been the perfect spot for sparring. It sat close enough to his forge for her father to see when a customer approached. And even though their little cottage stood nearby, the clearing was far enough away that Elora's mother wouldn't see her fighting—in a dress and corset, yes, but *without* the long-sleeved under slip she was *supposed* to wear at all times.

The tight corset only barely limited her movements now that she was used to fighting with it. But the under slip that covered her arms always got in the way when she had to move fast. Fighting without it always went smoother.

Her father had sheathed his sword. He stroked her cheek with his knuckle, wearing a smile that always made her feel proud. "I think you're better than me now."

The words came with a biting reminder. Her blade sang as she slammed it into its sheath. "I'll never get to fight in the tournaments as long as I'm a woman, though. How do I know how good I really am if I'm not even allowed to fight?"

Her father managed to stop himself from wincing at her words. Maybe he'd been practicing. Apparently, he didn't want to start a fight. He leaned up against a tree filled with leaves fluttering in the gentle wind. "You don't need to fight. I won hundreds of tournaments in my day, and you can beat me. That should tell you exactly how good you are."

That was all her sword fighting was allowed to be. A hobby. Something to pass the time, like needlework or poem writing. A woman could have a talent for others to applaud and admire, but it could never be something she earned money from.

Besides that, beating her father now didn't mean as much as it used to. As a child, she loved sitting on her mother's lap and ogling as her father easily defeated every sword fighter he went up against. But he was an old man now, with three daughters to provide for and only a forge in an out-of-the-way village to do it with.

He hadn't even ordered a new shipment of ore for several weeks.

From the corner of her eye, she noticed a flash of movement. Her head jerked toward it but only found the same tree that had always been there. After narrowing her eyes for a moment, she turned back to her father.

With a handkerchief embroidered by her mother, he dabbed at the sweat on his forehead. "I have something for you."

He must have been in a very good mood if he limited his lecture to those three sentences. Now he reached for the leather bag that usually held his business letters and a few of his favorite forging tools.

From out of the bag, he pulled a soft leather-bound book. The pages all poked out at different angles; a haphazard length of string seemed to hold the whole thing together. His silvery eyes brightened again as he pushed the book toward her. "It's from my friends who still work at the castle."

Her stomach danced a jig as soon as she touched the book. Her fingers buzzed as she struggled to open the buckle that held it closed. When the pages fell open in her hands, a gasp of sheer delight escaped her.

Drawings filled most of the pages, but many had descriptions too. The first section showed plants and flowers from the castle gardens. Another showed the layout and the quaint cobblestone paths between the different areas of the garden. The next section focused on clothing the courtiers and noblemen wore. One gave a detailed description and drawing of the king's favorite red velvet and gold crown.

"I explained to my friends how my oldest daughter is clever and always curious. I asked them to send drawings and descriptions so that you could see what the castle is like."

She turned over the pages with insatiable hunger, eager to devour the information at the greatest possible speed. But another part of her held her fingers back and forced her to enjoy each drawing to the fullest. The small details were always her favorite.

It didn't matter how quickly she looked through the book anyway, it would take her weeks to fully digest it all. Her eyebrows pinched as she neared the end. "Did they include any information about the food?"

Her father leaned forward, turning down one corner of his mouth. "I'm afraid I forgot to ask about the food. But I did ask about—"

Another gasp escaped her. If she'd had any control over it, she wouldn't have interrupted her father, but the final drawings were too great to suppress a reaction.

Luckily, he only smiled in response. "I specifically asked that they give detailed information about the guards' armor and weapons."

She stroked the page, sliding her finger over a drawn sword, as if her touch might convince it to leave the page and become real.

When her father swallowed, she tried to ignore how his fingers had stiffened at his sides. He cleared his throat. "What have you been thinking about marriage these days?"

The book suddenly felt heavier in her hand, like the pages had been forged from steel and the edges were sharp as blades. As much as she would treasure the book, she couldn't help seeing it for what it really was now. A bribe.

Her lips barely parted as she spoke. "I'm only seventeen. Isn't that too young for marriage?"

Her father dabbed his forehead again with the embroidered handkerchief. He seemed unusually sweaty in the cool air that surrounded them. "Many get married younger than seventeen."

She brought the book closer to her nose, specifically avoiding his eyes. "If you're ready for a wedding, why not wait for Chloe? She's fifteen and *dying* to get married. Can't you wait another year to arrange a wedding?"

"We can't wait that long."

He swallowed again. The lyrical sound of harp music drifted toward them from the cottage. Based on the speed of the scales, Grace was obviously the one playing. She may have been the youngest sister—only twelve—but she was still the most accomplished harpist of all three sisters.

While Elora and her father had been sparring, a cool, gentle wind kept her internal temperature perfect for fighting. Now it made the little hairs on her arm stand on end.

Her father lowered his eyes to the cracked dirt of the clearing. It had been too long since the last rain. Everyone in the village felt it. He stuffed the handkerchief into his pocket. "You know I had a butcher who commissioned that strange set of knives a while back. He never picked them up or paid. I've only been able to sell one of the knives since. The others used an alloy so strange, I can't melt them down to use for another weapon."

Tension caused her fingers to curl around the spine of the book. "You don't have enough money to buy more ore?"

He looked away. "Recent times have been difficult for many people in the village. My skills are great, but few are wanting new swords." His head hung. Sunlight pierced through the strands of his graying hair, making his bald spots prominent. "I can't provide for our family."

Her heart sank at his ability to speak such words. At one time, he never would have accepted defeat of any kind.

With a tender hand, he brushed her long, light brown hair behind her shoulders. "With your beauty, we've already had men offering small fortunes just to be with you. But your mother and I love you more than anything. I've made some inquiries and already dismissed several men who were clearly not worthy of our precious child." His hand dropped onto her shoulder, which he gave a strong squeeze. "I promise I will find you a good husband, someone who is kind and has the means to take care of you." Now his smile returned, but it carried a weight that hadn't been there before. "And he must allow you to practice sword fighting every day, or I will not even consider him."

When he pulled her into his arms, she buried her face in the safety of his chest. He had always been there to take care of her, to teach her. She had always known this day would come, but somehow, she had never been able to imagine another shoulder catching her tears. Maybe she'd have to embroider her own handkerchief to do the job.

Or maybe, she'd never feel safe enough to cry again.

A pair of boots had been stomping across the nearby path, but now they moved close enough to crunch the gravel in front of the nearby forge. Her father tightened his embrace. When he stepped back, he brushed his knuckles across her cheek again, but this time caught the falling tears.

He attempted a smile. "It seems the squire is here to have his swords polished. I have to go. Enjoy your book."

He swung the leather bag onto his back and started toward the forge. But then he looked back at her with a pair of tired eyes that she knew well. "And Elora, when you do harp lessons with your mother later, please don't give her too much grief."

His retreating form filled her with a rolling nausea. She'd always been his favorite. Chloe cared too much about epic poems and falling in love. Everyone loved Grace, but she acted so childish compared to the rest of them.

Elora and her father had always shared a special connection the others didn't have. His promise to find someone who would let her practice sword fighting every day had sounded simple. Truthfully, it wasn't simple at all. Most people looked down on her for knowing how to fight. Most people called it frightening and uncomely. Her father had taught her to ignore those comments just as he had taught her how to parry and strike.

For him to promise to find a husband who would allow her to continue sword fighting was probably the greatest gift he could possibly give her.

A hard lump formed in her throat as she pulled the book of drawings close to her chest.

Was it wrong for her to dream of something more?

Her lip quivered as she glanced through the woods at a path she had taken many times. At the end of it stood a tree she had often climbed. Yet, it in all her years, she had never managed to climb to the very top of the knotty tree.

It had always seemed like she'd have time someday. But maybe time wasn't as abundant as she had thought.

She glanced back toward her little cottage with blue-painted shutters. She had always intended to get through at least *one* music lesson with her mother without throwing a fit.

And what about the frame she had promised to buy for her sister Chloe to display her favorite love poem? And what about the harp duet she had promised Grace they would learn someday?

Unwittingly, her fingers clutched around the hilt of her sword, squeezing much tighter than she meant to. And what about the tournaments? She had always dreamed of disguising herself in order to compete. They couldn't turn her away if they thought she was a boy.

The thought of defying her parents' greatest wish turned her mouth dryer than the crusty dirt under foot. She let out a sigh and glanced down the path ahead.

Then her eyes narrowed, and her heart skipped a beat.

Perhaps fighting in the tournament was too big an adventure to attempt without careful planning.

But climbing that tree to the very top? That was dream she could finally fulfill. If she could accomplish at least some of her dreams, then maybe her marriage wouldn't feel so much like imprisonment.

She'd climb the tree that evening.

Visit kaylmoody.com/bitter for the complete prequel